"What are you doing?" Teon said, startling her.

"Trying to sleep," Revna lied.

"Most people close their eyes and lie down when they try to sleep, Revna. I suggest you do the same."

His velvety voice just a whisper away from her only intensified her feelings. She had the strange desire to reach out and touch him and tell him he could sleep in the bed, but she was too afraid of what his reaction would be. She knew she had to protect herself from further rejection and more disappointment.

"Just relax. You're safe with me. No one's going to come in here. I've got the door closely guarded."

But didn't he realize she wasn't frightened of who was out there? She was afraid of how he was making her feel inside this room.

Author Note

Thank you so much for choosing to read *Second Chance with His Viking Wife*.

Prince Teon cannot forgive his father, the king, for forcing him to marry an outsider to form an alliance with the Vikings and protect his kingdom—he has always despised the raiders from the North, ever since they attacked their lands and his mother was killed in battle. On hearing the news that she is to be wed, Revna is distraught. She is so young and does not want to marry a man she does not love. She doesn't want to be handed over to the Saxons to secure her father's lineage. Nevertheless, an arranged marriage takes place, but as soon as the wedding celebrations are over, Prince Teon leaves. He is determined theirs will be a marriage in name only. But six years later, when the king dies, Prince Teon must return to claim his crown—and his wife.

I loved writing this story, creating two characters who have such insane chemistry yet are reluctant to act on it, their prejudices holding them back. They are not willing to accept that they are perfect for each other. With them cooped up together in a fortress under siege, I had great fun exploring their relationship and watching it play out. I hope you enjoy reading it as much as I enjoyed writing it.

You can contact Sarah via @sarahrodiedits or sarahrodiedits@gmail.com. Or visit her website at sarahrodi.com.

SARAH
RODI

—

Second Chance
with His Viking Wife

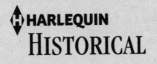

HARLEQUIN
HISTORICAL

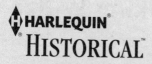

HARLEQUIN®
HISTORICAL™

Recycling programs
for this product may
not exist in your area.

ISBN-13: 978-1-335-59574-4

Second Chance with His Viking Wife

Harlequin Enterprises ULC
22 Adelaide St. West, 41st Floor
Toronto, Ontario M5H 4E3, Canada
www.Harlequin.com

Printed in U.S.A.

Sarah Rodi has always been a hopeless romantic. She grew up watching old, romantic movies recommended by her grandad, or devouring love stories from the local library. Sarah lives in the village of Cookham in Berkshire, where she enjoys walking along the River Thames with her husband, two daughters and their dog. She has been a magazine journalist for over twenty years, but it has been her lifelong dream to write romance for Harlequin Historical. Sarah believes everyone deserves to find their happy-ever-after. You can contact her via @sarahrodiedits or sarahrodiedits@gmail.com. Or visit her website at sarahrodi.com.

Books by Sarah Rodi

Harlequin Historical

One Night with Her Viking Warrior
Claimed by the Viking Chief
Second Chance with His Viking Wife

Rise of the Ivarssons

The Viking's Stolen Princess
Escaping with Her Saxon Enemy

Visit the Author Profile page
at Harlequin.com.

For Sarah, Fran and Amy
Bridesmaids and besties, always

Chapter One

~~~~~~~~~~

Kinborough Fortress—Ninth Century

As the shrill tones of the congregation's singing voices reached their peak Revna heard the rumblings of a commotion at the chapel door. Casting a furtive glance over her shoulder, she saw the wall of royal guards blocking the entrance, jostling for space, pressing their backs against the locked but rattling wooden doors. Her heart lurched. Was someone trying to get in? She had hoped this day would be memorable for all the right reasons and that the King's funeral would pass without incident.

Edmund had been a strong ruler, a man of great renown, whom she had come to love and respect like a father. But while he had lain sick in his bed, rumours of his imminent death had spread. It had prompted feelings of instability and unrest among his people, all watching and waiting to see what would happen next.

The King's line of succession was clear: power

would immediately be passed to his eldest child, his son, Prince Teon. Yet no one knew where Teon was—or whether he was even alive. He had last been seen fighting on their borders the previous winter.

When Edmund had fallen ill, soldiers had been sent to track down his heir, but even as the King had taken his last breath, Revna and the witan were still unsure of Prince Teon's whereabouts. Now, every day that the throne lay empty left them more vulnerable to attack—and upon hearing the disturbance at the door, Revna couldn't help but wonder if an enemy was at the gates, come to take the crown by force.

The battering sounds grew louder and louder and she turned back briefly to face the priest, sharing a wild look of concern. Just then, the doors unexpectedly burst open, icing her blood. The congregation cried out in fear, bringing the singing to an abrupt stop, as a group of warriors tried to storm the church. The lords and ladies huddled together, crowding down the far end of the pews, desperate to get out of the way. But Revna remained where she was, steadfast, despite her shock. She readied herself for whatever was to come, for she knew she had to be courageous for the young Princesses. She couldn't bear to think what would happen to them if they were captured and she pulled them into her arms, holding them close.

The royal guards were at least standing their ground and seemed to have the intruders surrounded, grappling with them, trying to halt their entry. But all of a sudden the King's soldiers seemed to give up and step back in reverential defeat as the leader of the group pushed past them. Catching a glimpse of his profile, Revna instantly understood why.

Her breath caught, her heart clenching in her chest. For a moment, she thought it had stopped beating. She *knew* that face. It was one that was hard to forget.

Her eyes narrowed as she watched the tall, powerfully built man, a scowl slashed across his formidable features, stride determinedly up the aisle towards her.

His presence had an immediate impact. The congregation fell into an awed hush, for the vision of Prince Teon was a sight to behold indeed, not least because the people of Kinborough hadn't seen him in—what was it now? Eight long winters.

Could it really be him? Revna had begun to think she would never lay eyes on him again, so she was as shaken as everyone else to see him here—perhaps more so, for the last time she'd been in the same room as him, it had been their wedding night.

An onslaught of painful memories crept out from their hiding place deep inside her heart… Images flooded her mind of being back in this very church. It was a beautiful, bright sunny day and the stronghold had been bedecked in flowers. She remembered hundreds of Saxons crowding into the grand hall, partaking in much drinking and revelry, and while she had been devastated that her father and his men hadn't come to celebrate with her, she'd been pleased she had at least made him proud, for he had wanted her to make a good marriage alliance since she was young.

Leaving their home of Greenland behind, she had been dragged across the ocean on his expeditions to the west. When she had been told she was to be married and discovered her betrothed was the handsome Prince Teon—the man who had once come to her rescue on the battlefield, showing her kindness among all the bloodshed—her heart had lifted in hope. But it hadn't taken long for her to realise how foolish her hope had been.

Her fingers crept up to her throat. She was glad for the sake of the realm that he was here, safeguarding the crown. The rightful heir had returned—and surely no one would dare to challenge Prince Teon and his men? But she couldn't be glad for herself— he was as dangerous as any enemy, for she knew he despised her.

Coming to a stop before the priest, Prince Teon placed his hands on his hips, his dark glare boring into the holy man. He was undoubtedly livid that he had been prevented entry into his own church. 'Who ordered this ceremony to go ahead, without me being present?' The sound of his harsh, authoritative tone echoed around the chapel, quickly followed by surprised, appreciative murmurs undulating through the pews, like ripples on a lake.

Revna bit down on the inside of her cheek, annoyed at the reaction he caused. But seeing him up close, she knew why. Prince Teon was the most devastatingly handsome man she'd ever seen, despite the heavy crease carved into his forehead, the frown furrowing his dark brow. But she didn't want to think him attractive. He was hateful—unreliable—not caring about crushing a young girl's dreams.

And the years had hardened him further, she thought. He looked even more forbidding, especially when his hand moved to the hilt of his sword upon barking out his question. He had left her as a young man and returned as a mighty warrior. Had he been defending his father's kingdom on the eastern borders all this time? Had he seen many battles? Suffered much pain? Still, that was no excuse to barge in here with his weapons, or to attack a man of the cloth.

'I did,' she said, bravely stepping forward, coming to the priest's defence. She certainly couldn't let Father Cuthbert take the blame for something she had arranged.

Prince Teon turned slowly towards the sound of her voice and, as his scornful eyes narrowed, a flicker of awareness sparked inside her. He was wearing a dark linen shirt beneath a gold-studded leather vest. The armour clung to his incredibly muscular chest and the rolled-up wet sleeves were moulded to his sculpted arms and broad shoulders. Was it still raining outside?

The dark clothes matched his windswept hair, which was longer than when she'd seen him last and had a slight curl to the ends. It was also soaking wet and much more dishevelled—no wonder the guards hadn't recognised him at first—but it didn't detract from his angular, striking face. Or his arrogant air of nobility. He looked like a man ready to take on his kingdom.

He gave her a long, hard look, making her insides quiver. An unwanted tremble started in her legs and she curled her fingers around the top of the wooden pew to steady herself.

'And who, might I ask, are you?'

His words were so sharp they pierced her heart, while bitterness—and unbearable humiliation—burned her throat. For the first time in a long time, she had the desire to flee, to escape far away from here and the people's prying eyes. She couldn't believe it. Her husband—the man she hadn't gone one day without thinking about—didn't even recognise her!

But why would he? It had been eight years. And even back then, it was as if he hadn't wanted to acknowledge she even existed. He hadn't been able to look her in the eye as she made the long, nerve-racking walk up the aisle towards him, or during their wedding ceremony, surrounded by a room full of strangers.

He had given her the briefest peck on the cheek when the priest had said he could kiss his bride and she'd been excruciatingly aware of his men suppressing their laughter in the background. He'd done all he could to avoid her at the feast afterwards—later lashing out and delivering his final blow, telling her he would never be able to forgive his father for forcing him to wed her.

She knew her appearance had changed beyond recognition over the summers and winters that had passed—she had grown into a woman—but still, upon hearing his words, the familiar feelings of hurt he had caused her before came rushing back. Mortified, she angled her face away from the congregation.

She had imagined this moment many times and couldn't deny there had been a ridiculous, romantic part of her that had hoped he would take one look at her now and think her beautiful. Because wasn't it only natural that she would want to show him what he'd been missing? That she'd want to make him regret rejecting her before?

But in a single comment he'd dashed her hopes once more, making her feel degraded, proving what she had tried to come to terms with—that their marriage was a sham. Because in reality, nothing more had passed between the two of them than the priest's words that day...

Prince Teon had been no more of a husband to her than a stranger passing her in the fortress square. He'd spoken his vows, not meaning a word of them, trapping her into this farce of a union, then he'd walked away, leaving her all alone—an outcast in his family's fortress. He was like the ice mountains of her home in Greenland—wild, imposing, dangerous. And now he was back to reclaim his crown, seemingly as cruel and ruthless as ever.

But her hurt—and her anger—returned with force, too. She shook her head slightly, as if to close off her thoughts. She knew they were being watched with interest and she refused to allow his cruel, casual dismissal of her to affect her position here. She was determined to keep her pride and maintain the respect of the people, which she'd fought so hard to earn while he'd been away. They were relying on her to sustain the fragile peace she'd been holding together since the death of the King.

And she had made a vow to Edmund that she would keep his subjects safe, so she refused to be intimidated. Not by Teon. Not this time. She was no longer the naive girl he had wed. She had become fiercely independent and could take care of herself.

She tipped her chin upwards defiantly, lifting her head to meet his smouldering gaze, and released a low, disapproving tutting sound. 'How remiss of you not to recognise your wife, Prince Teon.'

Teon felt an invisible punch to his gut.

He stared down at the woman before him, boldly daring to hold his gaze, a cold, cutting look of condemnation on her face, and he sucked in a breath. Her words caused the congregation to descend once more into quiet—and for a moment, they stunned him into silence, too.

Shock ripped through him, his eyes raking over her, trying to decide if she was telling the truth. Surely the heathen girl he had met just twice before—who he'd been forced to marry—was not this stunning woman standing before him now? Could it be true? He hadn't even recognised her. *His wife.* His enemy's daughter. Damn...

But she was like a different person entirely from the savage girl he had wed.

Her once mousy and tightly braided hair was now a pale, moon-like blonde and fell in loose, gentle waves around her face, right down to her slender waist. As for her body…once lean and straight and childlike, it had filled out in all the right places, making his mouth suddenly dry. But peering closer, her eyes were still that same unusual light blue—like crystals in the heart of a glacier, evidence of her northern heritage—and were just as guarded as they'd been back then.

Unable to help himself, he took a step towards her, needing to get a better look. 'My god. Revna?' Her name came out a bit breathless, as if the air was being pushed from his chest. She had thrown him off course, made him look like a fool in front of all these people! *His* people. And yet he couldn't bring himself to look away. She had captured his attention, the tendrils of resplendent curls framing her face contrasting with her black silk gown, which clung to the luscious swells of her breasts and skimmed the flare of her hips. His scowl deepened.

'Your Highness.' She nodded evenly, bowing her head just a little. The sound of her gently lilting voice and the way she pronounced her words washed over him. Was she mocking him?

Curling his hands into fists, digging his nails into the skin of his palms, he forced himself to remember exactly who this woman was. She was a heathen. She had crossed the sea on dragon ships and set ashore their beaches, like so many other Norse tribes before them.

These heinous warriors had laid siege to their farmsteads, scorching the earth of his homeland. He had never before seen men fight without armour, wearing animal heads and skins and using their weapons so barbarically. He had spent the past eight winters defending this isle from her kind, who came here to raid their homes, raping and pillaging, destroying everything in their wake. Those that stayed, wishing to lay claim to land here, were hated…

So he'd had to carry the shame around with him all these winters, that he, a man of royal blood, had had to marry one of them—a pagan girl, a nobody, from the remote icy islands of the north. And he was damned sure he wasn't the only one who viewed their union as discreditable, for a Saxon and a heathen marrying went against all conventions of the time. Despite how different she looked now, it didn't change what her people had done and how she came to be here.

He knew this wasn't the most normal of ways for a man to greet his wife after having been away for so many winters, and suddenly he was aware all eyes were on them. But theirs had never been a normal union—two adversaries fulfilling the duty their fathers had demanded of them. As they'd never really known each other, or been intimate, he couldn't exactly pull her towards him and embrace her now for the benefit of all these people, even if he wanted to. Which he definitely did not. Instead, he raked his hand through his thick hair.

'How you've…changed. I barely recognised you.'

He was fiercely proud of his Saxon heritage and could never forgive her for what had happened here. And yet, as his eyes burned into hers, he felt something pass between them—a sudden, unexpected flicker of attraction. He instantly wanted to stamp it out.

'I should hope so—it has been a while.'

She had been plain back then, when he'd last seen her—and practically still a girl. It had disgusted him that his father had married him off to someone so young, against his will, and despite his many protests. It had seemed so wrong, not least because her people were responsible for his mother's death…

'You remember your sisters, of course?' Revna said, arching a perfect eyebrow and gesturing to the two young girls standing behind her.

His gaze quickly drifted over them in silent assessment, his eyes widening at the revelation, and they tentatively stepped forward to welcome him home. He reached out to squeeze their shoulders and ruffle their hair, their faces breaking out into smiles despite the weight of the day's sadness.

'Edlynne, Eldrida,' he acknowledged. They had been just six and eight when he had left and, apart from having similar colouring to him, they were almost unknowable themselves.

'We are all surprised to see you here,' Revna said.

A streak of anger ripped through him. He could never comprehend how the King had made an alliance with the very people who had threatened the stability of the royal fortress. His father had offered them land to build a settlement in return for peace and protection and it had worked for a while. But the following winter, his mother had been killed.

Whereas Teon had made a vow of vengeance, proclaiming all-out war, his father had stepped in and put a halt to his plans. The King had gone on to make a second pact to save his kingdom from ruin—and this time, he'd offered his son's hand in marriage to his enemy, the Northman chief's daughter, to seal the deal. In the end, his son's happiness had meant nothing. It had widened the crack in their already ruptured relationship and Teon had never been able to forgive him for it. Or her...

'It shouldn't be. This is my home, *I* belong here.'
She didn't.

He saw her eyes widen just a little, understanding his meaning, and she took a step back. Good, he hoped he had wounded her. Just who did she think she was, burying the King without him being here? He and his father might have parted on bad terms—been estranged all this time—but he was still *his* father. This was *his* home.

Father Cuthbert gave a little cough, interrupting them, rescuing Revna in return. He motioned to the congregation behind Teon, bringing the Prince back to his surroundings and all the people watching, reminding him they were in the middle of a ceremony. 'Prince Teon, we are all gladdened by the fact you are here. But do you think...may we perhaps continue with the service now?'

Teon gave a curt nod, moving to the pews on the other side of the aisle. He was not finished with her yet, but he could tell this would have to wait. They had to bury his father first.

'Yes,' he said darkly. 'It seems we have no choice but to see this through now. We will discuss your oversight later,' he said to the priest. 'But for now you may continue.'

As the man tentatively recommenced his service, first in the church and then as they all moved outside, Teon forced himself to take some deep breaths, to calm himself down. He needed to be strong and lead his people through this commemoration of their sovereign. He had to put all thoughts of the past and his heathen wife aside.

The news of the King's death had reached him while he'd been resisting an attack from the latest Norse tribe who had crossed the seas, chancing their luck by coming here. But he and his men had been ready for them, as always. Upon hearing that his father had passed, he had felt a deep sense of sadness that they had not put aside their differences before now. But some wounds just ran too deep. However, the duty to his people that his father had instilled in him and that had kept him fighting on the frontline all these winters had forced him home. He had come as quickly as he could.

The long ride here had given him chance to think about what he wanted to say in his eulogy and, when the priest gestured for him to take over, he remained stoic and proud as he talked the congregation through the highlights of his father's reign. Despite his many faults as a father, he had been a good king and it was far easier to speak about him in that way.

As the people sang songs of praise for their late monarch, Teon and a few of his men began to shovel the earth, interring the King with his shield and armour, surrounded by food, jewels and coins, in the grand burial mound. His muscles began to burn, sweat and raindrops licking his brow, but he knew he couldn't stop until the barrow loomed large over the landscape. No matter how his father had wronged him, he owed him this final mark of respect.

At least his father was now reunited with his mother. They were together at rest, despite their relationship having been fractured in life. He wanted to honour and remember them, to focus on the priest's final words, and yet, frustratingly, his gaze kept being drawn back to Revna through the pelting rain. It was difficult not to look at her, she drew the eye like an exotic flower in an English garden—beautiful, but out of place here, her pale hair set against her glowing skin.

As the last of the earth was thrown on to the burial mound and the service drew to a close, he was glad when the deed was finally done, yet it seemed as if every lord and lady from Kinborough wanted to speak to him, to pass on their condolences, and he felt as if his brittle smile could break at any moment. He breathed a heavy sigh of relief when eventually, the people began to leave the burial site and make their way back to the keep.

Glancing over at Revna, he saw a tear slide down her cheek and she quickly swiped it away as she focused on consoling his siblings, offering them comfort, but it didn't soften his feelings. If anything, it hardened his heart against her, for he didn't believe her grief—surely she and the King hadn't been close?

He couldn't believe she cared for the passing of an old Saxon man. No, she was not to be trusted.

Teon's hand wrapped around the hilt of his sword, gripping it tight as he strode over to where she and his sisters were standing. 'You were quick to get him in the ground, weren't you? Were you that eager to take his crown?'

Revna lifted her head to face him. 'We waited as long as we could, but I'm afraid we did not know where you were, or how to reach you. As you were not here to oversee the arrangements, the task fell to me and the witan,' she said bitingly.

His cool gaze studied her. 'I understand my sisters are far too young to be making decisions for the crown, but since when have you been part of my father's witan?'

'Since he asked me to be.'

He could scarcely believe it—his father's council was made up of noblemen and thegns, those he chose to seek out their advice—yet, even as he was shaking his head, his sisters retreated like traitors to their position by her side, nodding as if to support her claim. Surely his father wouldn't allow one of her kind—*the enemy*—to be privy to all his most private discussions? He pursed his lips. He could see some changes would need to be made now he was home.

'Well, the *task* has been handled appallingly. The King's death should not have been announced until I arrived here. Instead, all you have achieved is chaos and unrest among the neighbouring burghs.'

Backing away from his wrath, Revna calmly focused her attention on his sisters. 'Edlynne, Eldrida, why don't you go on ahead and I'll catch you up? I don't want you catching a chill.' And dutifully, his sisters did as she commanded.

They watched them go before Revna turned on him, the tension between them as thick as the foggy afternoon air. 'If you had a preference over how things were done, then perhaps you should have sent word you were alive, or that you were returning to Kinborough…'

Pure, red-hot anger took his breath away. How dare she speak to him in this way? The girl he had married had been timid and shy. He'd almost felt sorry for her. Almost. Especially when she'd been ushered into his bedchamber on the night of their wedding, wearing a long, white tunic, her eyes cast down to the ground, her teeth sinking into her bottom lip… Now she was standing up to him, speaking to him in a sharp tongue, drawing his eyes to the sensual curve of that very mouth. It was maddening.

'I'm here now.'

'I think we can all see that.'

'I will take over from here. And I can tell I have quite the *task* ahead of me to get all of my subjects under control.'

He would have to be blind to miss the rigidity in her body. On hearing his words, she brought her arms up, wrapping them around her slender waist, holding on to her elbows, as if she was trying to form a barrier as thick as the fortress walls between them.

Her eyes flicked over him in disdain. 'Better late than never.'

His brows rose at her blatant disrespect. It shocked him—he wasn't used to anyone talking to him in such a critical way. Men and women usually hung on his every word, accepting his decisions to be trustworthy, willing to follow him anywhere—even into battle.

He took a step towards her. 'What did you say to me?' he said warningly. His body was thrumming with anger—and something else he didn't want to acknowledge.

'I said better late than never. I'm certain your father would be pleased you were here today, but I hope you'll forgive me if I can't bring myself to feel the same.' And with that, she picked up her skirts and turned on her heel, racing to catch up with his sisters further up the path.

A muscle flickered in his jaw... It was hard to think that someone so pleasing to look at had been the cause of the quarrel between him and his father. That she was the reason he had stayed away from his home all these winters. He'd decided leaving the stronghold would be more desirable than spending even one night with her as his wife, seeing his people look at him with pity, or mocking laughter in their eyes.

Revna was the reason he'd been absent as his sisters had grown up, she was the reason he'd missed seeing his kingdom grow and change through the seasons—and why he hadn't been there at the end of his father's life. And she was the reason his mother was dead. Just having to look at her brought back all the horrific memories. This woman had ruined his life.

He clenched and then unclenched his hand, turning away from her retreating back, which was disappearing into the swirling mist. He would now take up his seat and position here in Kinborough and he was determined this heathen—his wife—would have no more impact on their lives.

Chapter Two

The grand assembly room in the fortress keep was alive with chatter tonight, the lords and ladies all extremely excited about the return of Prince Teon and his men.

If only Revna felt the same.

As the leading woman in Kinborough, she had served the first ale of the evening, confirming Teon's rulership here, as she had often done for the King these past few winters. But now, glancing out across the crowded benches, she took in the familiar faces of Edmund's hall, yet found they offered no distraction from the formidable man who was working his way around the tables, exuding confidence as he reacquainted himself with all his subjects. Her husband. A fierce warrior. The future King. He was a man who selfishly behaved how he liked with no regard for others. A man she never thought she'd see again.

She took the opportunity to study him freely now, while he was preoccupied. She had always thought his looks were without fault—since the first time she'd laid eyes on him on the battlefield the day she and her father had arrived on these shores. Their ships had been greeted by vast blue skies, a patchwork of fertile farmland—and an army. Her father's men had launched themselves over the sides of their ships, waded through the shallow waters and reluctantly headed straight into battle, waving their axes and chanting for heroic glory.

She remembered all too well the rumbling of the ground beneath her feet as she had watched on, her father demanding she leave the sanctuary of the ship and take cover in the hedgerow. He had trained her to fight, yet she was in no fit state to do so after their perilous journey here. The native townsfolk were wailing in distress, trying to escape the fray, and as they ran, she got caught up in their movements, getting shoved and knocked about. It was a stampede—like those of the musk oxen of her homeland—and she fell, before being dragged and then trampled. Already weak from their long journey, she had thought the end was nigh and had been ready to join her mother and brother with their Norse forefathers on the other side.

Seeing a godlike figure in burnished armour on horseback coming towards her, leading a band of men, she'd wondered if it was Odin, come to fetch her himself, but as he drew closer, ushering the crowds away from her battered and bruised body, she'd realised it was a man. He'd descended from his mighty horse and spoken to the people, rallying the men to join his father's army and telling the women to seek shelter, and then his eyes had landed upon her again.

She had lain still, holding her breath, unsure what he was going to do. But to her surprise, he had stalked over, gathered her up into his arms and carried her out of harm's way, gently lowering her down on a bale of hay near a farmstead. Taking off his helmet, his shock of dark hair had fallen loose and he'd checked her over.

'Can you move, child?' he'd asked her.

She'd nodded, even though her leg and her ribs felt broken.

'I'd stay out of sight until this is all over if I were you,' he'd said. 'The battlefield is no place for a girl.'

And she'd tried to ignore her pain and smile, grateful for his kindness.

He saved her life that day. And when the King and her father had agreed terms, bringing the battle to an end, her tribe had been allowed to stay and build a settlement. But she had wondered if she could ever be safe here after that, knowing there was such ill feeling between their peoples. The animosity between them often tipped over into vicious skirmishes, before her father, or the King's men, put a halt to them. She had longed to return to her homeland.

Just under a year later, on hearing that she was finally to be wed, Revna had taken the news with a heavy sense of duty. She was only young and did not want to marry a man she did not love. She couldn't believe her father had arranged for her to marry a prince. That she might one day be his Queen. It was almost too much, too overwhelming. She didn't want that kind of power or responsibility, even if her father wished it for her.

But when she had gone to the next market in the fortress square, to get a look at her betrothed, and discovered the Prince was the handsome warrior who had saved her that day, she had relented. He had all the desirable elements, tall, dark, handsome, with mesmerising deep brown eyes, and she knew he was kind. Only when she had been brought before Teon again at the altar, he was like a different man—cold, hard and devoid of emotion.

Just like now.

She noticed he had discarded his sodden cloak and his sword, and his thick hair had begun to dry yet seemed untameable, especially as he kept raking his hand through it. She couldn't drag her gaze away as he weaved his way through the people, stopping to talk to the men, who each bowed their heads, offering their sympathies, before eagerly competing with each other for his attention. They were no doubt telling him how glad they were to have him home and explaining how they could assist him in his new role as their soon-to-be King.

Her heart floundered—a sudden thought making her chest pound with panic. How would *she* be expected to be of service to him? She had never lived with him in this fortress, not even for one night. But as they were married, didn't he have rights?

Her memories returned to the night of their wedding and those innocent, hopeful first few hours. Teon had been quiet throughout the bridal feast, barely talking to her, instead turning to speak to his right-hand man at his side, but she'd tried to make excuses for him, putting it down to awkwardness. The gods knew she felt the same—after all, they were strangers. She had at least enjoyed the dancing, while the men had sat around drinking ale.

Later, when the Saxon maids had removed her heavy silk gown, instead dressing her in a long, white tunic, she couldn't remember feeling afraid, just bemused. She hadn't really known what was expected of her—no one had ever told her. They'd escorted her to Teon's bedchamber, giggling and making a fuss of her, and when she'd heard the gentle thud of the door closing behind her, and their retreating footsteps, she'd gawkishly stood there before him, shuffling her feet, not knowing what to say or do. But she needn't have worried—when she'd glanced up at him, his face had been full of disgust, not desire.

Now he was back, would she be expected to fulfil all of her wifely duties? Surely not…she shivered. He didn't even seem to like her, let alone want to touch her.

While she should have been relieved that he was home and that they had given the King the magnificent send-off he deserved, she didn't think she could eat a thing as the bowls of wild deer and vegetables were served and the men and women began to settle down to eat. Her stomach was a tangle of knots.

Just then, Teon looked up and his reprimanding eyes clashed with hers across the room. She willed her heart to stop racing, schooling her face, knowing he was about to stride over, take up his seat at the top table and she would be forced to sit next to him for the duration of the meal. She told herself to keep calm—she could do this. All she needed to do was exchange a few words and be pleasant.

When he stopped beside her, placing a hand on the back of her chair, the tiny hairs on her neck bristled in anticipation.

'Who told you that you could sit here?' he hissed.

She straightened her spine. 'Your father. He liked us all to sit together, looking out over the hall,' she said, staring directly ahead. It was how Edmund had taught her to observe his subjects, gleaning information from watching who they spoke to and how they behaved. 'Why? Is something wrong?'

'Everything!' he muttered, before lowering himself down next to her, filling the space with his unrivalled, powerful frame.

His shoulders were definitely wider than when she saw him last, his chest much broader. She had never been so aware of a man before. His long, muscled legs took up so much space under the table that his knee brushed against hers. She pulled away sharply, despite the peculiar pang for an intimacy she had never known. He was near enough for her to feel the heat radiating from his body—and his barely contained seething anger—and with every stifled breath she took, she drew in his male, musky scent. He smelt of wild rain and woodsmoke.

His tankard was quickly filled with ale and he

reached out to wrap his large hand around it just as she tried to take her own. The movement caused their fingers to touch, like the striking together of two branches, sending sparks up her arm. She stiffened, snatching her hand back in surprise, and he turned away from her, ignoring her, to talk to his sisters on the other side of him—in a warm tone, she noticed, one that was not used when he spoke to her. No, when he spoke to her his voice was harsh, his eyes darkened with disdain—and something else she couldn't quite place.

She listened as his sisters excitedly filled him in on their studies, praising Revna for her help, and her heart warmed. When the young Princesses had begun to depend on her, she had finally felt as if she had value here—and over time, their needs had become more important to her than her own. When they revealed how Revna had been teaching them to swordfight, his gaze swung to look at her, incredulous, and she bit back a smile.

She shrugged. 'Surely a woman needs to know how to defend herself?'

He glowered at her. 'A woman has a man to do that for her.'

'Not *all* women,' she challenged. She had learned she could only rely on herself. He—and her father—had taught her that.

'My sisters will, for they are worthy of a man's protection,' he said, wounding her, and his unjustified dislike of her ridiculously made her want to rebel, to lash out and provoke him even more.

Instead she sighed, smoothing her kirtle over her

thighs. She knew she should try to take the higher ground—say something to try to cut through the tension—but what?

'I am sorry about your father,' she said genuinely. A deep loneliness had followed her around this fortress when she'd first come to live at Kinborough. Her mother and brother were dead, her father had left her here, not even returning for her wedding day, and Teon had deserted her, too. She had found herself among strangers, feeling utterly abandoned, in an enormous stronghold in a place far away from home. She'd learned a hard lesson over and again— that when you allowed yourself to care for someone, they always ended up leaving you.

Life had been constrained for a while, but King Edmund had gradually tried to ease her solitude, finding her things to do and people to talk to, and she'd come to care for him. She had been tasked with helping to raise the Princesses, and, despite her fear of one day losing them, too, she'd been determined to work her way into their hearts and those of Edmund's people. She would always be grateful to Edmund for giving her that chance. 'He was a good man.'

'I know that,' Teon said, staring stonily ahead.

'He spoke of you often.'

He turned, almost unwillingly, his breathtaking-ebony gaze in the lantern-lit hall looking searchingly down into her face, dipping to her lips. Under his scrutiny, her skin prickled with awareness. He was stunning up close—the stubble on his chin not detracting from his strong jawline or his proud, patrician face.

'Did he now?' he said, leaning back in his seat, taking a long drink of the amber liquid. 'Tell me, what else did the two of you discuss?'

She shrugged. 'He told me tales of your history here, your family… He was hoping to see you again before he passed. He struggled to understand why you stayed away so long.'

His brows knitted together and she regretted the words as soon as she'd spoken them. She didn't mean to sound so accusatory.

'I thought I'd made my reasons pretty clear the night of our wedding,' he said darkly.

His words took her back to the moment she'd discovered he'd never wanted to marry her. The moment she'd realised he despised her.

Standing alone, just the two of them, in his room, the air thick between them, he'd turned around and unleashed his wrath on her as he threw his belongings into a satchel. He dismissed the day and all the vows he'd spoken. He told her he never intended to be a real husband, that all he saw in her was a young girl descended from the pagans. And he had determined theirs would be a union in name only.

'You can't ever love me—you loathe me?' she'd questioned him, horrified, a slow curl of dread unfurling through her body.

And he'd coldly reached out and stroked a hand down her face. 'Not half as much as I loathe myself for succumbing to my father's demands and agreeing to marry you.'

'But you saved me once...' she'd gasped.

'I remember. I did not know then that you were a heathen.'

Her breath had lodged in her throat. 'So you would have left me to die had you known?'

He had shrugged and she'd been too stunned to say anything more. She wasn't sure what she'd done that was so bad to warrant such fierce rejection. She'd just watched him pull on his armour, pick up his satchel and leave, and managed to keep her devastation inside until he was gone.

She had berated herself many a time since for foolishly wanting to care for him and hoping that he might one day feel the same. Instead, he had ripped out her heart, saying he didn't want her. He had made it clear, in no uncertain terms, that he couldn't even bear to be in the same fortress as her, let alone the same room.

It had taken a lot of courage for her to get up the next day, swallow down her humiliation and tell the King that Teon had left, after the incredible wedding he had thrown for them.

The people had whispered about her, mocking her, those first few months, and she felt her difference to them in every bone of her body. She'd resorted to keeping herself locked away in her room as much as possible that winter. It was only when a mare had struggled to give birth one night and she had been the only person able to help that things had begun to change. It was around the same time that the first signs of summer began to bloom through the soil and she'd decided she was ready to cast off her cloak of negativity. Over the days and weeks that passed, she had gradually built herself back up again, trusting in whatever her Norse gods had in store for her.

Tentatively, some of the people had sought out her advice and she'd assisted them with the lambing and farming of the cattle that season. Back in Greenland, her father had taught her all he knew about the land and how animals could be of use to them, and she had been glad his teachings were finally coming into their own.

King Edmund had disapproved of her working with the animals at first, saying it was no task for a future queen, but, seeing it was helping to ease her solitude and improving relations between her and the people, he had relented and she'd been so grateful. The harvest that first year had been bountiful and they had celebrated with a huge feast. She had finally felt as if she'd been welcomed into the fold and had carved out a place for herself here. But she had vowed never to forgive Teon for his mistreatment of her.

A serving girl reached over Teon's shoulder and went to top up his tankard, but he covered the cup with his palm and shook his head, smiling up at her. 'I've had enough,' he said. The girl blushed—and Revna's stomach burned.

She had heard rumours of Teon's sexual appetites while he'd been away and she didn't want to acknowledge the peculiar jealousy that ripped through her at the thought of him with another woman. Were the rumours true? They must be! A virile man such as he wouldn't have remained celibate these past eight winters. And yet why should it bother her? She should be glad she'd had a reprieve, shouldn't she?

Bringing herself back to the present, she shrugged. 'Your reasons for leaving sounded more like excuses to me. Excuses that allowed you to run away and put your desire for glory before everything else.'

'Someone has to defend our lands against your people.'

'My people live in peace here. They have done for years!' she replied angrily.

'Now they do. It wasn't always the case, or have you forgotten…?'

Her father had been right about this island—it was a glorious place. The stronghold of Kinborough was built on a hill, dominating the landscape for miles around. She loved the uninterrupted views from the fortress ramparts, looking out over the untamed countryside, which gave way to the muddy creeks that fed into the dark, rolling ocean in the distance.

She enjoyed nothing more than to ride out on her horse, feeling the wind blowing in her hair, or to spend mornings with the animals in the stables. But most of all she liked the fact that she woke up to the same view every day. She had moved around so much with her father, she had craved stability.

'Is that where you've been all this time, trying to stop people coming to these shores who want nothing more than to prosper somewhere new after losing their own homes?'

'I've spent long winters at the eastern garrison, yes. I felt it my personal duty to build new forts against those trying to invade, guarding our borders from those who would seek to plunder or claim our lands as their own.'

'Well, I hope it was worth abandoning your father and your people for...' She had felt that loss as much as the rest of them, if not more, for she had pinned all her hopes and dreams—her future happiness—on him.

'I never abandoned my people, or my father. It was only you I couldn't wait to get away from.'

Her chest squeezed in shock at the disdain behind his words. How could he be so hateful? She wished she could get up and walk out of here, but everyone was watching.

'I was only young—' she whispered.

'Exactly! Just a girl. But one who was still willing to lie with me in my bed in return for wearing a crown.'

She gasped, launching herself from her chair, bristling at the injustice of his scathing words. 'That was never my intention! I didn't even know about such things...how things were between a man and woman...'

His eyes narrowed on her. 'And now you do?'

'Excuse me,' Revna said, moving past him to leave.

'Wait.'

Teon gripped her arm, a sudden and unwanted throb of desire—something he hadn't felt in a very long time—taking him by surprise. It was ridiculous that he should feel this now, with her of all people.

Seemingly stricken, Revna's eyes widened at the contact of his large hand curled around her wrist, but his touch had the desired effect—it halted her departure. Had she felt the same searing heat that had shot through his own body as their skin made contact?

He was no fool. He knew why Revna's father, Ravn, the leader of the tribe of Greenlanders, had facilitated the alliance between them. Ravn wanted to see his bloodline on the royal throne. The chief had agreed that if Revna and Teon married, he and his people would live here in peace, protecting Kinborough's lands rather than destroying them. And the King had conceded. But while Teon had had no choice in the marriage, he could make damned sure he didn't father a child of heathen blood.

'While you've been away, much has changed,' she said.

'Yes… I can see that,' he said, his eyes slowly roaming over her, in a way he had never looked at her back then, and he took wicked delight in seeing her face heat under his gaze.

'I have learned much from the things I've seen, or overheard,' she said. 'I was brought to your room that night by your people, not mine. I came to you in all innocence, hoping you'd be kind, unsure what was expected of me, and instead you were cruel.'

He blinked. Cruel? Who was she to talk about cruelty—when her tribe had delivered his mother's bloodied and lifeless body to the fortress gates? 'How can you say that when it was my principles that protected you that night?' he replied steadily.

His scruples that had prevented him from touching her. *His* values that had sent him away from his home, appalled.

But she was a woman now. And he couldn't deny his interest hadn't been piqued by the new, full swells of her breasts and the sensual curve of her lips. It had his groin hardening. He had the sudden desire to wrap her long hair around his hand and lower his mouth on to hers. And why shouldn't he? He was her husband. Her King. Nothing was stopping him from claiming her if he wanted to... Although the way she was looking at him, with intense scorn in her icy eyes, he had the feeling she would protest—and he wasn't the type of man to force a woman, heathen or not.

He couldn't understand her anger. It seemed unjustified. Surely he had every right to be furious—but why did she? He had saved her life—then protected her from having to bed a man when she was so young. Now she had a position here in the royal household, whereas he had had to suffer her clan attacking them. His mother had been killed. He'd been forced to marry her—a pagan, someone way beneath his position...

He turned her hand over to inspect her fingers. 'Where is your wedding ring?' he asked.

She fiercely pulled herself out of his grasp. 'Where I come from, it is custom for a man and wife to give each other swords, not rings.'

'Ah, but a ring represents our never-ending love. Our unbreakable bond,' he mocked darkly.

She made a small, dismissive sound. 'It signifies

our lives are tied to one another—a contract between our fathers, forged in a tiny gold band. Nothing more. And perhaps I'm not wearing it because I didn't want to see that constant reminder.'

'I'm hurt…' he said disingenuously, rubbing a fake wound in his chest, yet her words hit home. They were bound together, but their rings were more like bonds than tokens of love.

The night his father had told him he had to marry her, for the sake of the realm, had been one of the worst nights of his life. His relationship with his father had already been tested to its limits, like a frozen lake, covered in cracks in the ice, but this demand had been the final break, shattering their bond for good. He'd felt as if his father was trying to ruin his life. First, he'd put his title at risk and now his reputation. And he hadn't given a thought to his son's future happiness…

'Well, as you've made your feelings towards me clear—for the second time—I think it best that now you've returned, we agree to avoid each other whenever possible,' Revna said coolly, bringing his attention back to her.

His eyes blazed into hers. 'Do you?' He had been thinking exactly the same thing on his journey here, yet now he was here he strangely didn't want to let her out of his sight. The thought brought him up short. He tugged her elbow warningly. 'Sit down, Revna.'

He breathed a sigh of relief when she slumped back into the seat. For some reason, she unnerved him. She wasn't like the Saxon women he usually mixed with. She was reluctant to obey—unpredictable. He couldn't be sure how she was going to act.

He glanced around the room to see if anyone was watching them. It wouldn't look good to cause a scene on his first night back here. He needed to be seen to be in charge of his people—and his wife.

Arriving home today, approaching the huge wooden gates that hid the splendour of the stronghold within, he had had mixed emotions. Built on the site of an old Roman fortress, in a commanding position on the mouth of the river, he'd taken in the lone sycamore tree on top of the tower of the keep that had been there for generations, but he'd barely had chance to look around, keen to get into the chapel as soon as possible and make his presence known. But now he allowed himself a moment to draw in the familiar surroundings and relive the memories this stronghold held for him growing up here.

Although the great hall had new animal trophies on the walls, more fire pits smouldering, with some older and some new, unfamiliar faces filling the hand-carved tables around them, he could remember playing in here as a boy, and in the labyrinth of corridors and underground tunnels, his mother gently chastising him for getting his clothes dirty, while his father would allow him to help sharpen his sword. He'd had a happy childhood and had felt safe within these walls. He knew most of the people who lived within the battlements and on the surrounding lands.

But by the time he'd turned seventeen, he couldn't wait to leave. His relationship with his father had become strained and his mother had suddenly been taken from them, leaving a gaping big hole. He hadn't cared for the gatherings of the witan—instead, he'd longed for adventure and glory, wanting to prove himself on the battlefield as a warrior and leader of men. And he definitely hadn't wanted to be married—especially not to Revna. He could never care for one of their kind...

But her attack on his absence—on him not being there for his father—had cut deep. He'd wanted to demonstrate his worth as a king, so the people would think he was deserving of the crown when his time to ascend the throne came. But was she right? Had they all held him in contempt for staying away so long, as she clearly did? Why did she care?

It felt strange that his father was no longer among them. Grief had sent Teon away from here and grief had brought him back. The King had left a huge void and now everyone was looking to him. Even though the weight of that responsibility lay heavy on his shoulders, he felt a lot more ready to lead than he had eight years ago. Now he had the trust and loyalty of his men and he knew he could take on anything, even the woman sat beside him—in his mother's old chair.

She was looking everywhere but at him, absent-mindedly pushing the food around on her plate with her spoon, the beads around her wrists jingling, and she kept twisting her peculiar-looking necklace in her other hand. Sitting on the edge of the chair, her shoulders straight and back, her knees pressed together, he could feel the tension rolling off her.

As he ate his own meal, he tried to swallow down his anger—and the peculiar waves of lust coursing through his body. He knew that his main duty as monarch, as well as protecting his people and his kingdom, was to bear a son. His father spoke often of continuing their Saxon line, of leaving a legacy, creating a dynasty. 'Produce an heir. Strengthen our bloodline,' he'd say.

Despite his father having tainted the institution of marriage for him, Teon had imagined he would one day marry a respectable Saxon lady—the daughter of a great lord—and have children. He couldn't see how aligning their house with Greenlanders would strengthen them, so he'd stubbornly made a vow to himself. He had determined his throne would pass to his sisters when he died, for no child of his would be born of heathen blood to later take on the Saxon throne.

Yet frustratingly, knowing Revna was a pagan wasn't hindering his unexpected attraction to her now. It was strange... He'd tried to forget he was even married when he'd returned here, until Revna had stepped forward and he'd heard her softly spoken words in the church. Her voice was annoyingly appealing to the ear. And when he'd seen her, he'd done a double take.

Foolishly, he hadn't once considered that he would return to find her a grown woman—and a beautiful one at that. In his mind, she had remained a gangly, plain young girl. He'd thought perhaps he could push her aside, ignore her existence and their union. But, no, now he was suddenly—excruciatingly—aware of her. He didn't want to desire her, yet when their fingers or knees touched he burned. Perhaps he had just gone too damned long without a woman.

He sighed, trying to calm himself, and attempted to soften his tone a little. 'So what have you been doing here all this while?' he asked.

She turned to him, her eyes narrowing, as if suspicious of his question.

'How have you been spending your days?' he added.

'I have taken care of your sisters, raising them to be fine young maidens.'

'Fine young maidens who fight... Tell me, do they go to ale houses and ride their horses side saddle, too?' He smirked, unable to help himself.

'If I had my way they would.' She took a long, large sip of her drink, draining her cup, as if to prove it.

He raised his brow. 'I'm sure. Tell me, do you always wear your hair like that?' She had changed out of her mourning attire and into a bright, exotic-looking pinafore and tunic, and the colours, the material—even the detailing—screamed her difference, making her stand out. Yet she seemed unbothered by what others thought—even him. It irritated him. He had noticed the way the men looked at her with interest now, not mockery, and he didn't like it. It made him want to put her in her place.

'Like what?'

'As you're married, shouldn't you have it covered up?'

'I like it like this.' She ran her fingertips through

her loose curls, before defiantly flicking her long locks over her shoulder.

His eyes flashed.

'Have you *ever* tried to fit in here?' he asked.

'Actually, yes,' she said. 'I've studied your people and your customs, your language and religions, and I've helped to manage the running of your father's stronghold…'

'Yes, you mentioned sitting in on my father's witan.' His mouth formed a hard line.

'He felt it important I learn and…'

'And what…?'

'He wasn't sure you would return. He wasn't sure you had the predilection for kingship.'

'He thought you might rule in my stead?' he asked, his anger threatening to return with force.

'No,' she said, shaking her head, a tiny frown crumpling her smooth forehead. 'Of course not. But he thought it would be useful for me to be informed about things. I can't be sure why he made the choices he did.'

'He has been known to make bad ones before. Our marriage is a good example.'

She shook her head. 'I can't understand why you went ahead with it then, especially if you knew it would make us both miserable.'

She pushed out her chair, standing abruptly, her back rigid, and this time was quick to move out of his reach. 'I think I've had enough of all this for one night. I've got a headache. I'm going to go to bed.'

Visions of her lying on animal skins, her hair and

body splayed out on the furs, entered his mind before he could halt them and the irony wasn't lost on him. He'd turned her down on their wedding night, never wanting to see her again—and now he couldn't take his eyes off her. He wanted her, he admitted to himself—not that he would ever act on his desires. He'd made a pledge to himself—and his late mother.

'*Our* bed?' he mocked, flashing a cold smile of insincerity.

'There is no such thing,' she said. 'Fortunately, I had another room made up eight years ago. And you'll be pleased to hear it is far, far away from yours, so we can put as much distance between us as possible.'

Chapter Three

The light rapping sound on Revna's door had her sitting bolt upright in bed. Panic thundered through her. Was it Teon? Had he come to claim her?

She had barely slept, the noise of all the merriment in the hall going on long into the night, keeping her awake. Or was it Teon's deep, mocking eyes and his taunting words running through her mind that had made her toss and turn, thoughts of him coming along the corridor to find her in the dark hours? Suddenly her room didn't feel like such a sanctuary.

She couldn't believe she'd spoken back to him, tossed her hair at him, then walked out on him in front of all his people. But if she was honest with herself, she'd wanted to provoke him, to cause some kind of reaction. And she couldn't deny it hadn't pleased her when she'd seen his eyes widen in surprise.

Revna dashed out of bed and swiped up her robe off the floor, tugging it tightly around her. She padded over to the door and pulled it ajar slightly.

With relief, she saw that it wasn't Teon. Instead, Edlynne stood there, furtively looking up and down the corridor.

'Is everything all right?' Revna asked.

'My brother told me not to disturb you,' Edlynne said, blushing guiltily. 'But I thought you should know… He's called a meeting with the witan this morning. It's already started.'

Betrayal ripped through her. How could the witan have a meeting without her? Had they cast her aside so quickly now Teon had returned? She felt wounded. When her mother had died, she'd spent months in the company of her father and his friends as they'd crossed the ocean, visiting strange lands. She'd had to toughen up, fast, and learn how to deal with men. She had thought she'd won over the King's councillors, yet deep down, she knew it wasn't them but Teon who was to blame.

He hadn't always been this cruel. There had been a time when he'd been kind, when he had come to her rescue.

She thought back to what he'd said last night about her being just a child when they had wed. She had believed he was disgusted by her heritage, but had he also refrained from touching her because she was young? Had he really been protecting her, again? Even if that was true, he was more than making up for it by being mean now.

Well, she wouldn't stand for this. She had earned the King's trust and worked hard to command the council's respect—she couldn't let Teon ruin it. She had come to care deeply about the people of Kinborough these past few years. Where had he been while she'd felt the weight of responsibility for their safety these past weeks? Determination settled in her stomach.

Slipping on her mother's black silk kirtle and red *hangerok*, she quickly secured it with brooches and ran a comb through her long locks, before heading in the direction of the grand hall. She often wore her mother's clothes—they were bright and beautiful, made out of flamboyant, exotic silks she'd bought from a market in Hvalsey in Greenland—and it made her feel as if she was holding on to a bit of her heritage and her homeland. She never wanted to forget the woman who had raised her—and the garments made her feel less invisible, giving her the confidence she needed right now. She didn't care what Teon thought about them.

Sweeping along the corridor and bursting through the doors to the hall, she found twenty men, some of whom she had come to know well from the previous meetings of the witan, and some she recognised as Teon's warriors, who had been at his side as they'd erupted into the chapel the day before.

They all turned to stare at her, some guiltily rising out of their seats, giving her apologetic glances, and for a moment she wavered. But she dug deep for her courage and held her head up high as she approached the table and, one by one, she lanced each of the lords with a look. She would not allow them to dismiss her so quickly. She saved her last challenging glare for the

Saxon Prince sat at the head of the table and steeled herself, ready for a fight.

He was dominating the proceedings, his large, imposing frame commanding attention, and as their eyes met, his mocked her with condescension. A bolt of unexpected heat struck low in her belly and she thought it must be anger stirring within her.

He was dressed in the same clothes as last night, his hair still unruly—had he even been to bed? Surely not someone else's?

'Prince Teon. My lords. Good morning. Excuse my tardiness, but I don't believe I was told we were gathering.'

Teon's gaze bore into her, but she would not let him know he unsettled her. 'That's because it's unnecessary for you to be here. Not now I've returned.' He was determined not to recognise her position on the council.

'Nevertheless, I made a promise to your father. He asked me to be part of his witan and I shall uphold my promise until there is a new king—just in case the Prince should go missing again.'

Laughter echoed around the room, but she didn't move her eyes from his. A muscle flickered in his jaw.

'That's exactly what we were just talking about— Prince Teon's coronation,' Lord Cenhelm said, stepping forward to acknowledge her.

'Then do continue. There's no need to stop on my behalf.' She lowered herself into a chair and they all did the same, anxiously looking between her and the Prince.

Teon seemed to weigh up whether to proceed or

not, drawing a hand over his thickened beard, and then sighed. 'We are discussing bringing the ceremony forward. Disturbingly, we have received word from Harold of Karamble declaring he should be the next King of Kinborough,' he said, reluctantly filling her in.

'But that's absurd,' she said fiercely, sitting forward in her seat, slightly emboldened by the fact he had shared this information with her. 'You are legitimately the next in line.'

'Still, it seems Harold is prepared to fight for his right to be so, gathering support in many of the burghs, building an army.'

'Perhaps now might be a good time for me to mention that Lady Revna has been advocating for the witan to send for reinforcements since your father became unwell, Prince Teon. To unite our allies and strengthen our walls,' Lord Cenhelm said and she was grateful for his support.

Teon's gaze lanced her, his eyebrows raised in surprise. 'Reinforcements from whom?'

'My father, among others.'

In the eight years that had passed since she'd come to live here, she had only seen her father a handful of times—when she had ridden out to see him at his settlement, or traversed the old tunnels beneath the fortress. He had never been to the Saxon stronghold to visit her. That had hurt. At first, she had felt ostracised—she'd thought perhaps he'd been glad to be rid of her. But he was always pleased to see her when she went there. And she knew he would uphold his end of the bargain if they ever needed him and his men. Lost in his grief, he might not have known how to be the best father to her after her mother died, but he had always been a forthright and honest man. She liked to think she had inherited some of those qualities.

Teon scowled. 'We don't need or want your father's help. I'm home now, with my own army. My men, together with my father's, shall clear up the mess that you've made since the King became sick. It is just unfortunate that rather than taking the throne peacefully, I now have to subdue my rivals first,' he said, a superior, hard edge to his voice and she felt as though he'd ignore her opinion, refuse her input, whatever she suggested.

'That shouldn't be too hard for a man who has spent the past eight winters wielding his sword,' she retorted, the heat roiling in her stomach.

'It won't be,' he said, arrogance pouring off him. 'But it wouldn't be necessary if you had carried out the most important of tasks—to secure any usurpers and control their movements before something like this could happen.' He seemed determined to belittle her.

'It wouldn't have been necessary if you'd been here in the first place,' Revna snapped back.

'My lady,' Lord Cenhelm choked, standing suddenly, as if to put a barrier between them.

Teon turned away from her, purposely ignoring her, and instead directed his words at his men. 'My lords, would you mind giving my wife and me a moment alone?'

* * *

Teon clenched his fists as he dismissed the lords of the witan and they slowly made their way out of the hall, sharing uncomfortable glances, leaving him and Revna alone at opposite ends of the table. He still couldn't believe she'd walked out on him last night, showing everyone in the hall he wasn't worth her time or attention, and in return, he'd relished the small satisfaction he'd felt when he'd managed to gather the royal council together while she still slept. For some reason he wanted to annoy her, as she infuriated him. How dare she speak to him in that way in front of his council?

She made an exaggerated sigh, her beautiful blue eyes rolling in her upturned face. 'Was that really necessary? To send them all away?' Her direct manner, the strength in her voice, surprised him.

He hadn't missed the way the men had gawked at her as she'd determinedly walked in, her beads tinkling at her wrists, with an almost deliberate sway to her hips that had their eyes raking over her—and it bothered him. Yet he couldn't blame them—she was stunning. She looked different to all the Saxon women he knew—she had her own unique style, as if she was proud of her heritage. It drew attention. Was that what she intended? He had the feeling she knew married women were meant to keep their hair covered—and tightly tied in braids—yet despite this she wore her locks loose, flowing freely in gentle, cascading waves down her back. Why did she insist on standing out? And why did he find it so captivating?

'I think so, yes.' He couldn't have her being so blatantly disrespectful, yet he found himself battling feelings of both hate and longing all at once. Lack of sleep didn't help. He'd barely slept last night. The words she'd thrown at him about their marriage bed had made him throb with desire, knowing she was in one of the other rooms down the corridor and wondering how a woman whom he despised—loathed everything about—could trigger such heated feelings. Was it because he'd decided not to bed her that his body was taunting him so?

Even now, her intoxicating floral scent was wrapping around him, affecting him. And despite his irritation that she had barged in here, making an impact, he found her determination not to be pushed aside by him and the council admirable, although maddening. She was a stronger woman than he'd given her credit for.

But what were her motives?

'I don't know what you expected me to do. I couldn't exactly round up all the lords of the neighbouring burghs on the off chance they might steal your crown. I did send guards to watch Harold… But I don't understand,' she said, shaking her head. 'He may have a blood tie, but he is illegitimate, none the less.'

His whole body stiffened, the shame and humiliation his father had caused exploding inside him, causing him to rise out of his seat and take a deathly step towards her. 'And just how do you know about that?' he said darkly.

'Your father told me.'

He struggled to hide his shock. Such things were never discussed. He himself had only discovered that he had a half-brother when he overheard his mother and father in heated conversation one night. He had been on the cusp of manhood, wanting to be just like his father when he was older—and in a single moment his world had been shattered. He'd almost wished he hadn't crept along the corridor to the kitchen to sneak some bread, as then he wouldn't have seen their door was ajar, he wouldn't have heard their angry words.

He had wanted to put his hands over his ears like a child and shake it all away the moment he'd realised what was being said, but it was too late. He had uncovered his father's shameful secret. It had devastated him to discover the King had not just had a mistress, but one who had borne him a son.

His parents had turned to see him standing there in the doorway and his father had hung his head in shame, while his mother had stepped forward, attempting to make excuses for her husband, trying to console Teon. But her words hadn't helped. His father had a second family and it had felt like such a betrayal, the implications for the future stability of his kingdom great. In Teon's eyes, the great King of Kinborough had jeopardised his leadership, his family—and his son's title.

The King and Queen's relationship had seemed broken beyond repair after that and Teon had become closer to his mother, wanting to look after her and protect her. And he'd begun to see his father differently, all his flaws. He no longer thought of him as perfect or a man to look up to. His feelings towards him had been conflicted. He loved him, but had found it harder to trust and respect him.

He couldn't fathom how the King had chosen to spend time with another woman and their son over him and his mother. It had shaken Teon's beliefs about marriage and love and family. And he hadn't even been able to talk to anyone about it, as the whole situation had become their family's dirty secret that he was forced to keep. It was never to be repeated.

'That is not common knowledge. And never to leave your lips,' he thundered. 'Besides, my father always asserted it was untrue.' Publicly, anyway.

'Of course I wouldn't speak of such things... I would never give weight to the rumours. But I don't understand... I can see how an empty throne would be an appealing target, but why would Harold do this now you're here? He knows you are the legal heir and that his own prospects are limited. Children born out of wedlock can't claim the throne. Does he resent you for your upbringing?'

'Considering you seem to be enlightened to so many of my family's affairs, do you really not know why?' His voice was laced with danger as he came around the table towards her.

'No.'

He closed the distance between them, his hand coming up to take her chin between his fingers. 'Some would say a bastard son of the King might be a preferable choice for the crown to a legitimate son who is married to a heathen.'

Her perfect lips parted on a gasp of shock. 'What? No!' she protested.

'Yes. Many believe I should lose my right to succession because you're my wife, Revna.'

She shook her head, seemingly appalled. 'And what do you think?' she whispered.

'I think they have a point... People don't want to see you on the throne of England. It has aggravated tensions between the burghs.'

'But I don't even want to be Queen!' she snapped, jerking herself away from his touch. 'Despite what you might think, I never coveted the throne.'

'It's a little late to put up false protests. I believe that's all your father had in mind when he tethered you to me.'

She recoiled from his wrath. 'Don't judge me on my father's plans. His ambitions were never mine. I never asked for this. I didn't want to be handed over to Saxon strangers as a peace weaver, to secure my father's lineage in a place far away from my home. I did not want to marry a man I did not care for, only to be abandoned and ignored once I'd gone through with it. Like you, I had no choice!'

Her searing honesty and uncomplimentary words sliced through him, unsettling him, and he stood there, his hands on his hips, glowering down at her. He had never met a woman who hadn't wanted to marry him before—or at least one who had the gall to tell him so!

But when he stared down into her crystal-clear blue eyes, he knew she meant it and, for a moment, he felt off balance, stunned. Was she really just an innocent bystander in all this, as he had been? Had he judged her too quickly, believing she had a hidden motive for being here? He had always assumed she had had a say in her father's plans.

'Then why did you?' he asked.

'Probably for the same reasons you went along with it, too. In marrying you, I protected my people, giving them a safe home here. It was a small price to pay for my own happiness. And when I realised it was you—the man who'd saved me once—I wrongly believed you might be kind. But,' she said, swiping her hand through the air, as if to draw a line under what she had just said, 'if I am the cause of all your problems, then why don't you just let me go, release me? Send me away from here? It might be preferable to living with someone who can't stand the sight of me.'

He searched her face. That wasn't exactly true, he thought. The sight of her was most definitely troubling, but mainly because she was so exquisite, he couldn't take his eyes off her. She stirred something inside him, making him want to reach out and touch her. And he had—and her skin was even softer than it looked.

'I will not break the rules of the church,' he said.

She shook her head. 'I don't believe in your God or the laws of your church. I'm a pagan, as you keep reminding me.'

'You'd better not let anyone hear you say that,' he said darkly, reaching out to take the pendant of her necklace between his fingers, turning it over in his hand, inspecting it. It had three strands around the neck, with beads of multi-coloured glass and seashells. And hanging down in the middle was a peculiar-looking symbol. 'And you should keep such trinkets representing your heritage tucked away, out of sight.'

She snatched the totem out of his grasp.

'You and your father knew who I was when you agreed to the alliance. I will not apologise for who I am.' He could see that, in the way she wore her clothes and Norse jewellery with pride, the row of unusual bangles covering her delicate wrists, the jingling sound signalling her presence. 'Besides... I thought divorce was allowed in cases of adultery.'

He took a step towards her, invading her space, anger rumbling through him, causing his brows to knit together. 'Why, have you been unfaithful, Revna?'

'I wasn't talking about me!' she retorted. 'I have heard the rumours of...of...'

'Of what?' His voice was like acid.

'Of your disreputable sexual morals while you've been away!' She flushed.

Her words about sexual acts made his groin harden and he had the crazy desire to kiss her, to silence her enraging accusations.

'People always say sons tend to inherit the characteristics of their fathers,' she added, tilting her chin up.

'You shouldn't believe all you hear,' he said. He didn't think he'd ever been so incensed.

She went to protest and he put his finger across her lips, silencing her retort. 'No. There will be no divorce, Revna, for if I did so, I would be breaking the

alliance your father and my father made and your people would declare war on these lands…*again*. I would
simply be exchanging Harold's army for another…'

'And there I was, thinking the *King* could do whatever he liked…' she said, moving to brush past him.

In that moment, he wanted to show her he could.
He was so worked up, a mixture of fury and lust taking over his sanity. 'I can,' he said, taking her arm
and spinning her round, tugging her into his pounding
chest, hard. Before she could protest, his hot mouth
captured hers. He thought she might kick him, or hit
him—put up a fight and resist—and he told himself
if she had, he would have laughed and let her go.

But instead, the instant his lips met hers, his hand
delving into her beautiful butter-like hair to hold her
face against his, she seemed to sink into him, giving in, and as her yielding lips parted and his tongue
swept inside, her surrender rocked him to the core.

It had started in anger. He'd wanted to punish her,
to show her he was in control, but as he ravaged her
mouth with his, her pert breasts thrust against him,
his body ignited in desire and he knew he'd lost all
constraint. He couldn't be further from being in control. He didn't want to feel this way. He had sworn to
hate her. And yet he also never ever wanted the kiss
to end, wanting to get lost in it.

He held her fast around the waist, tugging her into
his stomach, crushing her lips harder as he captured
her tongue with his, until it felt as if the ground was
giving way, rumbling beneath his feet, breaking them
apart. Teon stepped away, staring down at her, his

breathing ragged. He felt disorientated. What had just happened? And then an almighty blast, followed by a loud boom, had them staggering backwards.

'What was that?' Revna gasped, her cheeks heated, her hand rising to her lips.

The kiss or the explosion? He wasn't sure, but he felt as shaken as she looked.

Teon's right-hand man, Bordan, came rushing in. 'Teon! Come quickly! We're under attack.'

Alarm escalated inside him. He instinctively reached for his sword and followed his man towards the doors of the hall, but he couldn't decide if he was more disturbed by the news of the attack, or the feelings that had sprung to life within him on taking Revna in his arms and pressing his body against hers.

He glanced back over his shoulder to order her to stay where she was, but he was too late—she was right behind him, following him out into the winter sun, into the courtyard and up the uneven stone steps. Reaching the top of the ramparts, he heard her inhale of shock as they took in the alarming sight before them. Stretched out across their lands, on the outside of the royal fortress walls, were hundreds of men in formation, heading straight for them. All around them in every direction, farmsteads and crops were burning and people were running for their lives.

Kinborough was under siege.

Teon felt his whole body tense, his blood ice over as he took in the imminent danger his fortress and his people were in. How had this enemy got here, unseen and unheard? In the eight years he'd been at the garrison, the barbican had never been overrun. Now, in the space of one day of him being in charge here, the fortress was under attack. Had he brought this upon his people?

Damn Revna, for she had distracted him—and now look what had happened. He had missed an entire army approaching his gates, such was her allure. Now his people were at risk.

He had been in many battles, but an attack on his home brought back images of the last time the stronghold had been ambushed—by the Greenland people. *Her* people. And he was disgusted at his weakness that he'd just kissed her.

Yet Revna, too, looked sickened, her skin turning ashen. 'Is it Harold?' she whispered, in horrified disbelief. 'Come already?'

'Yes,' Bordan confirmed.

'He's acted quicker than we thought.' Teon grimaced.

'We think there are at least a few hundred or so men advancing,' Bordan said. 'Perhaps fifty or so already here.'

'Why were we not warned by the nightwatchmen?'

'They're all dead,' Bordan said. 'No sentinel has been left alive to warn us. And Harold's men... They are calling for you to come to the bridge,' he said to Teon.

'Perhaps you can talk to him? Maybe he'll see reason?' Revna asked.

Teon nodded, his lips forming a hard, determined line.

'Let's go. But, Revna—keep quiet, lay low and stay out of sight. I can't yet be sure what his intentions are.'

They hurried along the battlement pathway and when they reached the parapet of the guard tower, above Kinborough's sturdy wooden gates, which were being pounded by an enormous tree trunk and twenty men, Teon called out for a ceasefire, announcing he wanted to talk to their leader.

He stood tall, courageously not even trying to conceal himself from view as he looked out over the expanse below. He couldn't believe the harrowing scene before him. He felt helpless, watching his people in trouble. And then he saw a lone figure, surrounded by a shield wall of men, come cantering across the burning fields on his horse, amid a swirling mist of smoke. Teon's eyes narrowed, trying to get a better view of the rider.

He stopped at a distance away, looking unfazed atop his mare, and Teon recognised him instantly. He hadn't seen him in many winters, but seeing his straight, prominent nose, just like their father's, there was no doubt about it—it was indeed his half-brother, Harold. Shock tore through him. There was no love lost between them, but how could he do this, especially when their father's body was not yet cold in the ground? How long had he been planning it, considering he'd raised such an impressive army? Anger unfurled in his stomach. How could all these men stand by him? Did they really want Harold to be King over him? Their disloyalty smarted.

Peering down at the man, Teon saw he was certainly no match for him. He was no fierce warrior. But his heavy brow showed no emotion—he was cold, unfeeling, not caring about the devastation he was causing around him. Teon couldn't believe he'd already burned down homes, destroying crops, killing innocent people. Women and children. Teon looked for any signs of resemblance between them and, fortunately, saw none. Evil must run through Harold's blood on his mother's side.

Teon stepped forward, bracing his hands on the crenelated wall. 'Harold, what is the meaning of this?' he asked, projecting his voice out over the landscape before him.

'Ah, *Brother*,' Harold said, pulling on the reins, trying to steady his horse. 'There you are. I had expected you would be hiding, cowering from me.' He sneered menacingly. 'For you must know I have come to take possession of your wife, your throne and your fortress.'

Teon saw Revna flinch beside him, hidden from view, and cold rage ripped through him. 'Your men will die trying. You cannot hope to take this stronghold by force. It has never been achieved.'

'Then it shall be a challenge I shall very much enjoy,' the man countered.

'You wish to throw arrows and rocks into the royal fortress? You wish to knock it down? Shame on you. The King will be turning in his grave.'

'Fortunately for me, I have never sought *our* father's approval. As Kinborough was never allowed to be my home, I shall get a great deal of satisfaction from watching it crumble.'

'You are no brother of mine. To come all this way

with such an army—it is treason. You will be hanged for this.'

'If I lose. But then again, you might… There is an alternative to us attacking the fortress, Brother.' He sneered. 'A way to save yourself and your people. Tell your men to stand down and hand over your crown— or your wife. You must know the people do not want a heathen on the throne,' Harold insisted.

Revna drew in a breath of dismay beside him and Teon felt a coil of dread spread through his own body.

'If you do so, I will leave your precious fortress and those within it unharmed. But until you comply, I will order my men to start tearing the place apart…'

And as if to prove it, he lifted his hand. When he lowered it, a cascade of arrows was released and came arching over the walls, whistling past their ears. Instinctively, Teon launched himself on top of Revna, backing her up against the granite walls, shielding her from harm, as they all looked down in horror at the people in the courtyard, oblivious as to what was to come. He saw Revna squeeze her eyes shut, unable to watch. They heard the gentle thud, one after another, of bodies falling under the force of the wooden darts.

Revna was so close, when she opened her beautiful blue eyes he could see they were dilated with fear. Her fingers gently pressed against his chest. 'Teon, you must hand me over,' she whispered. 'I don't want anyone to get hurt because of me.'

What? Surely she wasn't willing to sacrifice herself for his people?

'No!'

'But—'

'I will not give in to Harold's demands, I'm much too stubborn for that,' he bit out furiously. 'He will not be rewarded for threatening his King and the people with violence. Now stay down.'

'But I can't go through this again...' She shuddered beneath him.

'Again?' Had she been in a situation like this before? He realised he knew nothing about her. His wife...

'Not if I can prevent it...' she whispered.

He brought himself upright, determinedly deciding on his course of action, then turned his mutinous face back to the soldiers lining up on his lands, encircling the fortress under a troubled red morning sky.

'If I hand over my wife, you'll just leave?' he asked Harold, aware of Revna swallowing beside him. He felt her eyes on him.

'Yes.' Harold grinned.

'I don't believe you,' Teon spat out. 'And even if I did, that is something I'd never do.'

'Don't tell me you have feelings for the heathen?' Harold mocked.

Feelings... He didn't know how he felt about her, especially after that potent kiss moments ago, but he did know he wasn't prepared to give her up. He would not be handing her over to Harold or anyone else any time soon.

'I don't believe you'll stop until you get what you want, Harold. But then, neither will I. No,' he said, shaking his head, 'there will be no deal. If you want a fight, you shall get one, but be warned—you will never win this war you're waging.'

He turned on his heel, grabbed Revna by the arm, hoisting her up, and charged along the battlements. He needed to get her inside. He needed to get his men ready. He could see by the glint in Harold's eyes that he would stop at nothing to get himself on the throne. And before they'd even reached the steps, the sound of the battering ram came thundering against the gates again, even louder and more forceful than before.

'Will they breach the walls?' she gasped, moving quickly beside him.

'Not if I can help it. No one's broken through these walls in sixty winters. They're practically impregnable. Bordan, ready the men. Revna, go back inside,' he commanded her, turning to go.

'But I can help…' she protested. 'I know how to wield a sword.'

'No!' he said, turning back to face her, swiping a hand over his face. He could still taste her on his tongue, still feel the swells of her soft breasts crushed against him. He couldn't imagine her fighting. No. He needed to get her out of sight, out of mind, to safety, so he could focus. 'Do as I say. If they find you, they'll…'

She shuddered. 'Wouldn't that solve all your problems?'

He pinched the bridge of his nose. 'Just…stay inside, Revna.'

The morning had started off terribly with Teon gathering the witan without her, but Revna had never imagined how awful it would get. And there was no way she could just stand aside and do nothing. All about her, children and livestock were running around the fortress square in panic, searching for their loved ones, hoping for rescue amid the chaos and confusion. People were trying to escape falling buildings, salvaging what they could of their belongings, and she knew she had to disobey Teon's orders and help.

Racing down the steps and back into the keep, she ran to her room and found her mother's sword. Heading back to the courtyard, she beckoned the women and children into the hall, crowding them inside, lining the corridors, filling every space available.

Boulders were being slung over the palisades, blasting into farmsteads, bombarding the walls, causing the ground to shake. There was a constant rainfall of arrows and lifeless bodies already lay scattered about the place.

Thankfully, Teon had acted quickly—he already had his father's army lining up in the square, ready to greet Harold's forces if they were to break through the gates, and she held her breath as she saw his own men were firing spears from the battlements and pouring hot ale on enemy soldiers below.

It was like something straight out of her nightmares, ripped right out of her past.

When she'd seen Harold's army, those images of what could be flashed through her mind. She'd lived through a siege like this before and, once again, it was a scene that she'd never forget. One of devastation and destruction, the men fighting brutally for their lives, the fortress in a state of disarray, terrifying sounds coming from every direction.

She scanned the battlements for Teon and her eyes found him on the bridge. He stood solidly, at the ready, his legs wide apart, fiercely commanding his men. He held a large wooden shield with the symbol of a stag on it, symbolic of his power and authority—and she hoped the Valkyries were watching over him, for despite his harsh treatment of her until now, she still didn't want him to get hurt.

She felt shaken—she hadn't been in the midst of a fight like this for years, yet she knew her troubled feelings had a lot to do with the man up there fighting for his home and his people and the kiss they had shared in the hall. She had felt his anger behind it, of course she had! It had been meant as a display of power. He had wanted to show her that he could do what he wanted, that it was his right to claim her mouth with his.

She should have objected, pushed him away, but when his lips had met hers, she had been helpless to resist him. She had never been kissed before and it had felt…good. A strange excitement and pleasure had taken over and she'd opened her mouth and kissed him back, pressing herself up against his rock-hard body, as his hands had tightened around her waist, and she'd forgotten all else. But now look where it had got them.

She couldn't understand—if he despised her, why had he saved her once again, why hadn't he given her up?

Seeing a lone foal, stranded in the middle of the courtyard, its eyes wide and nostrils flared, whinnying in fear, Revna picked her moment between the showers of arrows to race towards it. Reaching the animal, she gripped the rope around its neck and guided it back over to the stables, out of immediate danger, securing him tightly.

When she made it back to the square, she spotted one of Harold's men trying to scramble over the top of the outer walls and her heart clamoured in her chest. She glanced across at Teon, but he and his men were looking the other way, oblivious. She realised with dread that if he were to succeed, he would be able to approach Teon and his men from the back of the ramparts, taking them by surprise. There was nothing for it—without stopping to think, she rushed up the stone steps to engage the man and stop his progress and he almost faltered when he saw a wild woman wielding a sword charging towards him.

She knew it was unusual for the women of these lands to be seen on the battlefield, but her father had taught her how to fight when she was young, and she'd had to put what she'd learned into practice when their home in Hvalsey had been attacked. But she was still afraid—of the things she'd seen and done before and whether she'd be successful now. But she had to try.

As the man's sword struck hers, she winced at the ferociousness of his blow as metal clashed against metal, but she quickly swung her blade and jabbed, then ducked, moving out of his reach. He was a large man, he could easily overpower her, but she was quick on her feet and skilful with her weapon. He brought his sword down hard again and she defended herself, managing to shove him backwards, but he was back on his feet in moments, bearing down on her, and she readied herself to go again. She raised her sword and steeled herself for another slashing, when he was pulled away with force and he disappeared over the side of the walls.

Teon's wide, astonished but furious eyes met hers. 'What the hell do you think you're doing?' he roared.

'Helping you! I didn't think you'd seen him! I didn't need you to come to my rescue!'

'You're unbelievable!' he barked in angry admiration, his hand curling around her arm and propelling her down the steps once more. 'He could have killed you! I told you to stay inside,' he thundered.

She fiercely pulled herself out of his grasp. 'And I told you I could fight.'

'I don't want you out here fighting! I don't need to be worrying about you when all this is going on. Why can't you understand that and do as you're told for once? Now go!' he said, flinging her inside the keep and forcefully pulling the doors shut behind her.

Resting her back against the wood, she took a moment to gather her breath and her bearings. She had never seen the hall in such disarray. Glancing around, she took in the frightened eyes of the women and children, huddled together, scared, crying for those unaccounted for, fearful for their men fighting outside, all the while listening to the incessant din of the battering ram hammering against the gate, weapons clanging and the guttural roars of the soldiers in the throes of battle. What would become of them all if the enemy breached the walls? If one man had achieved it, couldn't more?

Knowing she had to be useful and keep busy, trying not to think of all the awful possible outcomes, Revna tasked Edlynne and Eldrida with handing out blankets and furs to those who had lost all their possessions, passing round water and bread and tending to those who were hurt. But not knowing what was going on outside unsettled her far more than actually being able to see how the battle was unfolding.

The day dragged on and on, the tension thick and cloying, and when the doors finally swung open, families cried out in fear, thinking the enemy might have broken through. The people all seemed to sigh in collective relief when they saw it was Teon and his men, some wounded, being helped into the hall. Many of the soldiers sought out their women and children, embracing them, while others had to share news to those whose husbands or fathers had fallen amid the combat.

It was a poignant sight, but Revna was focused on Teon. Taking in the chaos of the grand hall, where many kings had ruled before him, he strode past all the people before stopping at the raised platform, unkempt from the day's fighting. Seeing the strain on his face, she sensed his mood was black. She thought he was going to leave the room and disappear down the corridor, when he hesitated, as if realising he needed to address the room and say something to his people. He gently brought the hilt of his sword down on a table, demanding silence so he could speak.

'People of Kinborough,' he said. 'In a surprise attack this morning, the castle was besieged by Harold of Karamble's forces.' He raked a hand through his hair. 'We have sustained heavy losses and their troops have our walls surrounded. For now, it seems we are imprisoned in our own stronghold.' Whispers and mutterings rumbled around the room.

'We have fortified the fortress and dampened our roofs in case of fire. We shall allocate duties and tasks imminently, but for now, I advise all women and children to stay inside.'

Then he turned and was gone, leaving the people to turn to each other and talk between themselves.

Cautiously, Revna followed him and saw him enter his father's library. Reaching the doorway, she watched as she saw him pull down a huge hanging of his father off the wall, tossing it to the ground in anger.

'Damn you and your promiscuity!' he raved at the portrait. 'Look what it's caused!'

'Teon?' she asked softly.

'Damn you to hell,' he cursed again, swiping all his father's writings and journals off the table and on to the floor. She could tell he was livid—and probably in shock. They all were.

'Teon, stop it,' she said, coming into the room, forcing him to notice her. 'The people are really scared. If they see you like this, it won't help. Teon, please.'

He swung to look at her, a wild look in his eyes.

'What happened?' she whispered.

'You saw what happened!' he raged. 'They killed a quarter of my men already! Destroyed their homes. And they were good men—with wives, children. None of this would have happened if my father had kept his hands to himself. If he'd remained faithful to me and my mother… But instead, his actions have rocked the stability of our kingdom, the safety of our people— and my title.'

'I'm so sorry,' she said.

'They've burned all our crops… All the villagers' farmsteads on the outer lands are gone—razed to the ground,' he said, shaking his head in despair. Just like that,' he said, clicking his fingers. 'It will take years to recover. There are bodies everywhere…'

'Are we completely surrounded?' she asked.

'Yes. They'll be sure to prevent food, water and supplies from getting in.' He dragged a hand over his face. 'I can't believe Harold—my father's own son— could do this. The day after his funeral.'

'Is it worth trying to talk to him again?' Revna asked carefully.

'No.' Teon shook his head, lifting himself off the table and standing tall. He turned to face her. 'It's too late for that.'

'He is your…'

'Revna,' he warned. 'He was never my brother. And he is already beyond reason.'

She swallowed. 'You could still hand me over.'

'No!'

'Teon, I don't want people to die because of me,' she said, taking a step towards him, placing her hand on his arm, trying to get him to listen.

He leaned back against the table, drawing a breath, and stared down at her fingers curled over his leather bracer. 'This is Harold's doing, not yours, Revna,' he conceded.

And she thought that was the nicest thing he'd ever said to her.

'You think he'll stop if I hand you over? He won't,' he said, his brow furrowing. 'If he gets what he wants, he'll just push for more. He won't stop until he's sitting on the throne.'

She threw her hands up in despair. 'There must be something we can do…' she said, turning away from him to pace before coming back. 'Why has the banging stopped?'

'We think they've retreated to set up camp.'

'That's good.'

'Is it? It means they're planning to stay. That they're here for as long as it takes.'

'It will give us time to regroup. I'm sure you and the witan can come up with a counter-attack.'

He nodded, running his hands over his thickened stubble, trying to regain his composure. 'Any great ideas?' He tried to smile, but it didn't quite reach his eyes.

She couldn't believe it—was he really asking for her opinion?

'What about the Roman sewers?' she said. 'Could we use them as possible exits—escape routes out of the fortress?'

He raised an eyebrow. 'How do you know about those? Were you planning an escape, Revna?'

She shrugged. 'It was tempting at times, but, no.' Yet when he looked at her the way he was looking at her now, with those intense deep brown eyes, making her legs tremble, it was still an appealing option.

His face darkened. 'No. I won't abandon my family's fortress. I need to stay here and fight. I have to see this through.'

She nodded. 'I had a feeling you'd say that.'

He relented. 'But you and my sisters could go. We could evacuate the women and children. Seeing them all out there in the hall, I feel as though I've let them down.'

'You haven't,' she said, shaking her head fiercely. 'You're doing everything you can. And we're not leaving you. No one would want to. We're staying here. We have to fight for our home. And now the people know they have a new, strong leader to follow, they will rally. We just need a plan.'

He nodded.

'My men will need to barricade the gates. I'll need to inspire every able person who can fight to do so.'

'You wouldn't let me...'

He came off the table towards her and her heartbeat picked up pace. 'I still can't believe you fought that man. Do you know what they'll do to you if they get their hands on you, Revna? Foolish bravery won't keep you safe.'

'I know, I know… I forgot you think the battle-field is no place for a girl,' she said, remembering the words he'd said to her all those winners ago.

'And rescuing that horse! What the hell were you thinking?'

'It was a baby—a colt. He's only a few weeks old. I had to help him.'

'I don't care what it was! It's an animal and not worth risking your life over!' he said, livid. 'I told you to stay inside. You could have been killed!'

Did he really care about that?

'Those animals were my only friends when I arrived here. They saved me from going crazy…' She had spent much of her days tending the animals in the stables, trying to keep busy. At first they'd been the only ones who would listen or interact with her. And it was through assisting the people with their animals that they had come to see her for who she was—as someone who was willing to help and that she wasn't too proud to work hard.

His gaze raked over her. 'Never do that again! I can't always be there to protect you.'

'I'm well aware of that,' she said.

He gave her a furious look. 'This is not the time to argue with me, Revna.'

She crossed her arms over her chest, but stood her ground, and he took a deep breath, steadying his hands on the table.

'It's not too late to send for my father's help,' she said.

'No.'

'Why not?'

'I don't want his help. This is a fight for Saxon soldiers, not Greenlanders.'

She shook her head. 'You're right. You are stubborn. When will you see that we're on the same side?'

'We've never been on the same side,' he said simply.

It was like a knife to the heart. Would he ever accept her? she wondered. What was holding him back from welcoming her father's support? Did he really hate their kind so much he wouldn't even lean on their alliance when he needed it most? Even if it would help his people? Now who was being foolish?

She noticed how he shut her down, changed the topic when her father came up, as if he refused to speak about him or even acknowledge him.

He bent down to pick up a few of his own father's things that he'd scattered on to the floor. 'If we can't get any supplies in, we will need to ration the food—make the most of what we have.'

She nodded, biting her lip. 'I might be able to help there. I've always been worried something like this would happen...and that the people might starve. I thought the only way to be safe was to be prepared. So I asked your father if we could keep a secret stockpile of supplies, just in case,' she said, flushing. 'There's a roof-covered shack near the stables full of food and ale... No one knows about it.'

'Why, Revna, you're a hoarder!' he said, gently

teasing her. 'We'll also need a safe supply of water. Perhaps weaken the ale so it lasts longer.'

'Otherwise we are at risk of disease,' she added, nodding.

He took another step towards her. 'Outside, this morning, you mentioned you couldn't go through this again. What did you mean?'

'I have been in this situation before. There was a great battle back in Greenland. My mother…' She knew what suffering was to come if this siege raged on.

His brow furrowed. 'What about her?'

She had been just nine winters old and her mother and brother had died. Was she really about to tell him that? He didn't need to know her tragic story, not now when his people were facing the same danger. It would hardly inspire him to hope.

Just then, Edlynne popped her head round the door, saving her from her dark memories. 'Revna, here is the box you requested. Are you sure you want to give them everything else?'

'Yes.' She nodded, stepping forward to accept the wooden chest. 'Thank you, Edlynne.'

'What's going on?' Teon asked his sister.

'Revna is giving up her room for some of the families and her royal wardrobe.'

His gaze swung to look at her, incredulous. 'Why?'

'These people have lost their homes, their belongings…they need them more than me. All I need is my mother's few dresses and the small mementos I have of her in this box,' she said, holding them protectively to her. 'Your people gave me sanctuary when I lost my home, the least I can do is give something back.'

He shook his head, as if he was confused. 'And where are you planning to sleep?' he asked, stepping towards her, as if giving up her bed was the only thing of importance.

She shrugged. 'In the hall. Or your sisters have said I can share with them.'

He scowled and reached out to take her necklace between his fingers. 'What is this?'

She wondered why her amulet fascinated him. She knew it was unusual. It certainly wasn't beautiful, like the jewels the other Saxon ladies wore. But her mother had given it to her when she was small, so it meant a lot to her. It was chunky—nothing more than a bent piece of iron on several strands of thread, which she'd filled with beads and seashells she'd gathered on her father's expeditions. The pendant was a circle with the ends twisted into loops underneath. 'It's a Troll cross. It's meant to prevent one from falling into danger, to ward off evil.'

He looked sceptical. 'It didn't work today, did it?'

'I don't know, we're alive so far...'

'Is that because of a superstitious belief or the power of our weapons and how we use them?'

'Maybe both.'

He dropped the metal from his fingers. 'I need to speak to the people again, try to reassure them,' he said, bolder now, as if he'd regained his composure. 'But first we should call a gathering with the witan.'

'We? Does that mean I'm invited this time?'

'Do I have a choice?' he asked, a smile playing at the corner of his lips.

Chapter Four

Teon looked around the masses in the hall, crammed into every corner, nook and cranny, sitting on tables, benches, bales of hay and the floor. Mothers were cradling their babies, holding their children close, their belongings scattered everywhere, while fathers were tending their wounds or sharpening their swords. How had it come to this? Why couldn't he have just ascended to the throne quietly? Peacefully? He was glad his parents weren't around to see it.

Earlier, he and his men had picked their way through lifeless bodies as they'd discussed the weak points of the stronghold and where they should place their men, coming up with a battle plan. He had tasked Revna and Father Cuthbert with looking after the women and children and his sisters with the salting and storing of food.

His men and his father's generals secured the defences—they were manning the walls at all times—and then they'd suffered the harrowing task of removing the dead and burning the bodies. The mood was sombre as they'd all set to their tasks and now the hour was late.

'My loyal subjects, I want to assure you the witan and I and our armies are doing all we can to keep you and our fortress safe. This stronghold hasn't been breached for sixty winters and I don't intend for it to be any different now. The enemy have stated their terms...'

His anger returned with force. How dare Harold make such demands? He glanced over at Revna, standing watching him from the side of the hall, chewing on her bottom lip. Her beautiful face looked serious and concerned. He'd underestimated her, he realised. He couldn't believe she'd suggested sacrificing herself for the people of Kinborough. Why would she do that? It made no sense. It challenged everything he'd believed to be true about her. Did she have no care for her safety?

He'd noticed her reckless display outside as she'd gone to save that foal, more concerned for the animal's life than her own. And he'd felt a pang of guilt when she'd said the animals had been her only company when she came here. Had she been that lonely? But that was beside the point.

Then she'd engaged that brute in combat, to help him and his men. He'd been shocked and horrified when he'd turned to see her fighting on the ramparts. His heart had almost stopped beating. He'd been stunned to see her skilfully wield a sword, fighting so fiercely—pure heathen warrior and not ashamed of it! But he had been so worried she was going to get hurt, or worse.

Her actions had been honourable, but foolish. Did she not realise that, if she were to be caught, Harold would have his fun with her before killing her? She was far too alluring for any man to resist. Hell, he himself was a man who had more self-control than most and she'd weakened his resolve to stay away from her in the space of one night. He hadn't been able to stop himself from kissing her this morning, despite his better judgement.

But still, he admired her bravery. And giving away her room and her wardrobe... He was surprised by her willingness to help. His sisters clearly doted on her—did she really care for them in return? Or was it just out of duty? There was a strength and kindness about her which had thrown him. He had thought the people from the north were barbarians. All of them. But she was challenging those perceptions at every turn. He was desperately trying to hold on to her anger against her. He didn't want to like her.

'Harold has his sights on the crown...but there will be no surrendering. I will die defending my family's stronghold. I hope that you feel the same about your home and that you are all with me. We are heading into a harsh winter and we could be confined in these walls for many months...'

Revna had impressed him when she'd known about the risks of a siege, revealing about their secret supplies and understanding about the likelihood of disease, proving she wasn't just a pretty face. He had expected she might agree with everything he said to please him—but no. He was quickly discovering that that wasn't Revna. And he liked her frankness— the fact she was honest, unafraid to suggest a counter viewpoint. It was refreshing. He needed people around him who would speak openly to him, not tip-toe around his feelings.

She had calmed him from his rage, grounding him. Had she done the same for his father? Was that why the King had allowed her to be part of his witan? He wondered what she'd been about to tell him about her homestead. Something about her mother... And he realised he didn't really know anything about her. That was his own fault, he thought. He'd left not wanting to know her. He'd never even tried to see past his anger and grief. He'd never stopped to think that she might be suffering, too.

'If anyone wants to leave, I'm not going to stop you, but you do so at your own risk. If you stay and you are able, I will find you a weapon and I will expect you to fight, to help defend our home and our people. Harold's army will try to make life unbearable, but if we stand together, I do believe we have more than a chance of winning.'

The people began thumping their hands and feet on the hall floor, in their support of his rousing speech and his actions, and he allowed himself to take a breath. The fact they were on his side meant a lot.

'Right now, our enemy has retreated to set up an encampment, but when they are done, their attack will start up again and we must be ready. Women and children are to stay within the walls of the keep during daylight hours while the combat is taking place.'

Suddenly, a group of men lunged forward, one of them grabbing Revna, violently overpowering her from behind, clamping his hands over her arms and mouth. The hall erupted in screams and cries of distress, the people backing away from the commotion.

What was this now—his own people turning against them? Teon recognised the man from his childhood. They had grown up together and now he owned a large farm out on the flatlands beyond the fortress walls. It had probably been razed to the ground today by Harold's army.

Revna tried to lash out, but the large farmhand restrained her, the rest of his gang brandishing their swords, but Teon and his men were just as quick, raising their weapons, and his sisters and Father Cuthbert, even Lord Cenhelm, were by his side in an instant, uttering their outrage, fearful for Revna's safety.

Dread pounded through him. Could this day get any worse?

He didn't know how he felt about her, but as he watched her struggle under the farmhand's hold, the man's large, dirty hands on her body, a strange feeling of possession tore through him. If any man was going to put his hands on her, it would be him. And he was both shocked and appalled by the direction of his thoughts. Since when had he wanted to lay a finger on her? Since she had blossomed into the most beautiful woman he'd ever seen, a little voice mocked him.

He tried to focus. Her brilliant blue eyes were

wide, clinging to his across the room—and her vulnerability struck him right in the chest.

'What do you think you're doing?' he warned the gang, his men crowding them. 'Let her go.'

'It's her they want, isn't it? Why should we all die trying to protect a heathen?' the leader's rough voice sneered. 'She's a *haegtessan*. A witch.'

Teon understood. He had spent eight years hating her kind. Why *should* his people die trying to protect her… Yet, there was something about her. She wasn't like other women, Saxon or Norse. She didn't seem to care for riches. She didn't even care for her own safety or comfort compared to that of others. And despite what had happened between her people and his, she had been just a child. It wasn't exactly her fault. Right now she was depending on him and he knew he had to help her. She was his wife. His responsibility.

'I do not wish to fight you, but make no mistake— if you try to leave with Revna in your grip, we will cut you down.'

He took a step towards them. He chose his words with care, trying to speak in an even tone. 'Think about this. If you hand her over to Harold and his men, do you think they will stop? No.' He could hear the anger vibrating in his own voice. 'Harold will just be one step closer to the throne. And do you think a man who does this—who is willing to cause all this death and destruction—will make a good king?'

'He has managed to gather an army…many others seem willing to stand by him. Why shouldn't we?' the man said, shuffling backwards.

'And I wonder how many of their homes and families were threatened on their way here. I wonder if they had a choice,' Teon countered.

The group began retreating, backing away towards the large doors, throwing them open and bundling Revna with them out into the cool night. As the leader lifted her into the air to carry her down the steps, she continued to kick and try to wrestle her way free. She wouldn't go down without a fight, he knew that of her now.

Teon and his men were right behind them.

He watched as Revna tried to prise the man's hands off her and wrench herself free, kneeing him between the legs, causing him to cry out, and Teon's admiration for her only grew. But then the man smacked her around the face, splitting her lip and making her crumple, allowing him to seize her again.

Cold fury lurched through Teon. By his father's decree, Revna had been made Queen-in-waiting here. No matter what he or anyone else thought, the late King's word had to count for something. He knew he had to fix this.

'To continue along this path is treason.'

'The way we see it, it's a queen for a queen,' the brute quipped. 'Her being here puts us all in danger. If we hand her over, maybe Harold will accept you as King and stop this madness.'

'You can't really believe that—that Harold would come all this way to remove a woman from a seat of power? No. He wants that throne and this fortress for himself.' He made slow, cautious movements, like a wolf stalking its prey. There was a tightness in his stomach and his heart was pounding in his chest.

He kept his sword trained on them, as they continued to back away. 'Look around you.' He motioned to the rubble-strewn courtyard, dust and debris scattered all about them, the devastation of just one day of fighting visible in the pale light of the moon. And it was only going to get worse. 'If you walk out through those gates, he'll kill her—and then all of you.'

The men seemed to falter, the reality of the heinous scene before them finally kicking in, the thought of their own deaths becoming a real possibility.

'Revna's people didn't do this. Our own kind did,' Teon added.

The farmhand finally halted his retreat. 'So what would you have us do?' the man asked gruffly. 'We've lost our lands, our farms, our livestock...'

Was he getting through to them? Teon hoped so. He wasn't sure how he'd feel if something happened to her. He'd tried not to think about her for eight long winters, yet today she'd consumed his thoughts while he'd been fighting. With every arrow he'd struck, he'd known he had to keep the enemy away for her, to keep her safe. He couldn't lose her to his own people now.

He sheathed his sword, taking a risk.

'And I'm sorry,' Teon said, trying to defuse the tension, hoping to placate them, reason with them. 'We all know how you feel. We have all suffered terrible losses today. But none of us here is responsible. We need to stand together against the enemy out there. Fight for what's right. Stand by me and I will do all I can to protect you. And your families. I promise I will find you new homes, new lands when all this is over. You'll be richly rewarded...'

The men looked between each other, uncertain. Perhaps they were worried to go back on their plan now, for fear of being reprimanded.

Teon turned to his men and gestured for them to lower their weapons, too. 'Return Revna to me and we'll forget about this whole thing. You can go back inside to your wives and children. We won't speak of it again.'

The farmhand nodded, accepting what Teon was saying, but still holding on to Revna, hesitant. 'We're all worried about our families,' he reiterated.

'I understand,' Teon said.

There was a pause.

Finally, the man released Revna, shoving her forward, and Teon reached out to grab her arm, bringing her towards him, tucking her into the side of his body. He allowed himself to release the breath he'd been holding. She was safe. Not unharmed, but all right.

'You've made the right choice. Now come back inside and warm yourselves by the fire. Let's forget this ever happened.'

Teon took Revna's arm and led her back into the hall, walking quickly. They picked their way through the people, ignoring the murmurs and mutterings about what had just gone on outside, out to the back corridor, and he hurled her forward, at speed, his blinding rage vibrating off him.

She wondered how he could be so calm when talking to those farmers, when clearly he was furious inside. And she wasn't sure if his fury was directed at her, himself or the men.

'Where are we going?' she asked, wondering how her trembling legs were still holding her up.

'My room.'

She came to an abrupt stop in the corridor, just past a group of people bedding down on the floor for the night.

'I will not!' she whispered, swinging out of his grasp.

He took her arm again. 'You're staying with me. That's an order by your husband and your King. I won't have the future Queen of Kinborough sleeping out in the hall. It is neither appropriate nor safe for you to do so.'

'Queen? I thought I was a heathen...'

He ignored her comment and she knew she should put up more resistance—but she was shaken by what had happened out there in the courtyard. The instant his fingers curled around her arm again, she relented, wanting his comfort and his strength, and she let him hurry her forward. Reaching his room, he launched her inside, finally releasing her from his grip.

'And I'll be safe in here with you, will I?' she said, turning to face him, as he shut the door and leaned against it, raking his hand through his hair.

The beat of her heart was rushing in her ears.

'What's the matter? Afraid I'm going to kiss you again?'

'As a matter of fact, yes.' The thought of him doing

so both scared her and excited her all at once. 'I've had enough of strange men manhandling me for one night.' But she was smarting from his touch, not theirs—his were the only hands that sent strange tingles through her body.

His brows pulled together as he came towards her. 'Did he hurt you?'

She shook her head. 'It's just a bit of blood—nothing too terrible,' she said, bringing her hand up to her lips to check if the bleeding had stopped.

He cursed beneath his breath, seeming to be angry for her, on her side—bewildering her. He was giving her mixed signals.

It had shocked her—that people were willing to use her as a bargaining tool to get them out of this mess. Maybe she *would* be safer in here with him. Yet if Teon thought it would save lives, she would walk out of here right now and hand herself over. She would do it for him and his sisters if he asked her to. Going by choice was different to being taken by force.

'I'm sorry he treated you like that,' he said, softening his tone. 'Despite our differences, I want you to know I would never put you in harm's way. And I'm starting to think you'll need to stay hidden, out of sight, not left alone until this is all over. The mood of the people will be changeable the longer this goes on. They might begin to feel desperate. I can't be sure they won't try something like this again.'

She wrapped her arms around her waist. 'I will not hide away like a coward,' she said. 'If I still need to prove to the people that I'm one of them, that I can help, then so be it. I thought I'd begun to do that until you came home. Until this happened.'

'I don't understand why you care so much. You are not one of us.'

'Perhaps I want them to like me, the way I like them.' She shrugged. 'I told your father I would do everything in my power to protect them. I will keep my word.'

'That is admirable, Revna, but you need to be aware of the danger.'

'Oh, I'm well aware,' she said, but looking around her, she suddenly wasn't thinking about the men out there in the hall, or the enemy at their gates. Seeing the huge bed in the middle of the room covered with animal furs and a large unlit hearth up the corner, she knew she'd made a mistake letting him bring her in here. She hadn't set foot in this room since the night of their wedding and it brought back unwanted memories, making her shiver. Perhaps the shock of everything that had happened today was finally setting in.

'Cold?'

She nodded and he went over to the fire, crouching down, beginning to light it.

'Sit down,' he said, gesturing to the lone chair to the side of the room.

She shook her head, wary, and instead began to pace. She was too on edge in his company to sit—he seemed to heighten her awareness about everything. And the way he was looking at her with concern in his eyes was far more dangerous to her than his usual coldness. It made her think he cared, when deep down, she knew he didn't. Not really. He was just act-

ing out of duty. Teon thought her father would attack
if something happened to her. And something nearly
had! She went over it again in her mind—the way
those men had behaved, the words they had spoken.

'What did that man mean, a queen for a queen?'
she asked, coming to a halt before him.

He stared up at her, from where he was crouched
by the fire. The flames flickered wildly into life in the
almost-darkness, lighting up the room, yet a shadow
crossed his features. 'You must know?' he said.

'Clearly I don't.'

'You expect me to believe that?'

'Why not? It's the truth.'

'You know your father attacked these lands, don't
you? But of course you do, you were there!'

'Despite what you might think, we didn't come
here to fight. Nevertheless, your army was waiting
for us when we arrived. We had no choice...'

'You came flying your raven banners, waving your
weapons. Why would we think you'd be any different
from all the other raiding parties that had bloodied
our shores before you?'

She knew other Norse clans had come here for
riches and spoils—that's how her father had heard
of this green, fertile isle, a world away from their
snow-capped mountains and gentle fjords. It certainly
explained the hostilities between their people—why
she had struggled to fit in here and why Teon had
spent years lying in wait to strike out every clan who
stepped foot on English soil. But still, they hadn't been
one of them. Bloodshed had never been their intention.

'My father came here to find a new home, not make enemies.'

'Your ships breached our beaches and we defended ourselves.'

'I can tell we aren't ever going to agree, are we?' she said, despairingly, shaking her head. 'But that's all in the past. Your father and mine made a treaty... I even met your mother, when she came to visit our settlement. Our people have lived in harmony for years. It doesn't explain the man's comment. Teon, what happened to her?'

He stood, his hand curling around a wooden beam as he stared at her. 'Considering all that you and my father discussed, I am surprised this never came up,' he said, suspiciously.

'He told me she died suddenly, that her death was an unsolved mystery, but he never went into detail. The subject always seemed off limits, as if he didn't want to discuss it with me or your sisters.'

Teon released the beam and came towards her. 'That's because it was your father and his men who killed my mother, Revna.'

'What?' She reeled, her throat closing in shock, her hand coming up to cover her mouth. 'No!' she said, shaking her head. 'He wouldn't! He didn't.'

'He did.' Dark fury washed over his features and she saw the cold hatred in his eyes. Suddenly, everything made sense. He didn't just loathe her because she was a Greenlander, because they'd dared to come to his shores. He hated her because he believed the worst had happened—that her father had murdered his mother, the Queen.

She felt her blood run cold in shock. Her knees suddenly buckled beneath her and she slumped down on to the bed. She felt as if the room was closing in on her. No wonder he didn't want to be near her. No wonder he could never love or even like her.

Revna felt sickened and held her hand up, as if to ward off any more information. But he kept talking.

'That's why the fighting erupted again. That day our people met yours on the treacherous ice and the snow turned red. I wanted vengeance. I led my men out there to seek victory and to rid our lands of your people once and for all. But our fathers demanded I put a stop to the fighting and instead they facilitated our marriage. My father said it's what my mother would have wanted—to prevent any more unnecessary death. I cannot believe those were her wishes. And I could never reconcile with him for it.'

'It can't be true,' she said, wringing her hands, a flutter of guilt in her stomach. 'There must be a mistake.' If it were true, the King could never have grown to care for her. He had even told her she reminded him of his late wife. And for all his faults, she didn't think her own father would murder Teon's mother. He had no cause. No reason. Surely the two men wouldn't have formed an alliance if such villainy had taken place?

She began replaying that period of her life back in her head. The Queen's visits to their settlement, speaking to the people and learning the way they did things. She never saw any hostility between Teon's mother and her father. She couldn't understand why he would do such an atrocious thing. He couldn't have known that it would lead to a marriage alliance, but he would have known it would have led to a war!

'I saw it with my own eyes—I saw your father bring her body to our gates, bloodied and broken. The rumours were rife that the heathens had hurt her...'

'I heard those, too, but I never believed them. Not for a moment.'

Still, pictures filled her mind of a young boy discovering his mother had died. Instead of being able to seek revenge, he'd had to marry his enemy's daughter. Her heart went out to him and she buried her face in her hands, trying to shake away the images. 'I just can't comprehend it,' she said. Had it been some kind of tragic accident?

'Well, it's the truth.'

She could see now, in the way he looked at her— the way he held himself away from her—that Teon blamed her. But why had no one ever told her before now? Why had they forced them together, knowing it would cause him such pain and resentment? She smoothed her hands over her kirtle. She was frustrated at the unfairness of the situation. They never stood a chance at happiness. Why did their parents do this to them? And she had the feeling that now she knew, nothing would ever be the same.

It would certainly explain why her father and his men hadn't attended the wedding. They wouldn't have been welcome here. *Helvete*, *she* hadn't been welcome here! She had thought it was because tensions were high, but she had never realised to what extent.

'So you really didn't know?' he said, his deep brown eyes assessing her.

'Of course I didn't!' She shook her head, still trying to think of a reason why her father would commit such a crime. 'But, Teon, are you absolutely sure?'

'Yes.'

'Then I can understand why you loathe me. *Us.*' Yet he had just rescued her from the hands of those men… 'It would explain why you hated me at first sight. Why I was treated the way I was when I came here.'

His brow furrowed. 'You were mistreated?'

'No worse than I deserved, by the sounds of it,' she said, fiddling with the bangles on her wrist. And yet to a young, grief-ridden girl, lonely, confused and afraid in a strange place, the people's neglect had cut deep. But no wonder it had taken so long for them to come to accept her. Some clearly still didn't, judging by the events of tonight. She only hoped the majority had come to realise that whatever had happened, she wasn't to blame.

When the people had started to warm to her, beginning to engage her in conversation, saying good morning as she passed them in the square, it had meant so much. Perhaps that's why she was so keen to maintain their respect now, as it had been so hard won. The Princesses had liked her from the start, too young to be aware of the differences between them.

And although the King had been harder to get to know, he had always treated her kindly.

She had been aware he was dealing with his own grief, but he never acted as if he held her responsible for the death of his wife. Instead, they had walked and talked together, him asking questions of her homeland, wanting to know about their farming methods and their ships, and their journey across the ocean. He was an unprejudiced man. He had an open mind and was always willing to consider new ideas.

She in turn had been curious to know of her new home here and the King's ancestors. He had even made many assertions that she was a good match for his son, if only Teon could see it, too, and that one day she would make a strong queen, and her heart had swelled with pride.

Teon pushed a hand through his hair, sighing. 'You were just a child.'

His conciliatory words caused a lump to form in her throat.

'But I know his blood runs through your veins. It's hard to…come to terms with it.'

She nodded and watched as he turned to stoke the fire. And she felt the need to apologise—not so much out of guilt but to voice the unfairness of the whole situation.

'If what you're saying is true, I am desperately sorry, Teon… I know what it's like to lose a mother at a young age. I wouldn't wish that upon anyone.'

'What happened?' he asked. 'To your mother? You started to tell me earlier, but we were interrupted.'

'Our settlement in Greenland was attacked by another tribe,' she said quietly. 'A lot like today.'

'No wonder you looked haunted when you saw Harold's army approaching the fortress… What happened?' he asked.

She was surprised he wanted to know. That he was showing any interest in her at all after what he'd just told her. Could it be that he might be as generous with his forgiveness as his father must have been?

'We were stuck inside, trapped, for months. People were starving—dying of hunger, or their injuries. It wasn't the fighting but the disease that ended up doing the most damage.' And that's what she was most fearful of here, now Harold had them surrounded. It's what she dreaded most of all. Cooped up together, with a limited amount of clean water and supplies, she knew how messy things could get. What if they couldn't keep the people safe? She had failed her family before.

'Everyone was just waiting for their time to starve or get ill,' she said. 'My brother died of the sickness first, followed by my mother. And all I could do was sit by and watch them suffer, waiting for them to go.' Her arms wrapped around herself in a self-soothing manner.

'Then I'm sorry, too, for your loss. It seems we have our grief in common, if nothing else,' he said.

Over the summers and winters that had passed, she'd kept reliving it, over and over, wondering what she could have done differently. Sometimes she wondered why she'd survived and they didn't. Shortly afterwards, her father had lost the will to fight and yielded their homestead. He'd decided there was nothing left for them in Greenland, so he and his men had packed up their belongings, threw them in boats and set sail for distant shores. She felt as if she had become a burden to him—he became so focused on her making a prosperous marriage and finding her a good home. But she hadn't been sure she could ever feel at home anywhere else. Then she was brought here and her father had abandoned her, and Teon had, too.

She struggled for something to say, to build a bridge between them. She stood and came towards him. 'Teon, I miss my mother desperately. Your father becoming ill brought it all back. I know how you must feel, having lost them both. I'm so sorry. And for today. Everything.' She thought about the devastation and destruction in the courtyard. 'Perhaps you should have let those men take me, especially if I have brought this upon us.'

He sighed, standing up, drawing a hand over his face. 'No,' he conceded, shaking his head. 'You weren't to know what Harold would do. You couldn't have done anything to stop him. And it sounds as if you tried to get the witan to take action and they didn't listen.' He placed his hands on his hips. 'Besides, I am as much to blame. I should have been here. I shouldn't have stayed away so long.'

He ran a hand round the back of his neck. 'It's been one hell of a day. I imagine you're shattered—and hurting. You're getting quite the bruise.' He reached out and drew his knuckles over her cheek, brushing her lips. 'Those men were right. I got a queen for a queen, whether I liked it or not. We'll just have to get through this as best we can.'

She nodded, reaching up to hold her cheek, concerned by the burning of her skin where he'd touched her.

'Why don't you get some sleep now, Revna?'

She glanced back at the bed, her heart beginning to pick up pace. 'In here? With you?' she asked, suddenly panicked, chewing her lip. She couldn't imagine he really wanted her in here. Not after all he'd revealed. And she didn't know how she felt about it either, especially after that kiss earlier. The way her body responded to him made her nervous.

'Yes. I'm not letting you out of my sight tonight, not with tensions so rife in the hall.'

It wouldn't look good for something to happen to the future Queen now, would it? That he couldn't protect his own wife. Was that all he cared about? she wondered. His reputation?

'And don't worry, you have your necklace for protection against me, don't you?' he said, his mouth curving into a smile.

'I'll take my chances on the floor, then,' she said.

He shook his head, bemused. 'Most women would jump at the chance to share my bed, yet my own wife would rather sleep on the floor… You can sleep in the bed, Revna. I'm not going to touch you. I promise.'

'Where will you sleep?' she asked, sitting down on the furs, stroking her hand through them.

'I'll take the chair.'

Tentatively, she lay down, fully clothed, curling up on her side, facing away from him. When she heard him walk across the floor, she held her breath. She only released it when she heard the creak of the chair as he lowered himself into it.

He moved about, as if he was trying to get comfortable. She had never been so close to a man before and in such a confined space. Lying beside him in the darkness, listening to his breathing, felt almost intimate. She was aware of his every movement and she wondered why she had agreed to it. It was frustrating. There was no way she could sleep like this...

Thoughts about everything that had happened throughout the day kept running through her mind. She was worried what the siege would bring, concerned for Teon and his men, Edlynne, Eldrida, the priest and all the people's lives. Then she kept thinking about her father, and whether he'd committed the atrocity Teon had accused him of. She was appalled, yet she couldn't believe it to be true. It just didn't make any sense. She didn't think her father could do that. He knew what impact the loss of a mother had on a child. But if he had, what kind of person did that make her? Did people see her not only as a heathen, but as the child of a queen killer?

And she thought about the kiss... She turned over, flipping on to her back, and her body ached. It was bruised from being restrained by that huge man out in the courtyard and her face stung from being hit. She had been afraid, but her eyes had sought out Teon's and she'd drawn from his strength, lashing out and kicking that man, hurting him in return. But she could deal with the aches and pains.

What was more disturbing was the frustration she was feeling at being in Teon's proximity—there was a restless irritability in her body at being so close to him, disturbingly making her want things she had never wanted before. She wanted him to take her in his arms again. She wanted him to comfort her, telling her everything would be all right. Things that she knew now could never be.

She tried to sneak a look at him in the darkness, propping herself up on her elbow. She could just make out his magnificent chest gently rising and falling, his head resting in his hand, his long legs stretched out in front of him. For a man who had a reputation of having a way with women, she thought how ironic it was that he didn't want to touch his own wife. He could overpower her if he wanted to and yet he had never mistreated her in that way. In fact, he had protected her innocence. She should have been grateful, but instead she'd been hurt by his cold rejection of her.

He was a decent man, she realised. He had been ruthless out there on the battlements today, doing what was necessary, and he had shown his strong leadership in the hall and in saving her. Looking back, he hadn't wanted to marry her, but had done it anyway—for his father and his people. And he had saved her life—twice now. He'd had every chance to claim her, but he hadn't. And now he was keeping his distance, possessing a restraint she hadn't expected him to. She knew that scorching kiss today had more to do with anger than desire.

'What are you doing?' he said, startling her.

'Trying to sleep,' she lied.

'Most people close their eyes and lie down when they try to sleep, Revna. I suggest you do the same.'

His velvety voice just a whisper away from her only intensified her feelings. She had the strange desire to reach out and touch him and tell him he could sleep in the bed, but she was too afraid of what his reaction would be. She knew she had to protect herself from further rejection and more disappointment.

'Just relax. You're safe with me. No one's going to come in here, I've got the door closely guarded.'

But didn't he realise she wasn't frightened of who was out there? She was afraid of how he was making her feel inside this room.

Teon was still livid about the mutinous way those men had behaved out there in the courtyard. Their insubordination had made him want to punish all of them. He couldn't believe they'd tried to take her, that they'd hit her and drawn blood. A possessiveness he didn't understand lashed through him. Thank God he'd got her back. He knew she must be scared and, for some reason, he wanted to reassure her that she was safe with him. It was absurd. He had never cared about her feelings before.

As they lay there in the darkness, Teon wondered if she was finally asleep. She was unnaturally still, her breathing unusually quiet, and he curled and unfurled his toes, trying to release some of the tension in his body. He felt the need to get up, move, or do something—his body reacting to his thoughts that just wouldn't turn off.

He kept second-guessing his decisions about today. He had never been responsible for so many lives before and was conscious his mistakes would mean the difference of life and death for others. It was one thing fighting alongside his men at the garrison— men who had willingly volunteered to be there— and another going into battle with men who had no experience of fighting, but were having to do so to protect their families and homes. The men out at the barbican were warriors, able to put up with terrible conditions, as he had for years, but he didn't want to subject his people, or Revna and his sisters, to that. He wondered how they'd fare.

He was still furious with himself for not realising Harold would lay claim to the throne—for not return-ing to Kinborough quicker and preventing the siege from ever happening. Had he brought this upon his people? And now that they were under attack, had he done everything he could? He felt as if his judge-ment was off—impaired. Was it because of Revna?

Now he knew she was in danger, he had to worry about keeping her safe. But he was surely treading a dangerous path, keeping her in his room. It could only lead to trouble. Hell, he was already suffering from that decision. His groin was rock-hard, knowing she was just inches away from him in his bed. All he needed to do was reach out and touch her… She was his wife—why shouldn't he?

He wondered how she would respond, especially after that kiss this morning, setting his body alight. But damn, he didn't want to be attracted to her—he hated himself for being so. It was impermissible. Distasteful. It went against everything he had fought against these past winters. It went against the vow he'd made to himself that he would never bed her and father a child.

Yet since he'd taken her in his arms, he couldn't stop thinking about how her body had felt pressed against him, how he'd stormed her silky mouth and her innocent, untutored tongue had tentatively stroked his back. What else could he teach her? And would she enjoy it? Yet he knew he mustn't. He'd made a vow to himself—and his mother.

If these eight winters had taught him anything, it had been restraint. He was the master of control. Yet he wanted her more than he'd ever wanted anyone. This was his come-uppance, he thought, inwardly groaning, trying to swallow down his desire—his punishment for rejecting her before. He could make out the lines of her body in the darkness—the curves of her pert breasts and her round bottom. Why was he so aware of her? he wondered.

All these years, his anger towards her had allowed him to keep his distance, but in just one day she had smashed down the walls he'd built up that had been keeping her at bay and had shattered his beliefs about who she was. She was like a different person entirely to the one he'd conjured up in his mind.

When they'd spoken earlier she had said her people had come here looking for a new home, not to rape and pillage, but he couldn't believe it. And yet she had been adamant. He thought of that young girl, who he'd rescued from the stampede that day, and how frightened she had been.

When his father had told him he must marry a heathen girl, he had ranted and raved. He had thrown every abuse he could think of at the man who had fallen short in his role as a husband and parent, affecting his security and trust. But if he was stubborn, so was his father and there had been no way out of it. The decision had been made. His father said it was vital for the stability of the kingdom and he had never been able to argue with that. It was what compelled him even now.

Waiting for his pagan bride at the altar, he had been shocked to recognise the young girl nervously walking up the aisle towards him as the one he had saved the winter before—only he hadn't known then that she was a heathen. He should have realised by the beautiful paleness of her eyes.

When she had reached where he was standing in front of the priest, she had tentatively smiled up at him and he had been blinded by rage, that she was the daughter of his mother's killer. That he was being tethered to a child. He had been so humiliated, he could barely look at her, let alone stand to kiss her when Father Cuthbert had told him he could kiss his bride.

And come the feast, he hadn't wanted to sit next to

her, he'd just wanted to get away. He'd made up his mind. He couldn't stomach this, he had to leave. He had found it almost abhorrent, when the maids had brought her to his room, that anyone would think he would want to take her. So he'd packed his satchel and left.

And from that day on, he'd been blinded by hate. He had turned his back on her, determined he would always hold her and her people to blame for his mother's death. He had sought solace at the garrison, the constant fighting and defending of their borders helping to rid him of his rage, knowing he was returning a little of the pain these invaders had caused him. But had he lost himself somewhere along the way? He'd become bloodthirsty, hellbent on revenge. He'd seen Revna and her people as the cause of all his problems.

But if Revna hadn't even known what had happened to the Queen, how could he hold her responsible? It hadn't been her fault, yet she'd offered him a heartfelt apology none the less. He would never be able to forget what her father had done, but was it possible he could accept Revna hadn't played a part in it, despite the fact she was one of them? Because it felt good to let go of his anger towards her. To understand her a bit better. To discuss their past and shared grief.

Now he felt bad for his own cruel treatment of her. A girl who had just lost her own mother and brother—who had lost her home and been brought over the wild ocean and straight into a battle. No wonder she'd hoarded all that food, worried something like that might happen again!

Then her father had sold her like property, against her will, and he, the man who was meant to protect her and look after her, had been cold, abandoning her, leaving her to fend for herself for eight winters. He'd been selfish, only thinking of his own misery. He'd never stopped to think that she had been suffering, too. He had ruined her trust. No wonder she despised him in return.

Most people would have been bitter, but Revna had thrived. She had blossomed into a beautiful, strong, clever and compassionate woman while he'd been away, now trusted by the people and the witan. She had taken care of his father and sisters.

Edlynne and Eldrida had told him she'd practically raised them, looking after them. They refused to believe any of the rumours they'd heard about Revna's father and what he'd done. They'd grown close, his sisters had said, and he had been surprised by the dart of jealousy that struck his chest. It was ridiculous. He should be pleased they'd had someone to take care of them after his mother had passed.

'Revna, are you awake?'

She turned slightly, raising her head off the furs. 'Yes.'

'Were you with my father, at the end?' he asked.

'Yes,' she whispered. 'We all were.'

'Did he suffer?' he asked, shifting in the chair.

'No,' she said, shaking her head. 'He slipped away quietly. And you must know, he was very proud of all your achievements, Teon.'

He swallowed. 'I doubt he would be proud if he could see the fortress right now.'

'He would know it wasn't your fault.'

He hoped it was the truth—that she wasn't just telling him what he needed to hear. But he knew she was too honest for that.

He felt his rage dissipating, almost slipping away, and it was unsettling. Without his anger, where did that leave them? Defenceless against the insane desire he felt towards her—that's where! Yet he knew he couldn't act on it. And he also knew he had to conserve his energy for Harold's army in the morning.

'Do you really care for them? My sisters… Did you care for my father?' he asked.

She moved her body about on the furs, making his muscles tighten. 'Perhaps I don't see our differences quite as much as you do. Your sisters are wonderful people. I love them dearly. And for some reason, despite all you have said, your father did seem to care for me and looked after me, and I was genuinely fond of him in return.'

'Then I am glad he had you for company, at the end. Was it you who organised the huge barrow for his funeral?'

'Yes. It was the least he deserved.'

He had known the answer, even before she gave it.

'Thank you,' he said, his voice gruff.

Damn, how did she make him feel this mixed up? He suddenly missed his hard bed at the garrison, the constant threat of the enemy, preventing him from feeling anything at all. It was unbearable being this close to her and not being able to touch her. Perhaps he should just take her and be done with it.

But he'd sworn not to do that with her. He hadn't planned to consummate this marriage—he intended to keep his Saxon lineage pure. Yet he could not stop thinking about claiming her, even in the midst of a battle for his throne. And deep down he knew there was only way he could rid himself of this insane lust that was tearing up his blood.

Chapter Five

By the time the sun began to rise, the fortress was alive with activity. A storm had raged through the night, the wind howling across the ramparts, and Revna hoped it had unsettled Harold and his men, who were sleeping under canvas. Perhaps it would give Teon and his men an advantage—not that he looked as though he needed it this morning. He looked strong, exuding a raw power and energy, ready for whatever was in store.

When she had woken this morning, she had expected to find him asleep in the chair beside her, but he wasn't there. The only sign that he had been in the room were the smouldering embers of the fire. She wondered what time he had left her and knew her disappointment was unwarranted, for he had an army to fight and a fortress to save. She mustn't get in his way.

Men were in position on the battlements, others were busy making weapons and distributing them and Teon and his warriors were attempting to train those who had no skills, before the fighting commenced.

Revna had made the breakfast of curdled milk and fruit go as far as possible and was now enjoying the honey rays of sun drizzle across her face as she went to collect cauldrons of rainwater for washing, knowing it might be the only daylight she'd see today if she was to behave and stay indoors. She passed the warriors on her way back and saw Teon drape a heavy chainmail vest over the head of a young boy before passing him a sword.

'Surely he's too young to fight?' she said, interrupting them, unable to help herself. She momentarily put down the heavy pots, slopping a bit of water over the sides.

Teon raised a single brow at her. 'Morning.'

'Good morning.' She flushed, aware she'd missed out that small courtesy.

'Did you sleep well?'

'I got some sleep, yes. You?'

'A little.'

It felt strange to exchange pleasantries with him, after their heavy conversation last night. She felt so awkward, her skin prickling with awareness as his gaze raked over her face.

Teon turned his attention back to the lad, who was excitedly, and dangerously, swinging the sword about.

'How old are you, boy?'

'Twelve winters.'

'See! He's far too young!' Revna said.

'What's your name?' Teon asked him.

'Ealfrith.'

'Well, Ealfrith, I shall train you myself. Right now,

we need every able person to fight and I think you can help us win this battle.'

The boy nodded, practising his jabbing in one hand, while attempting to hold up a heavy shield in the other.

'He's just a child,' Revna said, shaking her head in dismay.

'Exactly. Now you know how I felt about you, when we married.'

She tilted her chin up in defiance. 'But I'm not twelve now…'

He came towards her, his eyes glittering down at her, his lips curving up into a suggestive smile. 'What are you saying?'

Her breath hitched at his nearness, understanding his meaning, and a ripple of heat shot through her body. It was as if he'd relaxed a little around her, dropping his guard slightly, and it pleased and unnerved her all at once.

They seemed to have come to some silent understanding that they had both been forced into this situation and they had to make the best of it—she didn't want to ruin their fragile truce now. But this new Teon, who was light-heartedly teasing her, was all the more threatening, for she was in danger of liking him. He was making her feel things she didn't want to feel.

'I'm merely saying you don't need to treat me like a baby. I'm not twelve winters old any more. And if that boy can fight, so can I!'

'This boy won't be used as leverage to get the upper hand and win this battle. We've discussed this. I expect you to stay inside today,' he said. 'And stay away from those men who tried to take you captive yesterday. One of my men will be watching you—and guarding my sisters.' His lips pressed together in a slight grimace.

'I noticed I had a shadow since I left the room this morning. That man over there is following me around,' she said, nodding to a burly warrior with long, slicked-back hair, a sword in his hand—and watching her every move. 'Your doing, I suppose?'

Teon grinned fully then and she felt a responsive rush in her stomach. He was so incredibly attractive. Primal and perfect. 'Egeslic is under orders to keep you safe while I cannot be here to guard you.' He picked up the cauldrons she'd been carrying and made his way inside the hall, setting them down on one of the tables.

'Thank you,' she said, keeping up with him, grateful for the help.

'His name means Terror, so you'd better behave,' he said, a devilish twinkle in his eye.

'Funny,' she snapped, 'but I don't do well cooped up. And I need to be useful.'

'You can be useful inside. Do what I say, Revna. Promise me?' He reached out and took her chin between his thumb and forefingers. 'How is your face today?'

'I'm fine.'

He nodded. 'I don't need to be worrying about you while trying to lead my men.'

'Why would you worry about me?' she asked, suddenly finding it hard to swallow. Yes, he had saved her life last night—and kept her safe in his room. He'd made sure she was comfortable and had kept the fire going to keep her warm, but it didn't mean he cared.

'As I said,' he shrugged, dropping his fingers from her jaw, 'I don't want something happening to you and your father coming after me, now do I?' Yet he winked, as if to say that wasn't the whole reason, causing a warm, fuzzy feeling to spread through her. She knew she needed to keep him at arm's length. She could not allow herself to need him. She had proven she didn't. She must remember she could rely only on herself.

The battle began with Harold's men charging at the gates again and raged on all day. It was relentless, ruthless—a day never to be forgotten—and Revna had been frantic all morning, tending to the wounded. There was a constant stream of overwrought soldiers, their faces grim, carrying the injured inside, lining them up in rows in the hall, then bravely heading back out into the fray.

She felt the burden of the people all around her moaning, wailing, begging for help, while she tried to crush her concern for the men and what was happening outside. And with every body they'd brought in, her heart was in her mouth, fearing it would be Teon. Since when had she begun to care? she wondered.

While he had been away, although she had thought of him often, she had learned not to worry about him. But since he'd come home, he had consumed her every waking thought. She told herself it was because they were all relying on him to lead them to victory, to get them out of this situation, but deep down she knew it was more than that. She had wanted to care for him when she was a girl, but now she was a woman, she had more than foolish hopes and dreams.

She had needs and when he looked at her the way he had done outside, gently teasing her, her insides had melted. It both scared and excited her all at once. She knew she was playing with fire. Her innocence was no match for a man like him. And yet, she still wanted him to want her. Could he ever, after everything that had happened in their past?

She moved along the line of invalids, bone-achingly weary. She'd been on her feet all day and hadn't had time to stop to eat or drink. When she came before her next patient, she reeled, frozen momentarily in fear. It was the brute who had tried to take her hostage last night. She sensed Egeslic take a protective step towards her and, glancing over her shoulder at him, put up her hand, halting his advance. She took a deep breath and turned back to the man.

'I'm sorry. About before,' he said gruffly, holding his arm with his hand. 'I didn't mean it. It's just I have a wife. She's with child. And a boy. He's only five winters old,' he said by way of explanation.

She moved his hand away to see his wound, her heart softening, understanding his fear. 'We all do strange things when we're afraid for our loved ones,' she said.

'I'm not proud of it.'

'It's forgotten now.'

He nodded, hanging his head in shame. 'Is your face all right?'

'It's all better now. Don't worry. Thank you for standing by Prince Teon today and fighting. I'm sorry you've been hurt. What's your name?'

'Garren. My wife over there is Darrelle. And my boy, he's called Graeham.' She glanced over at where he was pointing to on the other side of the hall. She could tell he was proud of his family.

Revna set to bandaging up his arm with wool.

'How many months with child is she?' she asked him.

'Seven. But she's huge,' he said. 'We think it'll come early. I don't want her birthing a child amid all this.'

'Let's hope it'll all be over by then,' she said.

When she was done, he jumped down from the table and muttered his thanks, before turning back to her. 'I didn't mean what I said last night. I actually think you'd make a good queen.'

'Thank you,' she whispered. She turned around to her next patient and came face to face with Teon— and almost wilted in relief. Her eyes raked over him, checking for any injuries of his own. He had a cut to his forehead, but he seemed otherwise all right. But he had his arm around Bordan, holding him up, and she could see blood was seeping through the young warrior's chainmail.

'This man needs help,' he said, heaving him on to the table, and she could tell he was full of concern for his warrior. 'He has a wound to his head and his stomach.'

Quickly clearing space, she gestured for Teon to lay Bordan down and fumbled with the fastening of the man's leather vest, trying to get it off so that she could see what she was dealing with. She had no experience with undoing men's clothes and her face heated, realising Teon was watching her.

Dipping a piece of flax in a bowl of water, she washed the blood from Bordan's skin and saw he had a deep gash just above his hip. She reached for a jug of wine and salt and rubbed the mixture into the wound, and Bordan roared. Teon held down his shoulders, pressing him back down to the table, and his friend cursed him, making Teon grimace. He mocked him, telling him not to be a coward. Going by their easy banter, she could tell they were good friends, that he was important to Teon.

Revna was no healer, she had only learned some things from her mother during their own siege in Greenland, but she would try her best. For him. With as steady a hand as she could, she used a needle and thread to suture the cut. She found it difficult to stay on task, her hands trembling under Teon's gaze and Bordan's curses. It wasn't the neatest of jobs, but at least it would hold the wound closed. When she was done, she put an arm under Bordan's shoulder and helped him up.

Teon nodded at her in thanks, leaving her to go and wash his hands and check on his other men, while she cleaned up the smaller wound on Bordan's head.

'How are you feeling?' she asked him.

'As though I've just been stabbed and stitched up!

If it wasn't for Teon, I'd be dead right now. This huge beast came over the crenels and lunged at me from behind. Teon got there just in time.'

Just as he had for her yesterday. She shuddered, not wanting to think about the constant danger they were putting themselves in. And if Harold's men were breaching the walls and the combat was so up close, were the enemy making incursions into their lines of defence? Were they making headway? She hoped not.

'You and Teon seem close,' she said.

'We met at the garrison…' He shrugged. 'It's tough out there. You have to know the man beside you has your back. That was him for me and the other way round. But he doesn't let anyone get *too* close, you know? But he's the best, none the less.' He grinned.

She wondered why Teon was so private—did he find it hard to trust people? She imagined it came with the territory of being born royal and having a kingdom to take care of, living under constant threat of someone wanting to usurp your title, but did it also have something to do with the person whom he'd looked up to—relied on the most—letting him down? Edmund had spoken to her of his regret, how Teon had never been able to forgive him for his misdeeds. Had his father's affair tarnished his ideas of loyalty?

'Teon took me under his wing when I was orphaned. He gave me a bed and hot food, trained me and hauled me up through the ranks. He gave my life purpose again. I wouldn't be where I am now without him,' Bordan continued.

'You mean injured, fighting a war?' she jested.

'By his side. I wouldn't want it any other way,' he said, showing his support. And she could tell his right-hand man looked up to him, as most of his men did.

So he could take care of someone when he wanted to, she thought. Although hadn't he done the same with her last night? Yet she had relied on him to take care of her and he let her down before. She refused to rely on him again.

She held up her hand in front of the warrior, keeping her thumb and little finger in her palm. 'How many fingers am I holding up?'

He grinned. 'Thirty?'

She giggled. 'I think perhaps you need to rest a while, before heading back out there.'

'Yes…and I think you'd better go and check on our leader over there,' he said, nodding his head in the direction of the other side of the hall. 'The way he's looking at me right now, I think he's regretting saving my life.'

She turned around in surprise and saw Teon heading out of the hall and into the corridor, a scowl carved into his face. He slammed the door behind him with more force than was necessary.

Had she done something wrong?

She washed her hands in the bowl of water and made her way through the people covering every spare inch of space. Heading down the corridor, she heard sounds coming from the kitchen and found Teon in there pouring himself an ale. Egeslic had followed her, but when he saw she'd found Teon, he gave her a curt nod and disappeared back into the hall again.

'There you are. I wondered where you'd gone. Shall I take a look at that wound on your head, too?'

He reached up to touch it and frowned, as if he hadn't even felt or noticed his injury. 'Not necessary. It's nothing.'

'How bad was it out there today?'

'Hellish,' he said, downing the jar of ale in one go before pouring himself another. It must have been bad—she'd noticed he didn't usually drink much.

'Going by the rows of wounded people in here, I'd guessed it to be so.' She wiped her hands on her pinafore. She realised she must look a state with her hair pulled back into a band and her kirtle smeared with dirt.

'They've dug defence ditches. This is clearly just the beginning. We did put an almighty dent in his infantry though.' He smiled faintly.

He took another sip of ale and then turned round, leaning back against the table. He passed her the cup to take some. She accepted it gratefully and took a small sip of the liquid. It felt good against her parched throat as it slipped down. She handed it back to him and it felt as though they were two confidants, sharing something secret. She guessed he didn't know that sharing a cup where she came from meant you were creating an everlasting bond.

'Why were you talking to that man who hit you yesterday?' he asked darkly. 'I told you to stay away from them.'

'He was hurt.'

'So?'

'You promised we'd help him and his family, remember? I couldn't ignore his wound. Besides, his wife is with child. He's worried for her and his son.'

'That's no excuse for how he behaved.' He glowered. 'And Bordan?'

'You asked me to patch up his wounds,' she said, her brow creasing, confused.

'I didn't tell you to take off his clothes and run your hands all over his bare chest!'

'What did you expect me to do?' she asked him, exasperated. Her eyes narrowed on him. 'Wait, are you...jealous?' she asked, incredulous. But when his lips thinned and his hands tightened into fists, she instantly knew she'd said the wrong thing.

She tentatively stepped towards him and went to brush his hair out of his eyes, to see how bad his wound was, and with a force that surprised her, he gripped her wrist, halting her, making her breath hitch.

'Maybe I am. Bordan is my best man, but I felt like taking my own blade to him when I saw him making you laugh, your hands on his body.' She felt the pulse beating at the base of her throat and he must have noticed it, too, as he lifted his other hand to stroke his thumb over it. 'Because despite everything that's going on, I can't stop thinking about that kiss we shared yesterday. Can you?'

Caught in his vice-like grip, she didn't think she could move. She wasn't sure she wanted to. She was both excited and afraid all at once, wondering what he was going to do.

'Was it your first kiss, Revna?' he asked.

'You know it was,' she whispered.

That seemed to please him, releasing some of the tension in his shoulders, and he loosened his hold on her, instead taking her hand in his, holding it as he brought it down to his side. 'It's the only thing that's got me through today—that and the thought of doing it again.'

'Why would you want to do that?' She swallowed. 'I thought you didn't like anything about me.' Her tongue darted out to moisten her lips, nervous.

'That's not entirely true,' he said.

And she stopped breathing, going still in expectation as his molten brown eyes looked down at her, waiting for her to say something.

'Isn't it?'

He shook his head. 'No.'

Her heart began to pound faster as his other hand came up to cup her cheek, firm but gentle. Careful. And she realised this was what desire must feel like— to want a man to put his hands on you. To want him to kiss you. And unable to help it, she stepped towards him, leaning into him, wanting to get closer.

She felt her legs begin to tremble and was grateful when he released her hand and slid his arm around her back, holding her up and drawing her closer still. He brought her right up against his large, powerful body and her pulse leapt wildly as he slowly bent his head, bringing his lips down to graze hers, and her eyes fluttered shut.

With an intensity she wasn't expecting, his tongue swept inside her mouth, softer than before, gently stroking, caressing, and she gasped at the thrill that rushed through her body. She could feel her heartbeat thudding against his chest. She glided her own tongue against his, hoping she was doing it right.

His face felt cool compared to the heat of his mouth and he still smelt of rain and woodsmoke and today's battle. His hand drifted from her cheek into her hair, pressing her closer, and his tongue became more insistent, open-mouthed, hot and heavy, and her arms came up to his shoulders, clinging on for support.

He tipped her head back, exposing her neck to him, and he broke away from her lips and began to leave a trail of kisses down her throat. She savoured the sensations he was creating. She wanted this, she realised. She had been craving his touch—not only to satisfy her frustrating desire, but she wanted to get closer to him. To feel a connection with him, even if it was a dangerous idea. But hadn't she always wanted that, for as long as she could remember?

When his mouth reached the rim of her pinafore, nibbling and nipping at her skin, his thickening beard softly grazing her, his lips pressing soft kisses to the tops of her swollen breasts, every swirl of his tongue sent a fresh coil of heat down between her legs and she moaned softly.

Before yesterday, she hadn't ever kissed him before and now his fingers and his lips were on her, branding her skin, laying claim to her at last, and she just stood there, helpless, letting him do it.

His hand left her waist and skimmed up her ribcage, coming up to cup one of her breasts through her kirtle, his thumb flicking over her erect nipple that was straining beneath the material, and she wrapped her hands around his neck, pressing her hips harder against him, wriggling against him, seeking greater satisfaction. But then his large hands came down on her hips, holding her fast.

When he lifted his head away slightly, his dark hooded eyes stared down at her, a slow, questioning smile crossing his features, and she swayed, feeling breathless and unsteady on her feet.

'Do you even know what you're doing?' he asked her.

'No.'

And then with a soft curse, as if all restraint was gone, he was lifting her, carrying her until her back came up against the wall, and he began frantically rucking up her skirts, his hands trembling in urgency, his knee roughly parting her legs as his fingers slid up the back of her thighs. It was as if he was desperate with need, wanting to seek out her intimate places, and she was encouraging him, raising her leg to hook over his hip, allowing him better access.

When his hands curved over the rounds of her bare bottom and squeezed, she whimpered. She writhed against him again, feeling the ridge of him against her stomach, wondering if she had created that, and then her world was suspended as his fingers dipped between her legs, delving into her moist heat, and she cried out in surprised pleasure.

'Revna?'

They both froze.

'Edlynne,' she gasped, tearing her lips from his,

gently pushing at his shoulders, her face heating. His sister was calling her from somewhere along the corridor.

What was happening? She couldn't believe she was letting him put his hands all over her. Here. Now. After all this time. Someone could walk in at any moment. His sister... 'We can't do this. Not here.'

He growled and lifted his head from hers. 'Let's go to my room,' he said, his fingers lightly grazing her soft, secret places, not making any signs of retreating now they'd sought out their destination.

It made her blood heat, her legs feel like vapour. She shook her head. 'She needs me.'

'I need you,' he said.

They heard footsteps run past the kitchen and down the corridor. Teon dipped his head, kissing her neck again, and she succumbed, melting into him once more. His large hand covered her mound and his fingers plunged through her curls into her soft, wet folds, parting her, and as he began to stroke her, intimately, she whimpered into his broad shoulder.

'I don't understand,' she whispered, struggling to talk, the wicked sensations he was creating lashing through her. She clung on to him. 'One moment you hate me...can't stand the sight of me...' she stuttered, 'and now you're putting your hands on me, touching me, like this... I don't know what you want from me.'

'Don't you really?' he said, moving his finger purposely around her tiny nub.

'Oh,' she gasped.

He lowered his head, his lips trailing across the top

of her cleavage, teasing her while touching her with precision below. 'My body wants you, despite what my head says,' he whispered. 'And as we're stuck here together, in the midst of a war, we might as well give each other the satisfaction it seems we both require. I want the wedding night we never had, Revna,' he said. 'And I think you want that, too.'

'Tell me, would it be a duty or a pleasure?' he asked, tugging her knee higher over his hip, gazing down into her hooded eyes as he pushed his finger gently inside her.

She groaned out loud in shocked pleasure, her head tipping forward to rest on his shoulder. And a bolt of triumph tore through him at her surrender—that she was letting him take ownership of her body, even though it was only with his hands.

Seeing her beautiful fingers on Bordan's chest, soothing his friend's wounds, had sent him slightly crazy. He knew he was being unfair—he had seen how hard she had been working out there in the hall, looking after everyone. He had noticed how the people seemed to admire her leadership and kindness—the men as well as the women. She was holding them together. Hell, she was holding him together.

But seeing her laugh with Bordan, he'd felt a troubling feeling of possessiveness—that she was his, no one else's. He knew he was being irrational, irritable, due to the brutalness of today's battle and his pent-up lust, but as his finger pressed deep inside her, the breach of her innocent body felt like a huge victory. And he needed a win right now.

Why was she making him feel like this? He'd even thought he'd tried to pick a fight with her just to ease some of his frustration, but he'd ended up kissing her instead. Bringing his mouth down on hers, he'd wondered if she'd respond with the same eager passion she had at the witan yesterday morning. And she had.

But it was the impatient wriggle that had got to him, telling him she wanted more, that she, too, had had to wait too long for fulfilment, and his restraint had snapped. Now he had a desire to erase all distance and clothes between them. He was finally giving in to the battle his body had been fighting against his desire.

He removed his finger, stroking between her folds again, opening her up to him before plunging back into her.

And he knew she was close. Her breath was quickening against his neck, her fingers clinging on to him for dear life, and it was making him so hard, he wanted to lift her skirts, wrap her legs around his waist and thrust into her. He wanted to claim her at last. He needed that release.

But then he heard footsteps coming back up the corridor towards them and wondered what Edlynne wanted. And what the hell he was doing? He was the leader of this fortress. What would it look like if someone were to find them here, in an embrace like this, with everything that was going on?

He should be out in the hall, boosting morale, not

acting like the reckless boy he'd once been, finding a girl after one of his father's feasts and having a quick tumble with her in one of the stables. Only this wasn't some stranger, this was his wife… Yet Revna had never done this before—didn't he owe her more than a secret tryst in the kitchen?

But had he forgotten who she was? A heathen. So why the hell was he feeling like this—wanting her more than he'd wanted anyone?

Taking a deep breath, he took a step back. It was harder than he thought. She was looking up at him, her eyes wide, startled, her cheeks beautifully flushed, and it took all his resolve to remove his hand from between her legs, releasing her skirts. 'You're right. We can't do this now. Here.'

And it was just as well he did, as Edlynne suddenly popped her head round the door. She looked frantic.

'There you both are!' she said, distraught. 'We've been looking for you everywhere! The fortress is on fire. We can't get it under control. Please, come quickly.'

He sent Revna a look, but she avoided his gaze. Damn. There were other things he needed to get under control, too.

She went to follow his sister out of the door, brushing past him, the floral scent of her drifting under his nose, and he swallowed down another rush of desire, the hardness in his groin not abating. He gripped her arm, tugging her back.

'Come to my room tonight,' he whispered. 'Tonight, we won't be disturbed.'

Then he released her and she was gone.

Teon pushed his way through the crowds in the courtyard. The sky was darkening above and, all around them, flames were engulfing the palisades, spreading to the roofs of the farmsteads. Had Harold done this, or one of their own, wanting to help the enemy by putting an end to the siege?

Men were trapped in burning buildings and he raced to pull them from the wreckage as beams came tumbling down. How long had this been going on? All the time he'd been preoccupied, trying to quell the flames in his own body? Glancing over at Revna, he watched in awe as he saw her put out the flames on a young girl's body with the skirts of her own pinafore. She fascinated him.

People were racing to and from the well, carrying buckets of water to douse the flames, but the heat was overpowering, preventing them from getting too close. He was just beginning to despair, thinking their walls would be ruptured, that they'd be defenceless against Harold's men on the morrow, when the heavens opened and the rain came pounding down. The people cheered and he sent his silent thanks up above, thinking his parents must be watching over them. They really could do with some good luck right now.

Finally, as the rain thrashed against the blaze, the flames of the fire were quietened. For a moment, all was still. The people looked on, aghast, taking in the skeleton trees and blackened, charred timbers where buildings once stood. At least the stone keep and the walls were still standing. As long as they had those, they could still survive this.

Yet everything was in disarray—people were beginning to wail, having suffered more losses, clambering over burned wood and rocks to get to safety, and he didn't think he'd ever seen such a bleak sight. He felt so overwhelmingly tired. So responsible. Was he failing them? He began to pick up some of the wood, tossing it aside, attempting to clear a path, when he saw Revna by the well, her cheeks damp—from the rain, or had she been crying?

'Are you all right?' he asked, instantly dropping what he was doing and crossing the path towards her.

'I'm fine. It's silly really. It's just, this was my mother's kirtle.' She smiled sadly, smoothing down the singed skirts. 'I cherished it. It was something to remind me of her.'

'I'm sorry, Revna. But what you did out there…' he said, shaking his head. 'I saw you—you saved that girl's life.'

'I guess nothing matters compared to people's lives, especially an old dress,' she sniffed.

'I'm sure your mother would have been proud,' he said, swiping a little soot off her face. He inclined his head. 'You impressed me.'

She gave a half-smile. 'Oh, dear. I'd better be careful. I don't want to do that too often.'

He grinned, enjoying her humour, even at a time like this. He gripped her elbow, helping her up. He wanted to take her inside and finish what they'd started. Even this latest catastrophe hadn't dampened his hunger for her. He wondered what it was about this woman that made him want her so badly. Was it simply because she was his wife and he had rights he hadn't wielded over her? Once he took what he needed, would he finally be sated?

'Come inside and warm yourself by the fire. Have something to eat. You'll soon feel better. Let's leave this mess till morning, when we can see what we're doing. I don't have the heart to tackle it now.' And he turned and announced the same to the people, telling them to get some food inside their bellies and some rest before tomorrow. They all needed to keep up their strength.

As they reached the doorway, before they headed inside with the rest of the people, he hooked his finger beneath her chin. 'And I haven't forgotten we have other unfinished matters to attend to,' he said.

'Teon…perhaps it's a bad idea,' she protested.

'As I'm finding it hard to stay focused—can't concentrate on anything else, putting my people at risk as I'm distracted—I'd say it was a necessity, wouldn't you?'

Chapter Six

Revna's body had been a quivering mess all evening. She tried to tell herself it was because of the fire outside, the further destruction to their home, but it was the flames raging inside her body caused by Teon's touch that she had a feeling were to blame. He had given her a taste of what his hard, muscular body felt like pressed up against hers. And she flushed, thinking about how she'd encouraged him, wriggling against him, willing him to put his hands all over her… She was shocked he wanted to!

But she was no fool—she knew it didn't have anything to do with him liking her, he had said so himself. It was purely about a need that had to be satisfied. A desire for a consummation that had never taken place. Perhaps even a distraction to get through this horrendous siege. And could she really go ahead with it, knowing that was all it was? But perhaps this was for the best… Perhaps they could both take what they needed from each other and be done with it, like laying ghosts to rest. She'd just have to protect her feelings and defend her heart from getting broken again.

She hadn't seen Teon since the courtyard earlier this evening—when the flames had eaten into the very heart of the fortress, licking at the keep. If they hadn't spent so long in the kitchen, could they have stopped the fire from spreading? She felt awful about that. But Teon, like the fire, had been all-consuming. They had been fortunate it had rained when it did, otherwise it could have been so much worse. They might not be sitting here now.

She had made her way around the hall, trying to put a smile on all the forlorn faces of the people, checking to see if they had everything they needed. And now, sitting down to eat with Edlynne and Eldrida, she wanted to return to the past, to normalcy, when Edmund was still alive and all was well. But then Teon wouldn't be here and she knew there was no way she would wish him away again. Having him here had rallied the people and inspired them to fight. She saw how they all looked up to him, with respect and admiration. As did she. He was a leader to believe in.

She glanced around looking for him, wondering where he was. The anticipation of their late-night assignation was setting her on edge, the evening dragging on and on, and she was a bundle of nerves. She could barely eat her stew and was aware of the Princesses chattering away beside her, but she struggled to join in their conversation. She just couldn't focus, wondering what lay in store for her in his room later on.

Then, suddenly, he was there, striding into the hall with Bordan, looking more attractive than she'd ever seen him, the sleeves of his fresh tunic rolled up, his hair damp and combed through. Her mouth dried. He looked as though he'd washed, the blood on his forehead gone.

Their eyes met across the room and her heart exploded in her chest. As he headed towards them, she tried to get her pulse under control. Towering over their table, he asked his sisters about their day and thanked Edlynne for alerting them about the fire. How was he so calm and composed? Heat was soaring through her body. She felt panicked, excited and exposed all at once, as if everyone could tell what she was thinking.

When Edlynne stood and announced she was going to bed, Teon met Revna's dark gaze over the flickering flames. He gave her a knowing smile and she practically squirmed in her seat. What was happening to her? How could he make her feel these things? She could barely even mutter a goodnight to the Princesses.

When he announced he was retiring, too, her stomach flipped. She watched as he stood, slanting her a look, before turning and working his way through the people, heading out of the hall, but not before a pretty woman, about Revna's age, approached him, said something to him and he smiled. Jealousy erupted inside her, especially when the woman placed her hand on his arm. But then he carried on, only stopping to look back at Revna from the door before disappearing through it.

She sat there, not knowing what to do. She couldn't just excuse herself and make her way to his room, could she? What would people think? Would her shadow, Egeslic, follow her, knowing exactly where she was going and what she was going to do? She felt her face heat at the thought. But then, they were married. It wasn't as if she was doing anything wrong.

She wondered why he hadn't taken her with him. Wouldn't most normal married couples retire to bed together? But they weren't normal, were they? They never had been. And perhaps, a thought mocked her, he was still ashamed of her.

What if Teon had changed his mind and didn't want her to come to him? But what if he did? A deep tremble started in her legs. Once he'd got what he wanted, then what? He'd spoken no words of love... or even like. Knowing he didn't care for her, could she really do this?

She excused herself from the table, telling Bordan she hoped he would feel better in the morning, and slipped out of the door and into the courtyard, into the pelting rain. She needed to think, to clear her head. Or maybe she just needed to act. She wasn't sure. She went over to the well and washed her face, before going to see the horses in the stables.

She topped up their hay and stroked the colt's mane. She thought he'd grown in the space of a day. What a magnificent horse he would become one day. He had been so brave, with the battle going on around them. She gave herself a talking to, telling herself she could learn a thing or two from the animal and that she must not be a coward either. Finally, she headed back into the keep and quietly slipped through the hall and out the back, to Teon's room.

She knocked softly, before glancing up the corridor to see Egeslic standing there. She muttered her goodnight, her face burning, and he nodded in return.

Her heart was in her mouth, her knees shaking, and then Teon opened the door and everything but him was forgotten. He stood in his tunic and trousers, his feet bare, his eyebrows raised.

'What took you so long?' he asked. Then he noticed her wet and miserable appearance. 'My God. You look awful. You're soaked through!'

He took her hand and tugged her inside, closing the door behind him.

'I went for a walk.'

'At this time of night? In the rain? Alone?' He frowned.

'Well, you won't let me out during the day!' she said tartly. 'And don't worry, Egeslic was lurking in the shadows.'

He took a step towards her, his brow furrowing. 'I thought you might have changed your mind.'

She shook her head, unable to speak. And when he saw the quiver of her lips, the uncontrollable trembling of her legs, he must have taken pity on her because he took her chin between his fingers in that commanding, gentle way she was getting used to.

'Are you all right? We don't have to do anything

you don't want to do, Revna. We can just talk. And that chair is pretty comfortable.' He grimaced. 'I can sleep in it again.'

Taking another look at her, he tutted. 'You could have caught your death out there! I don't want to be forceful,' he said, a smile curling up the corners of his mouth, 'but you should probably get out of these wet things.'

She thought he was going to strip her naked right there and then—he was practically doing so with his eyes—but instead he turned and rummaged around for something in a trunk, before pulling out a blanket and using it to dry her hair, patting her arms, trying to soak up some of the moisture, while she just stood there, letting him. He draped it around her shoulders to keep her warm. 'Wrap this around you,' he said. 'Take those off. I'll put some more wood on the fire.'

She was grateful when he turned his back to her, and with trembling fingers, she unclasped her wet, heavy *hangerok* and pulled off her kirtle, placing them over the chair, before quickly tugging the blanket around her as tightly as she could, using it as a robe and securing it with a brooch.

'I'll have Edlynne bring your clothes in here tomorrow,' he said.

Chewing on her lip, she came to sit next to him by the hearth.

'I feel bad we didn't stop the fire sooner,' she said.

'I doubt we could have done any more than we did,' he said, reassuring her, the flames reflecting in his eyes. 'We were lucky the rain was on our side.'

'Do you think Harold's men started it?'

'I can't be sure. If they did, I think they would have stayed to attack while we were in a weak spot. It seems to me it might have been one of our own.'

She shuddered, holding the blanket tighter around her. 'Another deceiver. Can no one be trusted?' she said.

'Very few.'

'Have you ever met Harold?' she asked carefully.

'Once. On my father's request. But I felt as though I was being disloyal to my mother. After I found out about my father's affair, it was as if I had to choose between my parents, as if I had to pick a side.'

'That must have been difficult.'

'Of course I sided with my mother. I was hurt and angry. My respect for my father was gone, almost overnight.'

'Did you ever talk to him about it?'

He shrugged. 'He tried to talk to me. I wasn't too interested in listening. I stubbornly withheld my forgiveness. Instead, I used the affair against him every time we argued. To be honest, I'd lost trust in him completely. He said the affair was over, but I became obsessed that he was still seeing her, going behind my and my mother's backs. I was constantly searching for clues that he was continuing with his secret meetings. I felt so gullible and swore to myself I'd never be so ignorant again.'

'Perhaps there were problems you didn't know about between him and your mother? It takes two people to make a marriage work.'

He nodded, his eyes raking over her face. 'Perhaps. But there is no excuse for what he did. My mother tried to put it behind her, for my sake, I think…but they were never the same after that'

'What about your sisters? Did you speak to them about it? I wasn't sure if they knew.'

'I never did. There was such an age gap between us, I never felt it was my place. But they must have heard the rumours…and I do think the speculation impacted my father's reputation. It made him less popular, less revered. I'm sure some people thought that if he couldn't remain loyal to his wife, how could he be loyal to his subjects? I determined when I took the crown after him, I would be well regarded,' he said. 'That I would never ruin the people's trust in me like he did.'

'You want to be popular?' She smiled.

'Absolutely! Don't we all?'

'You seemed pretty popular with that woman out there in the hall… Someone you know?'

His eyes narrowed. 'That was Ealfrith's mother, thanking me for teaching him how to defend himself. Are *you* jealous, Revna?'

She knew she couldn't lie. Not to him. He was a man who expected the truth at all times. 'Yes. I didn't like the way she was touching you.'

He nodded. 'It's not her I've been waiting for in here, though, is it? It was you.'

She swallowed. 'Teon, you mustn't let your feelings about the affair stain your memories of your father as a parent over the years.'

He smiled sadly. 'I learned so much from him. I wanted to be like him in a lot of ways. I probably should have told him that before it was too late.'

'I'm sure he knew.'

He raked a hand through his hair. 'Maybe I should have been more accepting of Harold. There was no love lost between us and now look where we are. I certainly didn't know he harboured this hatred towards me, or had designs on the throne. I never thought he was capable of doing something like this.'

'Why would you? How strange the lure of power is. It must be hard, everyone wanting, desiring what you have…'

Kneeling before her, he moved nearer with intent, his eyes burning into hers. 'It is.'

Were they still talking about his crown?

'Desire…that's a very appropriate word right now. Because I want you, Revna. Badly. Is that what you want, too?'

Her mouth dried. She didn't think she could speak.

He stood, holding his hand out for her to take, and gently lifted her to her feet. 'I don't want to talk any more, do you?'

She shook her head, biting her lip.

'You said you understand the way things are, between a man and a woman?' he asked.

Her face heated. 'Only through glimpses of the things I've seen after your father's feasts, when some of the men and women had had too much ale…' she said. 'And from you…earlier…in the kitchen.'

He muttered a soft curse. 'I'm sorry. I was much

too heavy-handed. Much too in a rush. Forgive me? I promise I will take things slower tonight.'

She noticed he moved carefully and spoke to her softly. All thoughts of the day fell away as he took her face in his hands, bent his head and pressed his lips against hers. His lips slowly coaxed hers open and his tongue invaded her mouth again, kissing her unhurriedly, deeply.

He hooked his arm around her waist, holding her to him, his solid thighs pressing against hers, and her hands splayed out over his chest. That peculiar, responsive heat burned low in her stomach again and she let out a little gasp of pleasure. She couldn't believe he wanted her. And he had his answer—she wanted him too.

'I want to get closer. I need to see your body,' he moaned into her mouth and moved backwards, taking her with him, until they reached the bed. He lowered his big body down on to it, sitting on the edge, looking up at her. 'I want to touch you, explore you, everywhere. Is that what you want, too?' he said.

And she nodded, mute, her stomach a tangle of nerves. He had given her a taste of what lay in store, but she still didn't know what she was meant to do.

Slowly, reverently, and with trembling hands, he unclasped her brooch, setting it down on the end of the bed, before raising his hands to part the blanket, sweeping it open across her breasts. Curving the wool over her shoulders, he let it drop to the floor and she gasped.

Standing before him completely naked, she let out

a little strangled cry of protest at the sudden intimate exposure, trying to slant her body away from him, attempting to cover herself with her hands, as a tingling heat swept up the back of her neck and across her face. But his large hands held her wrists either side of her body, so he could look at her, and she shivered. Her nipples hardened under his gaze, her stomach tightened. She tucked her elbows into her waist and looked down at the floor, unable to meet his eyes.

He pressed a soft kiss to her stomach and she dragged in a breath. 'Teon,' she moaned, her whole body trembling. Was this the norm? she wondered. For a man to strip his wife naked and study her in such erotic detail? She had imagined a darkened room and that she could lie hidden beneath a pile of furs. She knew honesty was important to him…that he expected a level of openness…but this was almost merciless.

'You are so beautiful,' he whispered, his eyes raking over her. 'Incredible.'

His eyes dropped to the ink around her hip and he took an intake of breath. 'What's this?' he said, releasing one of her hands to trail his fingers over the dark feather-like markings.

'My mother did it for me. It's the wings of a raven— or a Valkyrie. My name means raven, after my father—' She cut herself off, realising now was not the time to bring up her father. She was babbling…

'A Valkyrie?' he asked and she let out a breath when she realised he was going to ignore her comment.

'A symbol of female strength and courage. We believe Valkyries are the protectors of death.'

'It's…'

She swallowed.

'Exquisite. As are you.'

He dipped his head and trailed his tongue over the dark plumes of ink and she felt heat and moisture pool at the junction of her thighs, so she squeezed them together. 'Teon,' she whispered. 'You promised slow.'

'It seems I have a growing interest in your beliefs,' he said wickedly. But then he relented and stood, releasing her wrists to curve his hands around her body, resting his forehead against hers. 'I'm sorry,' he said.

But his hands weren't acting as though they were sorry, as they smoothed down over her bottom, caressing her soft skin with his fingertips and drawing her closer to him, so she could feel the long hard length of him against her stomach, making her squirm with pleasure and anticipation, and he began plundering her mouth with kisses once more.

His other hand skated up her side, taking one of her breasts in his hand, cupping her creamy pink swell of skin, crushing her softly between his fingers and she groaned, arching into him. She fitted his palm perfectly and wanted more of the feelings he was creating. She wanted him to squeeze and crush and touch her everywhere.

She realised she probably needed to touch him in return, that she needed to remove his own clothes if she wanted to feel his skin against hers, but her fingers were shaking so much, she wasn't sure she was able. Reaching out tentatively, she struggled to tug his tunic free of his trousers and pull it upwards, and he broke apart for a moment to help her bring it up over his chest and his head and discard it. Her eyes widened at the magnificent expanse of his chest before her.

He was all hard, lean muscle, his arms beautifully built. He had various scars, some deeper than others, which only added to his allure, and a thin line of dark hair leading down the centre of his stomach, tempting her to follow its path. Her eyes roamed over him greedily, her hands following suit, her fingertips trailing over his skin, wanting to learn the lines of him, and he sucked in a ragged breath.

Then his lips were back on hers, his fingers toying with her nipples, and she had never imagined it could feel this good. Then he dipped his head, taking one marble-hard peak into his hot mouth and she cried out in pleasure, her hands delving into his hair, holding his head in place at her breast.

She closed her eyes to savour the sensations washing over her, wondering in amazement at the liquid excitement mounting between her legs. She wanted him to touch her there, as he had earlier. She couldn't wait any longer. And she knew, despite what was happening to Kinborough, despite the danger they were in, she didn't want to be anywhere else. She wanted to be right here, in this moment, with Teon, where the past and future didn't matter.

As if he was a sear from her homeland and could read her thoughts, knowing what she wanted, his large hand trailed down to steal between her legs, teasing over her thighs, and she parted them slightly, shivering against his fingers in anticipation, willing him higher. And when he moved his fingers along her crease, opening her up, she gasped out her pleasure, wrapping her arms around his neck for support, thinking her legs might give way.

Then they were moving. He was lifting her off the floor and then laying her down on the bed, pressing her down into the furs, spreading her thighs with his knee as he came to lie down next to her. Holding himself up on his elbow, she could feel the hard ridge of him pressing into her hip, making her slick with excitement, wondering what he was going to do, and then his hand was back working between her legs.

He pushed one finger deep inside her and she gasped, drawing his head closer, wanting him to kiss her on the mouth again. And as his tongue swirled against hers, his fingers stroked and rubbed her, plunging inside her over and again.

'Teon,' she gasped, wanting to warn him she could take no more of this euphoric torture, unsure what was expected of her, or even what was happening to her.

'Let go,' he whispered. 'Take your pleasure.' And she did, throwing her head back and coming undone against the pressure of his fingers. She thrashed around beneath him, allowing her climax to take over and she came apart, whispering his name over and over again.

Teon held her close until the aftershocks of her climax subsided. She brought her arm up across her forehead, shielding her eyes from him as she released a shuddering, shaky breath. He hoped that meant she had enjoyed it.

He bent his head to kiss her shoulder and her beautiful chest.

'Have you done this a lot?' she whispered, biting her lip.

'What?' He lifted his face to look at her as his fingers drew little circles over her silky thighs.

'Have there been many other women, while you were away?' she asked, lowering her arm and turning to look at him.

He frowned. 'You are referring to the things you've heard about me.'

'Yes.'

He flattened his hand over her stomach, his fingertips trailing over the wispy lines of ink on her hip. 'The rumours aren't true, Revna. I haven't taken a woman to bed since we married. My father may have tainted my ideas of marriage, shattering the idyll, but I would never do that... I'm not guilty of any infidelity, if that's what you're asking.'

'Why not?'

Her cheeks were pink from the pleasure he'd given her, her eyes bright and her features softened and relaxed, and she looked more beautiful than he'd ever seen her. 'I mean, it's been a long time, hasn't it? For a man like you...' she said. 'And you weren't exactly pining for me.'

He smiled, raising an eyebrow. 'A man like me?'

She shrugged. 'You know what I mean.'

'I'm not sure I do. But we were much too busy

fighting at the garrison. And there was your father to consider,' he said seriously. 'I knew if I was unfaithful, your father could break our alliance. I'd gone through with the damn marriage…'

'Of course! You're so complimentary.'

He shrugged. 'It's the truth. I have been celibate these past years, knowing I could not be intimate with anyone else in case it should bring war to these lands. My goal has always been to create stability, not cause more unrest.'

'So, what you're saying is, I'm your only option?'

He gave a short laugh, not even dignifying that with any words of response.

She frowned. 'Celibate…does that include…the things we've just done?'

'There has been nothing, no one, since we married. I assume there hasn't for you either?'

'You know there hasn't!'

And he grinned. He knew it was the truth. He could tell by the way she'd gasped in surprise and panted out her pleasure that she'd never been touched before. It had made him so hard and excited, so determined to make it good for her.

'What about before we were wed?' she asked.

His fingers stilled. 'Enough of the questions! I'm not a monk, Revna…of course there were women before, but none of any importance.'

For a time, after he'd discovered his father had had an affair, he had overcompensated for a lack of satisfaction with his life with too much ale and far too many women, yet there had never been any real intimacy. And he'd never thought of the consequences, the way he had to now. He'd never cared about any of them, or their pleasure. But it was strange…he did want to please Revna. Or maybe he just couldn't get enough of her beautiful body. He was achingly hard for her and her line of questioning was maddening, distracting him from the things he wanted to do with her.

He pressed a kiss against the corner of her mouth. 'But it has been a very, very long time. And you're right, I do have needs…' He pulled her closer against his groin, conveying his desire. His lips nibbled and nipped his way along her neck, then he pushed himself up so he was kneeling to her side. He took her hand and placed it over the hard ridge in his trousers. 'Can you feel how much I want you?' he whispered.

She bit her lip. 'Teon, I want to please you, but I don't know how. Will you teach me?'

It was gratifying to hear and made him grow even harder still. He shrugged off his trousers and stretched out beside her, rolling her over on to her side to face him. Taking her hand in his, he wrapped her fingers around his thick shaft and enjoyed giving her a lesson in how to touch him. 'Just do what feels right,' he whispered.

As she continued to cradle him in her tight, possessive grip, it felt glorious. Her unhurried pace was like exquisite torture and he knew it wouldn't take long. It had been too long. As her other hand reached round and gripped his bottom, squeezing him tight, drifting her fingers over his skin, he knew he was on the brink.

'Does that feel good?' she whispered.

'So good.'

He drew her body closer, resting his forehead against hers, his hand at the back of her head coaxing her mouth over his tongue. How easy it would be to stretch his body out over her and thrust into her, he thought. He knew she was soaking wet and ready for him and it was making him so hard he felt ready to explode. He wanted to possess her—take ownership of her body—more than anything, yet something was holding him back. Could he really cross his moral boundaries in his pursuit of satisfaction?

And then it was unimportant, the battle in his head and his body over, for everything went blank as she stroked him faster, harder, and finally he erupted beneath her fingers.

Teon rolled away from her, lying back on the furs, one hand behind his head, and he gave a deep, satisfied sigh. They'd merely touched each other with their hands—hadn't even had full sex—so why was he feeling as if something remarkable had just happened between them? Was it simply because he hadn't been with a woman for so many winters?

Under hooded eyes, he glanced at her, strands of her long buttery blonde hair splayed out on the furs. He watched as she pulled one of the furs over her thighs, covering herself a little, and he knew he should get up and pull on his clothes. Now they'd got what they wanted from each other, he should be putting some distance between them, perhaps making light of what had happened…and he should definitely go and sleep in the chair. But damn, he didn't think he wanted to. He didn't want to move.

When his eyes roamed over her soft skin and her beautiful curves, he was disturbed to discover his excitement taking hold all over again. So much for getting satisfaction, he grimaced. She was like a moonflower that comes into bloom at night, opening before one's eyes. And if he was lucky, perhaps she'd stay open till sunrise.

He rolled over to face her, reaching out to stroke her hip. 'Are you sleeping?'

'No.'

'What are you looking forward to when this is all over?' he asked. 'What do you like to do?' He was suddenly curious as to what made her happy.

'Well…' she smiled '…the first thing I'd do is go for a long ride, out across the plains to the estuary… then maybe we'd all have a huge feast, sitting around the fire telling stories, celebrating getting through this. What about you?'

'A feast sounds good. And a proper bath. I used to swim in the ocean each day back at the garrison. I miss that. Although I doubt there'll be much time for swimming ever again. I'm sure my days will be full of duties, gatherings with the witan and serious talk.'

'Do you *want* to be King?' she asked in the darkness. 'I mean, I suppose you've never really had a choice in the matter. The responsibility must weigh heavy on your shoulders.'

'It would be far easier not to be,' he said, his fingers tracing the lines of her waist. 'But abandoning my duties is not an option. I have grown up knowing this was going to be my life. I've been preparing for it since I was born. Nothing could force me to ever abdicate. I wouldn't be able to live with myself.'

'There'll be no running away, then. We're stuck here for good?' she jested.

'You want to run away?'

'No…like you, I could never abandon the people. They're relying on you. *Us*. But in secret I sometimes wonder what it would be like to have a little more freedom, to come and go as I please… I was not born for this, like you.'

She was full of surprises. He thought most women were ambitious, that they set their heart on being Queen. Or perhaps that was just the women he'd grown up with. It had always made him wary of what women wanted from him, wondering if their feelings were genuine or just an act. But strangely, his wife seemed to pine for escape and adventure.

He didn't like the thought of her daydreaming of leaving here. He drew her closer to him, sweeping the furs from her body so he could look at her again. Damn, but she was beautiful. The most beautiful woman he'd ever seen.

What would it take to satiate this need for her? he wondered. Would he be able to rid himself of his desire if he took her with his body? But what of the repercussions? What if he were to plant a seed in her body? A child would certainly help to secure his lineage here, wiping out Harold's claim for good. But he knew he couldn't. He couldn't bed her—it would break the purity of the royal Saxon line and he wasn't willing to do that. It would go against everything he believed in.

But there were other ways and means of seeking satisfaction...and he rolled her over on to her back and pressed a kiss to her lips, pinning her hands above her head. She gasped, opening her eyes, and he resigned himself to the fact they probably wouldn't get any sleep tonight, as he strived to rid himself of these desires once and for all.

Chapter Seven

Revna was helping Edlynne and Eldrida prepare the pottage for tonight's dinner, making sure they didn't use too much meat, adding more vegetables to bulk it out and using only a little ale. She threw herself into peeling and chopping, trying to distract herself from worrying about Teon and his men.

It had been just days since the battle had begun and sometimes it felt like madness, as though they'd lost track of what part of the day it was. During daylight hours, the men fought bravely for their lives and their home while the women and children stayed inside, trying to stay busy, but today felt worse, as she longed for the night, when she knew she could be alone with him again.

Last night, lying in his bed, she and Teon had touched and teased each other all night long, unable to get enough of each other. She could still feel his hands on her body, stroking between her legs, even now. She had never imagined it could feel so good. Or that he'd want to do such things to her. It was wonderful, incredible—it made her blush just thinking about it.

But this morning he had awoken her with the worst news. He'd gently stroked her arm and she'd begrudgingly prised open her eyes. He was fully dressed in his chainmail and boots, sitting on the edge of the bed.

'Is it morning already?' she'd asked sleepily, frowning.

'Not quite. Me and a small group of the men are going to go through the tunnels. We're going to approach Harold's camp from behind—try to sabotage some of their stone throwers, perhaps steal some supplies.'

'No,' she'd said, aghast, sitting bolt upright, fully awake in an instant. She didn't want him to go.

'We'll be careful.'

'It's too dangerous,' she said, shaking her head. 'What if they see you? What if they discover where you've come from and find their way into the tunnels and the fortress?'

'Shh, they won't,' he said, smoothing her hair and tucking it behind her ears. 'But we have to do something to hamper their attack. We can't keep fighting off wave after wave of his men, losing more of our own each day... We need to try a different tack.'

She hadn't wanted him to leave her. Especially after such an incredible night. She was glad he'd woken her and shared his plans with her, including her, but she hadn't wanted to be left here in this fortress again without him. What if he didn't come back?

He'd looked tired and she couldn't believe he'd

been up half the night pleasuring her, when he had this on his mind. How had he kept it from her? But it wasn't as if they had done much talking in the dark hours.

Lying back on the furs in a state of bliss, she'd wanted to praise him for the pleasure he'd given her. She'd wanted to tell him she wanted a real marriage… that she had always cared for him. But she'd bitten back her words, knowing he wouldn't want to hear them. She knew that he didn't feel the same. He had told her this was purely a necessity, like quenching his thirst…so once he'd drained every last drop of passion from their loins, would he leave her again? Or was this just the beginning of something? For as amazing as last night had been, they still hadn't consummated their relationship. She wondered what was holding him back.

'Careful!' Edlynne asked, as she sliced the knife into her finger, drawing blood. The Princess handed her a pile of chopped carrots, bringing her back into focus. 'Is everything all right?'

'Yes,' Revna said, taking them and tossing them into the pot, watching the water bubble up around them. 'I'm just worried about the men. I hope they return soon, before the dawn breaks.'

Edlynne's eyes narrowed on her.

'Did something happen between you and Teon?' she asked.

'What makes you say that?' She flushed. She felt as if she had his handprints all over her, but it wasn't as if Edlynne could see them.

'You seem more worried about him than usual. And he came to see me, asking me to move your few belongings into his room. He also asked me to help him with a surprise for you…'

Revna's breath hitched.

'Something must have happened for him to want to do something nice for you,' Edlynne said, continuing to pry. 'Especially when he has so many other things to think about.'

Revna shrugged, setting the pot down over the hearth. But deep down, the Princess's words had given her hope. Teon was plotting something nice for her? She could scarcely believe it. Surely he had too much on his mind?

But she mustn't do that. She had promised to protect her heart against him. He hadn't once mentioned his feelings towards her—or even taken things any further. No, she didn't want Edlynne getting her hopes up and she mustn't either.

The dawn dragged so slowly as she waited for signs of Teon and his men returning. She did the rounds, checking on the people in the hall, fed the animals and cleared up some of the singed wood that still lay scattered about from the fire. She served up the bread and milk for breakfast and entertained some of the children in the square, before it was time for them to head inside, waiting for today's battle to commence.

When it didn't, she began to pace. She asked some of the sentinels on the bridge to check for any signs their men had been apprehended by the enemy, or if anything was amiss. But there was nothing. And when the sun was almost fully up, she began to imagine the worst. She hoped they hadn't been captured or hurt.

Finally, the doors burst open and the small group of men came in, bloodied and bruised but triumphant. She almost raced over to him, wanting to fling herself into his arms in relief, but she didn't think he'd like that. Not in front of everyone in the hall. She didn't think he would want to acknowledge their newfound intimacy to anyone.

But all that was important was that they were back. And they had accomplished what they'd set out to do. They'd managed to destroy some of the enemy's catapults, setting fire to them, before they'd been seen. They'd fought thirty or so of Harold's men, dispatching them while the rest of his army slept, then made it back to the old sewers, unnoticed. It had been a success. Yet all Revna could focus on was that Teon was hurt. He was holding his arm and there was a lot of blood.

'Let me see how bad it is,' she said, stepping towards him.

'What? Don't I get any words of praise?' He grinned.

'No, you're a fool!' she whispered, suddenly angry with him for putting himself at risk. 'You're crazy to go out there. Tell me you won't be doing that again.'

'I can't promise that,' he said.

'Next time they might be ready for you. Waiting.'

'Are you concerned about me, Revna?'

'Worried you're going to leave us all alone here again, yes.'

His eyes narrowed on her. 'I'm going to go and change,' he said coolly.

She sighed, wrapping her arms around her waist, watching him go. She shouldn't have attacked him or brought up the past. It was just he'd put her through agony all morning and her concern had bubbled over. She knew she should probably go and apologise.

After quickly checking over the other men's wounds and patching them up, she headed down the corridor and found Teon in his room, bare-chested, washing his wound with wool and a bowl of water. She stood in the doorway for a moment, unnoticed, staring. He was an incredibly beautiful man—all hard muscle and burnished skin. He was perfectly sculpted and so dynamic. She thought she could stand there and watch him all day.

'Here, let me do that,' she said, finally making her presence known, crossing the room towards him. She took the wool from his hand. 'I'm sorry about what I said out there. It's just… I've been fretting all morning. None of us want you getting hurt. We need you.'

'I understand,' he said. 'But it felt good to give Harold a bit back, knowing we were taking action, rather than just defending ourselves. We'll have sent them into a spin—they won't know what's hit them and they'll need time to regroup.'

She nodded, her mood lifting at seeing him so exuberant. She began wiping the blood from his arm and he winced as the material grazed his open wound.

'I'm glad it was a success. But you're hurt. I can't be happy about that. What happened?'

'I took on three men at once. It wasn't pretty.' He grimaced. She had seen how he fought. He was lethal—no man was a match for him. But three against one? She shuddered.

'This is deep. It's going to need a stitch,' she said. 'Shall I go and get a needle?'

He nodded, his face grim. 'If you must.'

She returned moments later with a needle and thread and a tankard of ale.

'I can cope with the discomfort, Revna, I don't need the ale,' he said. 'I don't drink much. It clouds my judgement.'

'The ale's for me. I can't cope with causing you pain,' she said and downed the liquid in one go.

He threw his head back and laughed in surprise and it was the most glorious sound. She'd like to hear that more often. Then she laughed, too, wiping the liquid from her mouth. She felt the tension of the morning receding, like the rolling tide on the distant shore.

'Tell me about your scars,' she said as she began with the first stitch.

'Are you trying to distract me from the pain?' he asked.

'Am I that obvious? Just keep still,' she said.

He sighed. 'They're all battle wounds, save one.' He pointed to the one just above his right eyebrow.

'How did you get that one?' She wanted to know

the stories behind each and every mark. She wanted to know everything she could about him.

'It was the day my father's lords were swearing allegiance to him in the hall. The oaths were going on and on and Edlynne kept complaining that she was so bored. We managed to sneak out of the hall when no one was watching and went outside, to get away from the crowds. I was about fifteen.

'She dared me to climb the sycamore tree on the keep,' he said, shaking his head. 'She wanted me to tell her how far I could see on the horizon. And then she challenged me to say the allegiance oath that we'd been listening to all morning out loud, while I was at the top. I felt so powerful, on top of the world, making my sister giggle…until I fell.' He grinned at the memory.

'I bet that hurt.'

'Yes. My pride more than anything. Especially when they had to fetch my parents as I'd been knocked unconscious. But it didn't stop me doing it again. I love it up there. That top branch? It's my favourite place in the fortress.'

'I love the view from up there, too, not that I've ever climbed the tree!' She smiled.

She tugged the skin together and he cursed, drawing in a breath. She was all too aware of his warm breath fluttering across her cheek, his dark, steady gaze on her face, causing her heart to pound. She tried to tell herself it was because she was worried about hurting him, but she knew it had more to do with just being near him again. She couldn't seem to be in his proximity with her blood racing, wanting him to put his hands on her...

'Now I know how Bordan felt yesterday and why he needed your hands to soothe him.'

She slanted him a look. 'Don't start that again,' she scorned him. 'He told me you two are close. That you came to his aid when he was orphaned.'

He nodded. 'I met him in an alehouse while I was at the garrison. There I was, feeling sorry for myself for everything my father had put me through...'

'You mean marrying me?' she asked, raising an eyebrow..

His lips curled upwards. 'Then he told me his story. He'd lost both his parents to the fever—at least I had one, for all my father's faults. There's always someone worse off, isn't there? We've stuck together ever since. He's the only person I can rely on.'

She nodded, but his words stung, sending a pang of pain to her heart. She thought it might have even shrunk a little. She wanted him to feel that way about her.

'What was it like there?'

'Cold. Desolate. The conditions were pretty bad. And we were constantly on edge, waiting for invaders to attack, but there were also long periods of boredom, with only the ocean or the alehouse to keep you entertained.'

'And that was preferable to being here?' she asked.

'I thought it was... I might have been wrong.'

Her breath hitched. 'There, all done,' she said, as

she tied a knot in the end of the thread, pulling away to check it over.

He studied her work. 'Very neat. Thank you, Revna.'

She nodded, putting the needle and thread down and washing her hands in the water.

When she turned round, he was right in front of her, his broad, bare chest filling her vision. He took her chin in his hands, tilting her face up to look at him. A swirl of intimacy enveloped them, making her feel hot and needy, a pulse thudding between her legs.

'Did you enjoy last night?' he asked her, his eyes glittering down into hers, reminding her once more of the way his fingers had eased inside her, time and again.

'Yes,' she said simply. 'But if I'd have known you were going to do this today...'

'What? Would you have stopped me from touching you?'

'Yes.'

'I don't think either of us had a choice in the matter, do you?' He stepped closer, pressing his body against hers. And she rested her forehead against his shoulder, breathing him in.

'And I don't think I can wait 'til tonight to do it again, can you?'

She shook her head, before looking up at him. She couldn't seem to say no to him. She couldn't get enough of him.

His hands came up to cradle her face and he bent down and pressed a soft kiss to her lips.

'Go and shut the door,' he said to her and, with

trembling legs, she went and closed it, before coming back into his open arms.

'So you're glad you agreed to sleep in here rather than the hall?' he muttered, his hands smoothing over her shoulders and down, taking her brooches between his fingers and unclasping them both with one flick of his clever fingers, letting her *hangerok* drop to the ground.

She nodded. 'Is this what you had in mind all along?'

He smoothed her arms up into the air, stretching them out above her head, before gripping the silky material of her kirtle and lifting it up, pulling it off over her head and arms, discarding it on to the floor.

'Are you questioning my motives?' He grinned and held her hips as he suddenly bent his head to kiss her nipple, making her gasp out her pleasure as he swirled his tongue around her engorged peak, suckling her. She couldn't believe she was naked again, in his arms…and in daylight hours. Then his tongue was trailing downwards over her taut stomach and lathering her hips, making her squirm beneath him.

He dropped down on to his knees and pushed her thighs wide apart. 'Teon!' she choked.

'It seems, my blue-eyed beauty, that your passion is as insatiable as mine.'

She whimpered, looking down at him as he began to trail his tongue up the inside of her leg, his thumb delving between her folds.

'And I can't wait any longer, I need to taste you,' he whispered, moving his hands away from her moist heat to hold the back of her thighs, and as his tongue roved upwards, she suddenly realised his intent, where he was heading, and she gasped, trying to break away.

Teon held her hips fast, but his erotic seduction became his own undoing, because he grew so hard he became dizzy with the desire for more. And he was so close to his destination now, there was no way he was going to stop. He wanted to taste her and finally bent his head and flicked his tongue over her nub. She cried out, her body going still in incredulity for just a moment, her head rolling back, her eyes closed.

Her hands grappled with the rim of the table behind her, holding on to it for support, and he wondered if she did actually want him to cease what he was doing—whether she could stand no more of his potent torture—before she bucked, raising her mound to meet him, and he lost all restraint, ravaging her with his mouth, his hands roaming round to hold her bottom, so she could do nothing but accept his onslaught of pure, unbridled pleasure.

He was aware of her thighs beginning to tremble, of her wrestling with his shoulders, her body convulsing, and then he felt her sweet release coat his tongue as she cried out his name. He pulled himself up to hold her body close as the tremors of her climax ebbed away.

'When did you first realise?' he breathed into her hair.

'What?' she asked, shaking her head, as if her

thoughts were scattered after what he'd just done to her.

'That you wanted me?' He grinned, pulling away from her slightly to stare down into her piercing eyes.

'When did you?' she countered, defensive, vulnerable, as if he was trying to strip her totally bare.

'From the moment I saw you again in the church—but I think especially the moment you had all the witan laughing at me that morning. It made my blood heat with anger and lust. I wanted to take you right there and then on that table in the hall.'

She gave a small smile. 'Sorry about that.'

He shrugged. 'So when did you realise?'

She shook her head, not wanting to tell him, resting her forehead on his solid chest.

'Tell me. Or are you still not sure if you do?' he said, wiggling his eyebrows, making her laugh.

'I think you can tell that I do,' she said. 'And I remember the exact moment I *wanted* you, too. Perhaps not in the way you mean, though...'

'Go on.'

'It was the day you rescued me from that stampede.'

'What?' he asked, pulling away from her slightly.

'I was pleased when my father told me we were to be wed,' she said, biting her lip. 'I wanted to marry the handsome stranger who had saved me that day. I didn't know you were the Prince.'

He frowned, as if perplexed. 'I thought you said your father forced you to marry me,' he said, his one hand still curved around her waist, the other rubbing the back of his neck.

'Oh, I had no say in the matter. But that doesn't mean to say I wasn't secretly pleased with his choice.' She stared up at him, her blue eyes huge.

'I thought you said you didn't want to be Queen.'

'I didn't. I don't.' She shrugged. 'I don't need a crown, Teon. That had nothing to do with it. I knew it might not be a marriage forged out of love, but I thought you were a good man, after saving me, which is why I didn't argue it. The truth is, I wanted you in my life—wanted you as a husband—and now, like this,' she said, running her hands over his chest, down to the rim of his trousers, 'I want you as a lover.'

He shook his head, disconcerted. He had been talking of lust… He was trying to come to terms with what she was telling him. He had always thought their feelings of loathing were mutual. 'Why didn't you ever say anything?'

She sighed, sitting back on the edge of the table, realising he wasn't finished with his questioning. 'When could I ever say anything? You didn't exactly give me a chance. You saw me as your enemy—you despised me. And then, well…' she frowned '…you were gone.'

Could it be true? That she had always wanted him, even as a girl? If it was, it made his abandonment of her all the more cruel. That he had destroyed her trust and crushed her hope. It made him feel at a bit of a loss, unsure what to do with that new information. It added weight to their connection here, the things they were doing together, and he wasn't sure that was a good thing. He'd thought they were just trying to rid themselves of their desire.

'I had no idea,' he said, shaking his head.

She sighed. 'Well, now you do,' she said, running her fingers over the hard ridge of him. And then she was pushing down his trousers, in desperate urgency, breaking through his serious thoughts, making him laugh, as he, too, was glad to be free of his clothes at last, wanting the skin-on-skin contact. But his smile faded when she ruthlessly took the long length of him in her palm and he groaned, resting his forehead against hers.

'What do you do to me?' he whispered. He needed her, wanted her, all the time.

His hand came out to stroke her hair behind her ears, taming it, pushing himself between her knees. He took hold of her bottom, pulling her closer as she stroked him up and down between their bodies.

Her hand was wrapped tight around him, the way he'd shown her how to touch him last night, and she curled her feet around his thighs, holding him in place.

She wiggled forward on the table, wanting to get closer, and then he was right there, against the moist heat of her entrance as she continued to pound his shaft, and she squirmed against his silky tip, as if she needed greater satisfaction, pressing herself against him as if she wanted more of him, encouraging him on, but not sure what she was doing.

'I want you inside me,' she whispered. 'More than anything.'

And he wanted that, too. He'd never wanted anything so much. And it would be so easy...all it would take was one smooth thrust.

The tip of his cock pressed into her entrance, making her whimper. She was pushing him, testing him, to the limit of his control. And he wanted to give in. He wanted to get closer. As close as could be. To bury himself inside her. He wanted to surrender...

'Please, Teon,' she muttered, in a desperate whisper. 'I can't wait any longer. Please take me. Make me yours.'

His eyes snapped open.

'Revna, stop.'

With a violent shove, he pushed her away, fiercely removing himself from her arms and her legs and launching himself across the room. His actions were so sudden, they shocked them both.

He stood, naked, leaning over the hearth, a scowl carved into his features. She still sat on the table, her eyes wide, wrapping her arms around her body.

'What is it?' she asked. 'Did I do something wrong?'

'No. Yes.' He was so conflicted. He dragged a hand across his jaw. 'We can't do this,' he said, raking in a breath, trying to get his desire under control. He had come so close. He had been a breath away from impaling her beautiful body with his, taking her completely, helpless against her beautiful body and whispered pleas.

But her final words had cut through his desire, reminding him why they had waited. Why he was keeping her at a distance. Why he couldn't slam into her. She had whispered 'please' so desperately, it sent a warning through him.

'Why not?' she whispered. 'We're not doing anything wrong. We're married...'

What were her motives? Why was she so desperate?

He knew his inability to trust was causing him to doubt her. But his father had taught him to be wary, especially where women were concerned. His father's head had been turned by a mere peasant woman and he'd betrayed his family just to seek a few moments of pleasure with her. And it had had repercussions. The woman had had a son, binding the King to her. They were still feeling the ripples of that bad decision even now. That bastard child was laying claim to the throne.

Was Revna trying to bewitch him, like that woman had his father? Was he really going to believe what she had said, about always caring for him? Surely that couldn't be true? It was far more likely she was conspiring with her father, trying to get their bloodline on the throne.

There was nothing for it. He had to tell her the cold, hard facts and see how she reacted.

'I don't want children and, if we go any further, that is a very likely outcome.'

He saw her reel, her knees come together, shocked by this new information. 'You don't want children?'

'No.'

'Not now? Because of the siege? Because we're at war?'

'No. Not ever,' he said, turning fully to look at her, his hands coming down to rest on his hips.

'But…why?'

'I just…don't.'

She frowned and he knew she didn't think it was a good enough answer.

'So you don't want me?' she said, slipping off the table and walking towards him.

He groaned, trying not to swallow his tongue.

'You're planning to remain celibate for the rest of your life?' she asked.

'Until now, that hasn't been a problem.'

'So let me get this straight,' she said, bending over and swiping her kirtle off the floor. 'You're planning for us never to consummate our marriage?' she asked. 'You want to touch me, tease me, drive me to distraction all night long, but you don't want to make love to me?' The colour was high in her cheeks, her frustration clear.

He sucked in a breath. This was harder than he'd thought. Because he did. More than anything. And he felt so damned frustrated with her and himself. It was all that he wanted, to hold her against him, to plunge deep inside her—to seek the release they both craved. But he didn't want the fallout. The trauma of his past was holding him back.

He hated that he wasn't being honest with her… He wondered if he should tell her the awful, hurtful truth—that he wasn't sure he could ever trust her. And he couldn't give himself fully to her because he didn't want her child, a heathen child, because if he hurt her, she would no longer want to do this, would she? She would no longer try to tempt him into breaking his vow.

But he had always thought their Saxon bloodline should be kept pure. He hated her people for the things they'd done to his lands. Her father had killed his mother and that man's blood flowed through her veins. What a betrayal that would be to his mother, if he had a child with her.

No! He wanted to ensure that his successor was a Saxon. Was that so wrong? And if that meant he couldn't have children, so be it.

He had resigned himself to ruling here with Revna at his side—he'd come to realise she was beloved by his family and his people, and if he let her go now, it would create much ill feeling. Besides, he was starting to think she would make a good queen, but it didn't mean they had to have a family.

Instead, he hoped his eldest sister would marry a Saxon noble and produce an heir of their own, strengthening their dynasty, should anything happen to him. There had been a time when he might have considered his half-brother as a potential successor, but now he had proven he wasn't a worthy ruler and he was illegitimate in the eyes of the law anyway.

Yet staring at Revna's beautiful face, looking up at him, waiting for answers, he couldn't bring himself to be cruel, to cause her unnecessary hurt. Lying was the greater kindness. But he could also never let Revna's father win. He had to keep control over his lineage.

'Why are you pushing this, Revna?'

'I just think I'm entitled to know, one way or the other—don't you think?' she said, exasperated. 'Does it always lead to children? You said you'd slept with women before and they weren't important to you— your words, not mine. Have you already fathered a child?'

'What? No!' he said, incredulous. 'I was young and foolish then. I was messing around, not giving the consequences a second thought. And thank goodness there weren't any.' He stepped towards her, raking a hand through his hair. 'So, no, it doesn't always lead to a child…but it could. And I don't want to take that chance.'

He couldn't risk it. He couldn't be swayed, he thought, reaching for his trousers and tugging them on. He had to stick to his beliefs.

She gave him a curt nod, pulling her *hangerok* up over her kirtle, fastening her brooches, as they dressed beside each other in silence. 'We'd better get back to the hall.'

'Revna…' he said, but she was already opening the door and walking through it.

He knew that he had hurt her, badly. That he probably hadn't been fair. He had started this seduction and she had surrendered to his desires, keeping up with him every step of the way. He couldn't have asked for more. And then when he'd driven her so crazy she'd asked him to take her, he'd pulled away from her, withdrawing from her body, rejecting her for the second time in their married life, and he wondered if she would ever forgive him.

Chapter Eight

Revna felt as if someone had reached into her chest and ripped out her heart. She was still trying to comprehend what Teon had told her. When he'd removed himself from her grasp, launching himself across the room, she had been shocked. She didn't know what she'd been expecting him to say by way of an explanation, but it wasn't that. How could he not want children? It was a tragedy. For him, for her and the realm.

It was his duty, wasn't it, as a prince, to produce an heir to secure his crown? And how on earth could he abstain from sex for the rest of his life? At least he had called her a temptation—that was something. But he obviously didn't long for her the way she did for him, for she hadn't thought she could wait another moment to have him inside her. She had practically begged him to take her, desperate with need. She had thought she'd go insane if he didn't. And she blushed, wondering who this brazen woman was that she'd become. She'd spread her legs wide, the slick wetness of her excitement on her thighs, wriggling against him, willing him to impale her with his body.

And he had rejected her. Again.

He had even asked her why she was pushing it, as if she was the one instigating it, and she winced, cringing at her behaviour. But she wanted him to take possession of her. She wanted them to be joined, intimately—to make him feel the way she felt about him. That was what she was spending her days thinking about. That was what she desired. Because he had always had a place in her heart.

But he obviously didn't care for her like that.

She thought they had what it took to make a successful marriage—a family later on—but he wasn't giving her a proper chance.

She kept herself busy at the meal that evening, serving everyone their bowls of pottage and making the task last, even willing to scrub the cauldrons outside, just so that she could avoid Teon as much as possible. The men were all exhausted from their early morning excursion, so perhaps they'd be heading to bed soon and she could breathe easily, away from him.

Bordan had told her that when the combat had got underway this afternoon, it had been more deadly than ever before, Harold no doubt furious that his stone throwers had been destroyed. And the mood in the hall had been sombre tonight, the successes at dawn already a distant memory.

She carried the pans back into the kitchen, storing them away for the morning.

'Do you ever stop working?'

Teon. She spun round, dropping a pan that came tumbling to the ground with a loud clatter.

He stooped to pick it up.

She hadn't been aware of anyone coming up behind her. She was surprised to see him here.

'Revna, can I talk to you?'

'I have a lot to do.'

'At this hour? I have something to show you,' he said, his arms hanging by his sides. His handsome face looked drawn and serious.

She raised her eyebrows at him. 'I thought we were finished with all the "you show me yours, I show you mine", Teon…'

He slanted her a look. 'It's not like that,' he said. 'Would you come with me, please?' He ran a hand around the back of his neck. She was starting to realise he did this when he felt uncomfortable, and he looked so tired, she didn't have the heart to say no. Taking pity on him, she threw down the cloth she was holding and nodded.

He led her down the corridor. When she realised they were heading to his room, her footsteps faltered. He saw that she'd stopped and he turned round. 'I have something for you, come on,' he said, taking her hand in his and leading her the rest of the way.

He pushed open the door and she stepped inside. There, lying on the bed, was her mother's dress, repaired and dried. She couldn't believe it. She gasped, rushing over to it, gathering it up and inspecting the intricate needlework.

'Teon, it's wonderful,' she said, incredibly touched. 'How did you…?'

'I got Edlynne to mend it for you. You're not the only one who's handy with a needle and thread,' he said, trying to smile, but it collapsed halfway. Was he nervous? Perhaps wary of her mood. 'I know how much it meant to you,' he said.

Her eyes shone up at him. 'Everything. Thank you so much,' she said. 'That was such a thoughtful thing to do.'

He stepped towards her, drawing a hand over his beard. It had grown fuller over the past few days. It suited him, she thought. 'And I wanted to say sorry. For earlier. I should have told you sooner, about my plans not to become a father. You had a right to know.'

She looked at him, startled. She couldn't believe he was apologising. Surely the King of Kinborough never needed to express his regret. And in that moment she thought perhaps they could be happy even if he didn't want children. It would be a great sacrifice not to become a mother, but a lifetime spent with him might just be worth it. He was a good man and she still wanted him. Whatever he was offering, she knew she would take. She loved him. Perhaps she always had.

She nodded, accepting his apology.

'Try it on,' he said. 'Edlynne had to cut some of the damaged material out and sew it back together. See if it still fits.'

She hesitated and he rolled his eyes. 'I'll turn around,' he said. And, true to his word, he did.

'How is your arm?' she asked, while his back was turned towards her and she changed out of her plain kirtle, swapping it for her mother's vibrant red one.

'Not so bad.'

'I'll need to change the dressing later.'

'I shall look forward to it.' He grimaced and turned to see her struggling with her brooches.

He stepped forward and took the metal pins from her fingers, helping her to fasten them. It was the opposite of what he'd done earlier, before they'd almost made love. Before he'd told her he didn't want to be a father. He had become an expert with her brooches, she realised.

'You know, I wasn't sure I liked the way you dressed when I first got home. I thought your clothes were far too exotic, different, drawing the eye. But they're growing on me. You're growing on me...'

She smiled then. 'I'm glad. It's only taken eight years,' she jested. And then she glanced down. 'Oh, Teon, it's perfect,' she said, giving him a twirl. 'I must go and thank Edlynne. It really is wonderful. The nicest thing anyone's ever done for me. Thank you.'

But as she went to leave his room, he gripped her arm, tugging her back. 'And we're all right?' he asked, his gaze boring into hers. 'Friends again now?'

Friends. Is that how he'd describe them? Husband and wife perhaps. Almost lovers. Never friends. Was it possible? It was he who had said they'd never been on the same side.

She nodded, biting her lip.

* * *

She found the Princesses in their room and they smiled with delight when they saw her in the dress. Revna told them how grateful she was, patting the skirts in delight.

'I was happy to help. But it was all Teon's idea,' Edlynne said. 'He was always a romantic growing up. He always wanted to be like our father. He wanted the whole thing—a wife and a family. When he went away, I thought he'd given up on that, but now he's returned…'

Revna's breath caught in her throat. She felt as if Edlynne was twisting the knife Teon had pressed into her chest earlier, making the wound hurt even more. 'I'm sure he's got far too much on his mind for romance,' Revna said, her voice sounding forced.

But could it be true? Had Teon always dreamed of having a wife and children when he was younger? When had that changed? Was it when he'd discovered his father's affair? Had it put him off somehow? It made her think he was holding something back from her. What wasn't he sharing? He demanded honesty from her. Was he being as open with her? She so desperately wanted him to feel he could confide in her, as he confided in Bordan.

Suddenly, they heard shouting coming from the hall. Racing along the corridor and through the doors, they saw there was some kind of commotion going on. When Revna realised the farmhand, Garren, was at the helm of it, her heart sank. Was he causing more trouble? But as she glanced past him, she knew why he looked so stricken. She saw his wife was lying on the floor, clutching her stomach, and a wave of dread swept through her. Surely the baby wasn't coming. Not now.

She pushed her way through to where the woman lay on the ground, writing in agony.

'Help her, please,' the man said.

Revna nodded.

She saw Teon push his way through to the front of the crowd and he came down beside her on his haunches. 'What can we do?'

'We need to find her a bed. Somewhere private. Make her as comfortable as possible. I will try to help her through this. Edlynne, can you look after their boy, Graeham, until this is all over? Darrelle doesn't need to be worrying about her son while birthing another.'

Edlynne nodded, finding the small boy who was stood staring at his mother, looking distressed. She took the small child's hand, leading him away.

'Have you done this before?' Teon asked Revna, helping her hoist the woman up under the arms.

'I helped my mother birth my brother.'

'You did? You're full of surprises, you know that?'

They quickly cleared Revna's old room for Darrelle and fetched water, blankets, needles and thread. Garren sat by his wife's side, holding her hand, while Revna offered words of encouragement and little sips of water. She was aware of Teon standing by the door. She'd noticed he'd removed his armour and rolled up his tunic sleeves. From time to time she asked him to send someone to fetch ale for the farmhand and more blankets for his wife, but he did so himself. She thought he'd want to remove himself, to get as far away from here as possible, but he remained by her side, as if he wanted to help.

The woman's pains continued all through the night. When they began to come closer together, Revna knew it was almost time.

'I can't do this,' Darrelle wailed, struggling with the pain.

'You can,' Revna told her, mopping her sweat-licked forehead. 'You've done it before, you can do it again. Be strong. You're going to meet your baby soon. Focus on that.'

And Revna began to hum.

'What are you doing?' Teon whispered, handing her another blanket.

'It's a Norse galdr song my mother taught me. We always pray to the goddesses Frigg and Freja and ask them to protect the mother and child. We're not all crazy barbarians, you know,' she mocked him.

When Revna told the woman to push, she did and, finally, Darrelle's screams gave way to a baby's cries. Revna held the newborn up in her hands for everyone to see, laughing, tears shimmering on her face. And Teon and Garren leaned over to take a closer look. He obviously didn't hate babies that much, Revna thought, as she saw the look of awe on Teon's face. That wasn't what was holding him back. It was something more.

She pushed her thoughts away and passed an exhausted Darrelle her baby to hold and it was a wonderful moment, the four of them celebrating the miracle of a new life. She felt elated.

Watching Garren come down beside his wife, to cradle their baby together, she met Teon's gaze over the bed. 'I should perhaps give you some time alone,' he said, his voice gruff. 'Congratulations to you both.'

She watched him go and wondered if this experience might have changed his thoughts on becoming a parent. Probably not. She knew how stubborn he was. But still, it was a night never to be forgotten. She was exhausted, but the excitement was still thrumming through her—she wasn't sure she would be able to get any sleep.

After cleaning up the baby and making sure Darrelle was comfortable, nursing her son at her breast, Revna went to leave the new family alone.

Garren stopped her by the door. 'I will never be able to repay you for what you did,' he said. 'But thank you.'

She smiled. 'I am very happy for you both,' she said and headed out into the corridor, bumping straight into Teon, who was leaning against the wall, waiting for her.

'I need to get some air,' she said, wary. What could he want now?

'Mind if I join you?'

She shook her head. People were still asleep in the hall, as they crept through the rows of snoring bodies, making their way outside. Now they had one more life to protect in this fortress.

Revna headed up the stone steps towards the sycamore tree at the top. She sat herself down on the stone under its branches, looking up to the morning sky.

'I have never seen you up here,' Teon said.

'I told you, like you, it's my favourite part of the fortress. But I've barely had a moment to come and ponder my life these past days. I've barely seen daylight.'

'Is that what you do up here, ponder your life?'

'When I first came to live here, I used to sit here and watch the people down below, longing to be included in whatever games or conversation they were involved in. I used to feel closer to my gods up here. Closer to the sun. Not so alone. It's good to see the light,' she said, looking at the orange ball of sun breaking through the morning mist, the golden glow cascading down on to her face, lighting it up. Still, she shivered. 'The view used to be worth braving the cold for,' she said. Now it looked out over enemy soldiers and devastation.

Teon pushed himself away from the wall and came towards her. 'Hopefully things will have improved here by the time the good weather returns. Perhaps it will all be over,' he said, then he sighed. 'Were you so very lonely when you came here?'

'I guess I felt as though I didn't belong. No one came near me at first, as if I was a leper. I was afraid of not being wanted. I felt disconnected from my people and my home. And I wasn't sure if my being here would be temporary. I didn't unpack for a while. I think it was made worse by losing my mother, then my father leaving me, never visiting. And you'd left me, too. I felt as if no one wanted me.'

'I am sorry for the things I said back then, on our wedding night. It was wrong of me,' he said. 'It wasn't you, but my father—and yours—whom I was angry with. I took it out on you. It was wrong of me. And I'm sorry I left you here all alone.'

She shrugged. 'It's all in the past now. Do you plan to stay this time, once this is all over?' She smiled.

'Well, I do have a kingdom to rule over, among other things I need to take care of.' He raked a hand through his hair.

Was she one of those other things? she wondered.

'You know… I have a new admiration for women after witnessing what went on in there,' he said, gesturing with his head to the keep. 'Are Darrelle and the baby all right?'

'They'll both be fine if they can avoid any fever in the next few days. I shall keep an eye on them.'

He nodded. 'You were incredible, the way you helped her… Your generosity with people never ceases to amaze me, Revna. Your limitless empathy despite how these people have treated you in the past is admirable. I have never met anyone like you.'

'Someone had to help her.'

'It always seems to be you.'

She shrugged. 'Perhaps I was the only one who knew how—skills garnered through assisting my mother and helping my father to birth and rear animals growing up.'

He crouched down in front of her, taking her chin between his thumb and forefinger. 'Do you want one of those?'

'A baby? That wasn't what was on my mind in your room yesterday, no,' she said. But if she was honest with herself, the events of the night had made her see she really did want to be a mother one day. She wanted to grow a baby in her belly and give birth to it. She wanted a family. With him. 'I don't want a baby right now, Teon, but one day I'd like a family.'

He nodded. 'I asserted my wishes to you yesterday and realised I hadn't even asked you what your thoughts were on the matter. What your hopes are.'

Did he really care? A glimmer of hope lit up inside her. She knew right now, she had to respect his wishes about not wanting to be a father, but she wondered if she might be able to change his mind about having children in the future. The way he had looked at the baby this morning...

'I don't think I could watch you go through all that pain,' he said, shaking his head. 'That was bad enough,' he said, pulling her towards him and resting his forehead against hers, his hands coming up to hold her neck.

Her heart was in her mouth. It felt like real intimacy, but with him she could never be sure.

'You know it's considerably warmer in my bed. The view's better in there, too,' he said.

She looked up into his hungry face. She knew he

was trying to rekindle the connection between them, but she pushed at his chest, turning away from him. He was giving her mixed messages. She didn't know what he wanted. One moment he was hot for her, the next he was pushing her away, cold again.

'I think I'll sleep in your sister's room from now on,' she announced coolly, trying to restore some of her pride.

'That's not necessary,' he said, shaking his head, his brow furrowing.

'I think it is.'

There was a small silence. He ran his hands through his hair. He looked tired, she thought. Frustrated. 'You know, we can share the same room and just talk, Revna. We don't always have to touch each other—we're not total animals, are we?'

That was unfair! She felt as if she'd taken an arrow to the chest. How did he do that? How did he make her feel as if she was the one to blame? That she was the one lusting after him and that's all she wanted? He was the one suggesting she return to his bed, insinuating the things they could do together. 'No, but...'

'Maybe I want to know more about you,' he shrugged, standing to pace away from her, before coming back. 'I know so little.'

'And whose fault is that?' she snapped.

But still his words brought her up short. Was he really interested in getting to know her rather than just getting to know her body? She would give anything to be in his bed again. She wanted him to put his hands all over her, even if that's all he was willing to do. But wasn't this better, in a way? That he wanted to *know* her. She had wanted that from the start before he'd begun his ruthless seduction of her.

'What do you want to know?' she said, relenting.

'I don't know—anything. Everything. I know nothing about where you've come from. What your people were like. What your home was like.' He sat back down, taking her hand in his, resting his back against the tree. 'You have learned a lot about my way of life. Perhaps it is time I learned some of yours.'

'Well, if you really want to know, my people are not the monsters you think they are. They don't deserve to be persecuted to extinction, as you believe.'

'Some of them do.'

'But we're not all like that. You wouldn't say you were like Harold, would you? And you're both Saxons. It doesn't make you the same as him, does it? Why do you think Greenlanders all have the same bad qualities as those from Norway? Or Denmark?'

He nodded, as if hearing her point.

'My people are farmers mostly. We raised cattle and lived by a beautiful fjord at the bottom of the mountains. My brother and I spent our days catching fish and paddling in the freezing water. We used to dream of catching a giant whale and becoming heroes. We imagined our settlement would feast off the meat for many months and everyone would know our names,' she said. It was a wonderful time, enshrined in her memory.

'What was his name, your brother? And your mother?'

'Bo. My mother was Gertrude. Legend has it, Gertrude was a goddess who turned into a bird. Sometimes I imagine the birds visiting this tree are her, that she's come to visit, looking out for me. As for Bo…perhaps he's out at sea somewhere, riding the back of an enormous whale,' she said, raising her gaze to the expanse of ocean in the distance. 'Neither of them would have gone to Valhalla, as they didn't die in battle.'

'Valhalla?'

'A little like your heaven, but it's only for our greatest warriors.'

'Speaking of which… How did you learn to fight like you did the other day?' he asked.

'My father taught me. There was lots of fighting between our tribes in Greenland, mainly over land or cattle, and he felt it essential I knew how to defend myself.'

'Going by the looks of how you fought that man the other day, he taught you well,' he said. 'Revna, my warrior Queen,' he said, tucking her hair behind her ear.

And she smiled.

'Where else have you been? Where did you go, before coming here? I envy you and your adventures.'

'Lots of places.' She shrugged. 'I don't know all their names. Some lands had nothing but birds and water. Others had large bustling cities and huge buildings. It was all incredible to see. But I don't think I really appreciated it at the time. I just longed for home.

To stay in one place. I hated moving around all the time.'

'I have always longed to travel. I should have loved to have seen some of the things you saw,' he said. 'How did you fare crossing the ocean in those ships? Surely they were no match for the ocean waves? Were you not scared?'

'I was scared of the nauseous feeling mostly!' She pouted. 'I was so sick I couldn't keep any food down. It's why my father told me to hide when we arrived here. I was too weak to fight. The waves had been huge and terrifying, but I had to be brave. I was among my father's men. In our culture, it is expected that you show courage at all times. It is shameful not to.'

He nodded. 'That explains a lot.'

'Now I'm older, I look back and do wish I'd explored some of those beautiful monasteries we'd seen.'

He grinned then, as if a thought had occurred to him. 'You know, when I discussed being married to you with Bordan, at the garrison, he did come up with a way out of my troubles,' he said, his eyes twinkling in sudden mischief.

'Oh? What was that?'

'He suggested I move you to a convent.'

She gasped. 'You wouldn't!'

'There's a very nice one on the peninsula in Rainhill,' he said, his grin widening, offering her a conspiratorial wink.

She gently punched him on his chest.

'Don't worry, I don't think you'd fit in very well,

do you?' He let out a deep chuckle, unable to help himself, and it eased her tension a little.

'No, but you might,' she said, raising an eyebrow.

He rolled his eyes and tugged her towards him. This time, she let him, resting her head on his shoulder, looking up at him. She studied his face. Just a week of living like this had made him pale—the strain of the responsibility for his people, and lack of sleep, causing more lines to appear around his eyes. He looked tired—but no less attractive. He was carrying the weight of the world on his shoulders, and right now, he needed her at his side. She wouldn't abandon him.

A determination settled in her stomach. She would be there for him, in any capacity that he needed her. She knew he struggled to trust, as did she, so she would just have to show him that he could rely on her. That they were good together. That theirs could be a successful marriage, despite what happened between his mother and father.

Teon's emotions were in turmoil. He was finding he wanted to talk to her, touch her, all of the time. He wanted to make her smile and hear her laugh.

Revna had been incredible throughout the night, assisting that couple, keeping the woman calm and helping her breathe through the pain. She had been kind to the farmer, even after the things that man had called her, after he'd hit her, hurting her the other day. She had so much compassion. She was a far

better person than he was. He couldn't so easily forgive and forget.

She had even accepted his apology for yesterday
morning and for leaving her here on their wedding
night. She was such a generous person.

He wrapped his arms around her, pulling her closer
into his chest, tucking her head under his chin. He
breathed in the scent of her hair—she smelt of wild-
flowers and herbs, whatever tonic she had given Darrelle to ease her ailments. She slid her hand up to hold
his jaw, running her fingers into his beard, and she
pulled away to look up at him. He bent down and
placed a soft kiss on her lips.

He just wanted to be near to her, closer to her—
but would she ever let him caress her body again?
He wanted her back in his bed. The thought of her
sleeping down the hallway in Edlynne's room was
unacceptable to him. Unbearable. He wondered if it
would help if he told her he was miserable. That he
was nearing the edge of his restraint?

'Come back to my room,' he whispered.

'The sun's almost up. The people will be waking.
The day is just beginning.'

'But I want you so much I can't think straight.' He
groaned, resting his forehead against hers. 'I don't
think I can get through another day without you. Do
you still want me?'

'You know I do, but you said…'

'Forget what I said.'

There was one other option—and damn if he hadn't
considered it yesterday. They could take it as far as

they could, yet he wasn't sure he would be able to stop. The things she did to him, the way she made him feel, it made him lose control. He would be blinded by pleasure… But he was willing to try.

He bent his head and crushed her mouth with his, tasting her fully, kissing her hard.

'But, Teon, are you sure?' she asked, pulling back, breathless. 'We don't have to…we can wait.'

'I want to. Let's just see what happens…' he whispered.

'All right,' she said. 'But on one condition.'

His eyes narrowed. 'What?'

She pulled away from him slightly, trying to keep a straight face. 'I want to see it.'

'What?'

'The climb. You can make an oath of allegiance to me, from the top of the tree.' She grinned, giggling.

'Now?' he asked, incredulous.

'Scared?' she goaded him.

'Never!'

'Just…promise me you won't fall.'

He shook his head, smiling, as he began to remove his tunic.

'What are you doing?' she asked.

'It's easier to climb without my clothes getting caught,' he said, passing her his top.

And then he was gone, heaving himself up to the first branch, swinging his legs over it and sitting on it, before pulling himself up to the next one.

'It's quite high…' She swallowed. 'Perhaps this is

a bad idea. I was only jesting. Please be careful,' she called out to him.

'I will.'

He looked down at her through the branches, the sunlight dappling through the tree, on to the tiny new buds that were forming. Soon, it would be a new season, welcoming new life. He determined this war would be over by then. He could not allow it to continue. They would have to fight harder. Deadlier. He glanced around, checking there was no sign of the enemy. There was no movement yet.

Looking up, he was nearly at the top. He navigated a few more branches and then he was there, swinging up on to the highest one, his muscles flexing, his long powerful limbs supporting him. 'Made it!' he called down to her, grinning arrogantly.

'I never doubted it.' She laughed, looking up at him, shielding her gaze from the sun. 'Go on then, let's hear it.'

He took a deep breath, trying to remember the words. When his lords made this oath of fealty to him, this time, he would not be able to escape and he would be listening to their every word, wanting to know they meant them.

'According to the laws of God I, Teon, Edmund's son, Prince of Kinborough, swear that I will be loyal and faithful, and bear true allegiance to Revna, my warrior Queen-in-waiting, according to the Almighty Lord's law. I will uphold justice and mercy where she is concerned, fulfil *all* my duties—' he grinned down at her '—and hold the peace for the length of her rule.'

'Hear, hear!' She smiled, clapping her hands together, laughing. 'Now get down from there, please. You're making me worried.'

He nodded, chuckling to himself. He hadn't felt this alive in a long time. She brought out the best of him, he thought, swinging himself down from branch to branch.

He was halfway down, out of danger, when he heard her giggle. He found her face looking up at him between the branches.

'If you still want me, Teon, you'll have to catch me,' she said, gripping his tunic tightly in her hands and making a run for it, taking him totally by surprise. He laughed at her sense of fun, then she was gone, and he felt the sudden, urgent need to catch up with her, his groin hardening at the game she was playing.

She had his shirt. He made it to the top step on the ramparts just as she landed in the square, charging across the pounded earth towards the doors of the keep, and he saw her glance back over her shoulder, heard her squeal.

He thundered down the steps, desperate to catch up to her. He was right behind her, coming after her.

She had to stop to pull open the door, as quietly as she could, allowing him to catch up with her, but then she escaped through the entrance and began zigzagging her way back through the sleeping people again. When he tripped over a satchel of belongings, she stifled a giggle, but then he sped up, more determined than ever to catch her.

She ran down the corridor, laughing and breathless, but he reached her at his door, trapping her between his hands, and he didn't think she minded a bit about being caught. Especially when her arms came up over his shoulders, her hands delving into his hair, and she kissed him, passionately, on the lips. He pressed his groin into her stomach, giving her a sign of what was to come if they went inside. When he pulled his lips away from her, they were both breathless.

They broke apart momentarily to open the door and fall through it, then she was back in his arms and he was kissing her as though he was mad for her, as if he would go insane if he didn't have her. He turned her round in his arms, his hands coming up to cup her breasts, her bottom nestling against his groin, as he pulled her back against his body.

He fumbled with the brooches on her dress, his hands trembling so much he found them tricky. If he hadn't known the dress was so important to her, he might have been inclined to rip the material from her body, so desperate was his need. When the pins finally came loose, the material dropped away, sinking to the floor at their feet.

Then his hands were back on her hips, drawing her back against him again, as he began to ruck up her tunic, his hands sliding up over her thighs, over her bare stomach, making all her muscles tighten and fire burn in his own stomach. He pressed himself harder between the crevice of her now-bare buttocks and she wriggled, as if she wanted him to touch her between her legs, but he didn't. Not yet. She deserved a bit of payback for that little prank she'd played outside.

'Teon,' she whispered, as if he was trying to torture her.

He slid his hands further up, underneath her tunic, to hold both her breasts, squeezing them in the palms of his hands as he kissed her neck. Then he lifted the material up and over her head, sending it away across the floor, and once again she was naked in his arms.

She grappled behind her, wrestling with his trousers, and he wanted to feel her bare legs against his. He helped her push them down and he sprung free, his cock pressing insistently into her buttocks. She reached around and gripped him tightly in her hand and he let out a hiss in her ear.

Then he was moving her towards the bed, holding her hips, staying right behind her as she clambered on to the furs. He pressed her belly down into the silky animal skins, his knees spreading her legs, coming down on top of her. She turned her head, seeking out his mouth, and he stroked her hair away from her shoulder and kissed her again, explicitly, holding her mouth open with his, his tongue stroking deeply inside.

Then his hand was tugging at her hip and she raised her body slightly to allow his hand to curl beneath her stomach and down. He knew he was giving in too easily, but he wanted to touch her, too. His fingers stroked between her folds, opening her up to him.

'Does that feel good?' he asked.

'Yes.'

He sat back, away from her, removing his hand, and she cried out in protest. She tried to turn, wondering what he was doing. Had he changed his mind? But then his hands came around the front of her legs, as he bent his head and his tongue trailed up the back of her knees. She trembled, her body tensing with need. His tongue wickedly teased the back of her thighs and up, kissing the curve of her bottom.

'Don't move,' he said, as the tip of his tongue drew a line up between her buttocks to the base of her spine.

'Teon,' she gasped.

It was like some kind of torture, and Revna wanted more. She wanted him to lose all restraint. She wanted him to give up his cool control and take her.

And as if her prayers were being answered, his large body came over her, pinning her down, holding her hands above her head and parting her knees with his body, spreading her wide, and then she felt him, right there where she wanted him—she felt the tip of his cock at her entrance.

'This is what you want?' he whispered into her ear, his voice hoarse.

'Yes,' she whispered. 'Do you?'

And with a groan of surrender, as if he had no choice, that he had to put an end to this torture, he slid halfway inside her. 'Yes,' he groaned. 'Oh, yes.' It was a single thrust, as far as her tight heat would allow, making her gasp, making him groan, shocking them both that he'd finally done it.

He stilled and she tried to keep a hold of her splintering thoughts.

'Are you all right?'

'Yes.' She nodded beneath him, their bodies prickling with sweat. 'Are you?'

'I don't know. Ask me later.'

He pulled out, and for an awful moment she thought he was changing his mind, but then he was turning her, flipping her over beneath him, so she was lying on her back, looking up at him, and he settled back between her legs.

And then he thrust again, a little harder this time, his eyes locked on hers, and she gasped at the invasion, at him nudging against her inner wall.

'Revna,' he whispered, bringing his forehead down against hers, her leg up around his hip. 'Try to relax. Let me in. I'm not going to hurt you.'

She forced herself to take a breath, to try to relax around him, and she felt him slip further inside her, sinking deeper. He withdrew slightly, before plunging all the way in and this time she cried out in wonder. Yes! This was what she'd wanted. This was where she'd needed him, buried deep inside her body, and she never wanted him to leave her.

She felt her emotions rise up inside her, her arms gripping his arms, needing to hold on tight, trying to prepare herself for the next wave of pleasure as he thrust harder, moving deeply, intimately, while kissing her forehead, her mouth, her neck.

'You feel incredible,' he choked.

He gripped the edge of the bed with his one hand, anchoring himself in place, as his other stroked down over the side of her body, and under her bottom, holding her tightly to him.

She felt whole, at last, as he filled her up inside. 'So do you.'

And then he began to surge harder, faster, giving her less time in between thrusts to prepare herself for the next onslaught of pleasure, as if his own excitement was mounting. She began to thrash beneath him, not sure how much more of this she could take. She tried to keep up with the pace he was setting and began to tug at his shoulders, holding him under the arms, wildly grappling with his buttocks, trying to haul him closer still, to cling on.

His chest rubbed against her breasts, their bodies now slick with sweat, and she felt her body begin to convulse beneath him, the pleasure so intense she began to spiral. She wanted him to give himself up to her completely, too.

She wrapped her legs tightly around him, wanting him to lose himself inside her body, and he groaned. And as he thrust one last time, deeper and harder than ever before, it had her screaming his name. She clung on in desperation as he roared out his own climax and she felt the warm rush of his powerful release inside her.

They lay like that, limbs entwined for a while, and Revna started to wonder if he'd fallen asleep. She didn't mind. She wanted to lie like this for ever.

She never wanted to move. She didn't even think she could move.

When he finally lifted his head and stared down at her, his eyes were guarded, his lips a thin line.

'I'm going to pull out. This might not feel pleasant,' he said.

She nodded, her gaze widening. She had hoped he might look down into her eyes and whisper something kind, say it had been amazing and tell her he was falling for her, but she knew she was being foolish.

When he removed himself from her body, it felt brutal and she gasped at the loss of him. She was glad he'd warned her, it played havoc with her emotions. She had wanted to tell him she loved him and never wanted to be parted from him. Instead, she bit down on her lip, unsure of his mood.

One moment they had been joined together and it had felt so intimate. Now he was rolling away from her on to his back, staring up at the roof above them, and she didn't like the distance between them. It wounded her, especially after what they'd just done. She glanced across at him, wondering what he was thinking. She hoped he didn't regret it. She knew she didn't. It had been amazing. Life-altering.

She truly loved him—she knew that now. She always had. He had plunged inside her body and made his way all the way to her heart. She wondered how she'd got so lucky. Her father had made a good match for her...had he thought they'd be well suited?

But the instant the thoughts filtered through her

head, she tried to shake them away. She'd promised herself she wouldn't do this. That she wouldn't allow herself to care. She had vowed to protect her heart from getting hurt, because she couldn't be sure if Teon felt the same and, all of a sudden, she felt vulnerable.

She pulled the furs over her body, covering herself up. Yes, they had this insane attraction chemistry between them, but did he feel anything else? Had he made love to her because he felt something for her, too, or just to rid himself of this attraction between them? She wished he would say something, anything, so she could gauge how he was feeling.

Teon felt at a loss. So much for being celibate for the rest of his life. She had driven him half-mad. She had broken down all his defences and he hadn't been able to fight his desire for her any longer. He'd lost his control. And as he'd entered her body, surrendering to his desire, his submission had felt glorious. It had never been better. It couldn't get any better.

Yet even as he'd initiated his seduction of her, he'd thought he could pull out before it was too late, not finish inside her. But she had felt too damned good. It was as if she was made for him, which was totally absurd. They had fit together so perfectly, so tightly, like the way his sword slipped snugly into its sheath. A tight, silky fit and it had been exquisite.

As he'd surged inside her, breaching her wall, thrusting deeper and deeper inside her body, all thoughts of his kingdom and his lineage had disappeared. All he could think of was her.

His release had completely and utterly overwhelmed him, the force of it taking him by surprise. There were no words to describe how good it had been. He'd almost lost consciousness. When he'd rallied, even then he hadn't wanted to move. He'd wanted to stay buried in her body, between her legs, for ever.

He glanced across at her, her beautiful moon-like hair splayed out across the furs, and he wondered if she was sleeping. She had tugged the covers over her body, hiding away from him, and he didn't like it. But he knew he was to blame. After he'd spilled his seed inside her, he had struggled to speak, to find the right words. And now he felt bad...

But he couldn't tell her how it had made him feel. He didn't understand it himself. He was still trying to work it out. He just knew he couldn't whisper sweet nothings into her ear. Now that he had claimed her, he should be distancing himself from her. He had got what he'd wanted. His lust had been sated. That had to be enough now. To do it again would be dangerous.

He saw her roll over and get off the bed, walk across the room and pick up her clothes.

'Where are you going?' he asked, incredulous, sitting up in the bed.

'The sun rose a while ago. We need to get on with our day. You know we must.'

'Do I?'

He was like a rock eel, floundering about in the

shallow offshore waters. How could she just up and leave him—walk away, after the things they'd just done? Had it not been as good for her as it had been for him? Was she not going to offer him any words of praise? Yet how could he be angry, when he'd just been thinking he must do the same?

She was right. They needed to get on with their day and their lives. But he wasn't ready to face the people in the hall or his enemy, he just wanted to lose himself inside her body again. And he wondered how the hell he could still want her? He should be spent.

She was stepping into her kirtle, pulling it up over her creamy thighs, and the sight was making him angry, and hard, all over again. Damn, she was so wilful.

He threw back the furs and launched himself out of bed, standing in front of her, his hands on his naked hips. 'You're just going to leave, without discussing what we just did? Without telling me if you even enjoyed it, without saying anything, given it was your first time?'

She looked up at him, wary, bringing the material over her bare breasts. 'I didn't think you wanted to talk,' she said, her eyes flicking over his body. 'I thought... I thought maybe you might be regretting it.'

A muscle flickered in his jaw. 'Not yet...'

Her lips parted on a small gasp. 'You mean not unless there are consequences?' she said, stepping away from him, fiddling with her brooches. 'That's a hateful thing to say.'

He gripped her hand and tugged her back into

his body, surprising her, his arms coming across her back, holding her tight against his throbbing groin.

'I didn't say that. Don't twist what I'm saying,' he said into her ear. 'I don't regret it, Revna,' he said, repeating her words, and, as if to prove it, he began to ruck up her skirts.

'Teon,' she gasped.

'You still haven't answered my question,' he said, gently pushing her down, bending her over the bed, lifting her the material up over her bottom, and spreading her legs with his own.

'Did you enjoy it, Revna?' he asked.

'Teon,' she groaned. 'You know I did. It was… incredible.'

And that was all he needed to hear, before he surged inside her again, all the way in, causing her to cry out in ecstasy.

'I want to know it was as good for you as it was for me,' he said.

'Yes, yes,' she panted.

'To think I had settled on a lifetime of celibacy, what I would have missed out on,' he groaned, his groin curving round her buttocks as he filled her up once more.

'Teon…' she whispered, in wild, desperate surrender, grappling with the furs.

He spread her legs wider, quickening his pace, gripping her hips to tug her closer, pressing harder, and he felt her coming apart, whimpering, panting beneath him, her hands bunching into fists. He felt himself splintering, powering himself deeper and deeper until he lost all control, collapsing on top of her as he exploded inside her once more.

Chapter Nine

Teon wanted to get some hot food inside him, wash off the dirt of the day's fighting and then take his wife to bed. It was all he'd thought about all day long, as the arrows had rained down on them once more, as new machines, which had been built for one purpose only—to destroy his father's fortress and his people—had been used to inflict wave after wave of explosions and pain upon them. They'd been lucky to survive the day and now he longed for gentler, softer explosions of his own, inside Revna's body.

It was amazing. He'd been dissatisfied—unhappy with his life—for so long. And now, in the midst of a battle for his stronghold, his crown and his people, he had found this incredible thing between him and Revna. His wife. The woman he'd vowed to hate.

He thought how strange it was that, in the short space of a week, he had discovered that he would sooner be married to her than anyone. He realised now that no matter how many times he took her, no matter how many times he tried to rid himself of this desire, it would keep coming back. His need for her was insatiable.

Slipping out of the hall after the meal that evening, he went to his room to change. He rummaged around, lifting clothes and blankets from the table, the bed, the chair, thinking he hadn't taken her on there yet, perhaps he could suggest it later, as he looked for a fresh tunic, when he saw one of Revna's brooches on the floor.

He reached down to pick it up and caught sight of that little wooden chest Edlynne had handed over to Revna on the first day of the siege. She had said it contained all her memories of her mother—all her worldly possessions she cared about—and he wondered…did it contain the wedding band he'd given her? The one he'd slipped on her finger the day they'd been bound together? Had she kept it?

Curiosity getting the better of him, he reached under the bed and his hands closed around the edges of the box. He pulled it out and sat on the bed, gently opening the lid. He lifted a few bits of material out of the way and carefully moved some beads and pendants around, then he found the ring and was feeling pleased.

Then he saw something else—not the ring, but a necklace—and went completely still, his whole body rigid in shock.

He held up the necklace between his fingers, taking a closer look at it in the light. It was a beautiful, unique gold chain, with a tiny amber bead at the bottom, which he knew was the only one of its kind. It matched the flickering flames of the firelight in colour and he knew it was believed to have healing powers. The reason he knew that was because his mother used to own this very necklace.

Revna entered Teon's room laughing, wanting to tell him about Garren and Darrelle naming the baby. She couldn't believe it. They'd decided to name him Hræfn after a raven, after her—as a thank you to her and Teon. She was so touched. She couldn't wait to share the news with him. She felt as if it was another sign of her acceptance here, especially by the people who had seen her as a threat just days before. She was starting to feel as if this place really could be a home, with people she cared about all around her. And with a man who looked after her at her side.

The instant she saw him, she knew something was wrong. He was sat on the bed, unmoving, a grim twist to his mouth, a grave expression in his eyes—and she went cold all over. In his hands was her wooden trinket box and she frowned. What was he doing with that? Between his fingers was a necklace.

When their gaze met across the room, his brown eyes were full of cold judgement and wary apprehension ebbed through her. He didn't look like the same man who had helped her birth that baby last night, or the man who had made her laugh up by the sycamore tree, pledging an oath of loyalty to her, before making love to her this morning. No, this man was a dark and dangerous stranger, like one of her Norse gods carved out of stone...

He lifted up the necklace, letting it dangle between his fingers—it was the gold one, with the little amber gem pendant.

'Why do you have this?' he asked, his lips curling in disgust. She had never heard him sound like that, not since the night of their wedding. His voice was devoid of emotion.

'It was given to me,' she stuttered.

'Impossible,' he said, slamming shut the box and discarding it on the bed. He stood, still holding the necklace before him. 'I won't be lied to. This was my mother's necklace.'

She shook her head, her brow furrowing. 'That can't be possible,' she said, voicing her confusion. 'It was a gift. I don't understand.'

His formidable anger was clouding her ability to think coherently. She didn't like his accusatory tone. She suddenly felt exposed.

'Did you take it from her dead body, after your father killed her, like the ravens of the battlefield, scavenging on whatever they can find?'

She reeled. 'What? No!' she said, shouting her denial. 'How can you even think that?' She felt as if he'd plunged a knife into her chest and was ripping it open. How could he say such hurtful things? Did he think so little of her? She knew he struggled to trust, but did he still doubt her loyalty, even after the things they'd done together this morning? Even after the way she'd stuck by his side this week?

Why had he even been snooping in her trinket box? That itself was testament enough to the fact he didn't have faith in her.

'My mother was wearing this necklace the day she died,' he spat, his voice simmering with anger. 'When her body was returned to us, the necklace was gone.'

Revna raked in a breath. That couldn't be true. This couldn't be happening. Not now, when things had been so good between them. Her hand splayed across her chest in a display of innocence.

'So where did you get it?' he said, stepping towards her, his big body dominating the space, where this morning he had been gentle and kind, taking care of her body, pleasing her in ways she'd never thought possible. And now...

He was unleashing his wrath on her, just as he had the night they had wed. It was as if this was his perfect get-out, almost as though he'd gone in search of something to accuse her of, so he could put an end to their relationship. She had been a fool. He would never be able to see past her heritage. He would never be able to love her the way she loved him.

She looked up at him, wary. Her head whirled with scrambling thoughts as she tried to find an answer she knew she could not give. She began sifting her memories to support her innocence and to challenge his awful accusation. 'My father gave it to me,' she said and it felt like an admission of guilt. 'But I had no idea it was your mother's, Teon—'

Why was he making her feel so ashamed, when she was blameless? 'You can take it. Keep it. I don't want it. I only need this one that I wear from my own mother.'

'I don't believe you,' he said coldly, slashing the air with his large hand, and she felt her hopes and dreams shatter around her, just like the fortress this past week.

'You're only believing what you want to hear. You're making up a story in your head,' she said. 'I've proved my loyalty at every opportunity.'

'The fact you even have this makes you his accomplice.'

'What? No!'

This was his excuse to leave her, she thought. And she felt her anger erupt inside her. She had known this was inevitable, yet she'd fallen for him anyway. She had hoped things would be good between them this time.

'When you look at me, you see my difference, don't you? You see him. You'll never see me, for who I really am,' she said, realisation seeping through her body. 'Just the fact I'm his daughter. When are you going to stop punishing me for something you think my father did?'

'He is the foundation of who you are...'

'So he's a killer, I'm a killer? Is that what you're saying?' she said, despairing. 'So if your father was a cheater, does that mean you'll be one? Is your infidelity an inevitability, too?'

'Possibly. Someone like you certainly couldn't keep me interested for long.'

Pain, like she'd never experienced before, lashed through her, the force of the blow making her legs go weak. And in her stomach she felt a slow curl of dread. For she knew now that they couldn't recover from this. If there had been any hope before, it was gone now.

Then an awful, dawning thought struck her. He had told her he didn't want children. Was that the truth? Or was it that he didn't want *her* children?

'So that's why you told me you don't want to be a father, Teon…because you don't think you'll have the staying power to raise them?'

'No,' he said, closing the distance between them, hooking his fingers under her chin. 'I don't want to be a father because I don't want to bring a child into this world if it's going to be a heathen. If it's going to have your father's blood running through its veins!'

She felt sick, bile rising in her throat. She held up her palms, slowly shaking her head, removing herself from his grasp. She felt unsteady, as though her whole world was crumbling around her. She wanted this to be over. She put her hands over her ears, wanting him to stop, wanting to end the agony of the moment.

Then everything around her began to sway and she stumbled forward. She clutched her body with her arms, as if to hold herself together, her heart clamouring dully in her chest.

She righted herself against the wall, taking a deep breath and standing tall. This morning, there had seemed as though there was a path through their tragic past. That their desire for each other could evolve into something more. But now it was as if an almighty avalanche had descended from the mountains, blocking their route, and there was no possible way out. She felt numb—she knew this was the end. He would never forgive her for this. He'd made up his mind. He was leaving her, withdrawing from her again. And the pain was worse than anything she'd ever experienced.

'So all those words you spoke this morning…the oath of allegiance you made to me didn't mean anything?'

'No. We were just jesting, Revna.'

'I see. So this is you "upholding justice and mercy where I'm concerned", is it? Well done, Teon.'

She tried to swallow the lump of emotion in her voice and lifted her chin, trying to keep in her tears. She would not let him see her cry.

Once again he was abandoning her. Once again he'd proved he wasn't dependable. She had anticipated this, like the Valkyries she'd told him of, and he had fulfilled her prophecy. She had lost him. She had lost her hope. Love is only temporary. In life, and through death, she thought, people always leave you.

'Teon, Teon!'

He glanced up from where he was sitting at the table, discussing the battle plan for the day with his men, when he saw his sisters rushing towards him through the hordes in the hall. The people parted, making it easier for them to get to him, and he sensed everyone in the room was watching them.

'It's Revna—we can't find her anywhere. I think she's gone!' Edlynne said.

He was up and out of his seat with the power and speed of an arrow. 'What do you mean, she's gone?'

Revna hadn't slept in his room last night—she had sought refuge from his rage in Edlynne and Eldrida's room. And he had been so furious after their fight that for once, he had let her, telling Egeslic to guard all three women through the night. But Teon hadn't got a moment of rest, he'd just tossed and turned, thinking about everything that had been said between them.

'Last night she said you had an argument. That you were angry with her. She was deeply upset,' Edlynne said. His chest burned at the memory. 'And this morning I woke to find her gone. At first, I didn't think anything of it, thinking perhaps she'd headed out early to the stables, or to sort the morning's food, but I've looked for her everywhere. I can't find her. And there's no sign of Egeslic either.'

Had their disagreement sent her cowering away from him, hiding? He wouldn't blame her. He knew he could be formidable. And he cursed himself now, for causing her any kind of fear. He hadn't meant it. He was a damned fool.

He turned to Bordan and the rest of his men. 'Has anyone seen her?' He was desperately trying to hide the fact that his chest was exploding in panic. What had he done? But surely she wouldn't do anything foolish, just because they'd had a fight? Hell, married couples had lots of those, didn't they? But then, he'd accused her of some pretty rotten things.

Tossing about in his bed last night, when his anger had begun to cool, he'd known he'd been too harsh on her. He'd sensed it in his bones and in the heavy weight in his chest. Just because she had the necklace, it didn't change anything he didn't already know. It might prove her father's guilt, but not hers.

'How long ago did you realise?' he asked his sisters.

'I don't know,' Edlynne said. 'Not long.'

'Everyone, spread out. Look for her. Find her,' he commanded, the skin on his forehead turning clammy. 'She can't have got far. And I would hope wherever she is, Egeslic is with her, too. He should be easy to find, he's a giant! Go!'

Teon strode out the doors and headed up the stone steps to the sycamore tree—it was the first place he thought of, but when she wasn't there, his panic escalated. He could see Harold's troops moving around their camp and knew the fighting would start up again soon. He didn't have long. He had to find her before then, or his aim would be off. He wouldn't be able to concentrate.

He glanced up at the tree, remembering the fun they had had here yesterday, before he'd taken her body, making her his. And he couldn't bring himself to regret it, despite what had happened afterwards. Claiming her had felt so right.

But then, seeing his mother's necklace lying there in Revna's little wooden trunk, his heart had slammed in his chest. It had made him think what he'd done was wrong, confusing him. It made him think that he'd been weak, that he'd broken his vow to his mother, tarnishing her memory, and he'd loathed himself for it.

He had instantly thought the worst of Revna, the way he always had. He'd berated himself for not seeing this coming, for misplacing his trust in her. He'd run over their past conversations in his mind, looking for missed signs she'd betrayed him. It was as if that had been what he'd been waiting for all along, to prove he was right about her kind. But was he? And it had come much too late, after the things they'd done together…

He had been wrong to accuse her, smashing what little trust they'd built up between them. Perhaps it was his way or pushing her away, knowing she was getting too close. Because, deep down, he was afraid. Afraid of the feelings she stirred inside him after closing himself off from people for so long. Afraid of them having a proper marriage, in case it went wrong, like it did for his mother and father.

The insults he'd thrown at her afterwards were now filling him with dread. He wanted to take them all back. How could he make love to her and then go and ruin it all like that? How could he say the hurtful things he'd said? He'd callously accused her of having a hand in his mother's death. He'd called her a liar. He had told her she could never keep him interested, when that couldn't have been further from the truth. He felt sick.

He raced down the steps to the stables. Perhaps she'd gone to feed the horses. He knew how fond she was of that handsome foal. Then he realised he was jealous of a horse! If the moment hadn't felt so desperate, he might have laughed. What was happening to him? He was losing it. But his hope was dashed when the stables were empty, like Edlynne had said, the horses whinnying at him as if they could sense something was wrong. As if they were missing her, too.

Then an awful thought lanced him. Surely she wouldn't walk out of the fortress gates? She'd be caught straight away. But images of her face last night entered his mind. She'd looked forlorn, her voice choked with emotion. He was a brute for making her feel that way. Would she ever forgive him? But no matter how bad she was feeling, he didn't think she'd hand herself over to the hands of the enemy. Not now they'd come this far. And she certainly wouldn't do it for him now, after the things he'd said.

Then he had another idea. Would she have gone through the tunnels? Surely she wouldn't be so reckless? Would she really just leave him in the middle of a fight for the fortress?

A cold claw of dread clutched his throat. If that's what she'd done, he just hoped she'd gone under cover of darkness, for who knew what trouble she would find herself in at the other end. If he'd sent her running, putting her in danger, he would never forgive himself if anything happened to her.

He stormed across the courtyard and round the back of the keep to the little trapdoor leading down to the old Roman sewers. Peering down into the darkness, nothing was amiss. There was no way of telling if she'd come through here.

Looking up, he saw Bordan and the rest of the men coming back from the ramparts and the grain stores. They were all shaking their heads. There was no sign of her, or her burly shadow. He felt lost, uncertain of how to move forward, for the first time in his life. He didn't know what to do. He wanted to go through the tunnels and look for her, go after her, but he knew he couldn't leave the fortress now, not with Harold's men approaching.

He didn't care how she had come to have the necklace. He should have believed her when she said it was a gift and she didn't know where her father had got it from. She had only ever been honest with him. But seeing the necklace had brought up all his past hurt and ill feeling. He knew he would need to put that aside for good if he was to move forward with her in his life. And now he was determined to do that. He would do anything. He just wanted her back. He just needed to know she was safe.

Heading back into the hall, he looked up hopefully as his sisters entered from the corridor. Had she been in one of the back rooms? Perhaps she'd been tending to the farmer's wife and his baby? She had rushed into his room last night, a look of excitement on her face. Had she wanted to tell him about them naming their baby after her? He had heard the news this morning. It was another sign that the people had accepted her as their Queen. She had wanted to share her joy with him and, instead, he had crushed her. Again.

'She's not here,' Edlynne wailed. 'Her mother's sword is gone. I don't understand. Why would she

do this? Why would she leave us now? We need her.'
Then she turned on him, frowning. 'What did you
do, Teon?' she said, poking a finger into his chest.

He'd reacted before thinking, that's what. He'd
been an absolute idiot.

He'd done his worst.

He'd served the fatal blow when he'd told her it
wasn't that he didn't want children—he just didn't
want children with her, because he was ashamed of
who she was. He didn't think he could have said anything more hurtful. And he had seen the pain ripple
across her face, as if he'd thrown a boulder into a
pond. He had abandoned her again, just as he had
when she was young—and now she had left him in
return.

Had he lost her for good?

His sisters were miserable without her. Hell, he
felt miserable without her—and it had only been a
moment? An hour? What joy would there be in anything with her no longer here?

Looking around the hall, he saw the concern
etched on the people's faces, the bleak mood that had
overtaken the fortress—like a huge cloud of melan-
choly hanging over them. It was as if their ray of hope
and light had gone out. Everyone was still looking for
her, without him asking them to. It seemed as if they
really cared for her.

His people had hated her kind for years and they
had good reason, but he was starting to see the error
of his ways. She had shown him that not all Norse
people were the same. Just like all Saxons were differ-

ent. He'd regarded them all as having the same faults, declared them all evil, but Revna wasn't that—she was someone who was willing to help others before herself, someone strong yet compassionate.

Slumping down into his chair, he turned to Edlynne. 'The people. They seem…almost sad. I think they could grow to like her, think of them as their Queen.' He had a thick lump in his throat that he couldn't dislodge.

'Oh, Teon. How can you be so blind? They already do. It's you who's been playing catch-up with the rest of us. She is the heartbeat of the fortress. How can you not see that? You need to stop punishing her for who she is, where she's from. You need to stop blaming her for our mother's death. It wasn't Revna's fault. Father knew that—he accepted it. He loved her. And Eldrida and I do, too.'

'They were close?' he asked. 'Father and Revna?'

'He adored her. He said she was a lot like Mother in many ways. He didn't always like her working the land with the people, or rearing the animals—he said it was unbecoming of a future queen—but he relented over time. He saw what good it was doing that the people got to talk to her.

'He had nothing but respect for her, Teon. I wish you had known him in his later years. He had decided to let go of the resentment and anger towards those who had hurt him. He wanted to live out his days in happiness and peace. And Revna was a loyal companion to him, like a third daughter, and a huge source of his contentment.'

He swallowed. His father had been able to do something he hadn't, for he had been hanging on to his anger, unable to forgive. He hadn't been himself since he'd found out about his father's affair, then losing his mother had been a devastating blow. He'd been furious with the world and his numb heart had totally frozen over like ice.

He had been unwilling to open up to people, distancing himself from all he cared for. He'd spent most of his years immersed in fighting, only feeling pain. He'd held on to his hatred against the heathens, it'd given him something to live for: revenge. So how strange it was that one of them could thaw his heart. But now he'd ruined everything and he didn't think he'd ever despised himself more than in this moment.

'I was a fool. I didn't give her a chance, did I?' he said, rubbing his chest as if to ease the pain that had taken up residence there. He felt cold all over, hollowed out.

'It's never too late to make amends. Did you know Father and Mother put aside their differences before she died? She forgave him.'

'She did?'

'And Revna will forgive you, for whatever it is you've done. She loved our father, Teon. She loves us. Is it so hard to believe she could love you, too?'

Revna knew what she had to do.

She and Egeslic raced through the long, dark tunnels as fast as they could and her legs were burning from the exertion. They had been moving all morning, knowing they needed to reach the other side before dawn, otherwise they would be exposed to the enemy. Thankfully, she knew from the few times she'd made this trip before, on the occasions she'd visited her father, that they were nearly at the end. Her heart was in her mouth at what lay in wait for them on the other side of the hatch. And she was suddenly relieved to have Egeslic, her shadow, with her.

As the Princesses had slept last night, the walls of their room had begun to close in on her. She had stared out of the smoke hole and watched the wings of a bird soaring high into the night sky, wondering if it was her mother, envying its freedom—and she'd made her decision. She had to leave.

She had known she had to go as soon as she'd heard Teon's words. She couldn't stay there a moment longer, knowing he thought the worst of her. She could no longer look into his eyes and see his cold hatred of her. It would tear her apart inside. How could she continue to be his Queen, to help rule his people, when he didn't respect her, but despised her?

What he'd said about having a child with her… She shuddered. Suddenly, the truth had hit her between the eyes. He was ashamed of her. Totally and utterly ashamed. He always had been, from the moment she'd walked up the aisle towards him in the church. He couldn't differentiate between her and all the other Norse tribes that had attacked them.

He had been mortified, she realised now. He hadn't wanted to be bound to her, he had felt it would reflect badly on him. He hadn't been able to dissociate her from his mother's death, blaming her family. He had hated her so much he had stayed away for eight winters because he didn't want to be near her.

When he'd returned and seen her again, he'd felt the same attraction as she had, but it had been lust, not love. And he'd been fighting it every step of the way, trying not to consummate their relationship.

Slowly, she'd thought she'd managed to change his opinion—that he'd come to see she wasn't like all those tribes who had attacked his lands. That her people wanted peace. But deep down, she now knew he would always be unable to accept their differences.

When he'd finally succumbed and made love to her, he'd wanted to bed her, to rid himself of his lust for her, but he didn't want to cherish her or have a family with her. She wasn't good enough in his eyes for that. He was a prince and she was a heathen, and she saw now that he was disgusted with himself that he had let himself down by bedding her. He must have regretted it, then he'd found his perfect way out. He'd used the necklace as a way to break them apart, before casting her aside once more. He had taken hold of her heart and shattered it into a million tiny pieces.

But she was as much to blame. This was her fault, too. She had known she couldn't rely on him. She'd known if you opened yourself up and let someone in, they would hurt you. They would eventually leave you.

Yet she'd done it anyway—she had fallen in love with him. She had opened herself up to him, completely, making herself vulnerable. And now he had done exactly as she'd first expected, what she should have been guarding herself against, and she was crushed. Her chest ached with the pain. It hurt to breathe.

And the most awful thing about it was she could feel the memory of him inside her, the raw sensations of where he'd taken her, reminding her on every stage of her journey now.

She'd left in the middle of the night. She'd had the sudden, urgent need to get away and to see her father. She needed to look into his blue eyes and ask him if he had done the awful thing that Teon had accused him of. She couldn't understand how he'd come to have the Queen's necklace and passed it on to her. She couldn't bear it any longer, she had to know the truth. She must prove her own innocence—somehow.

Poor Egeslic. She had crept up on him in the corridor, holding her mother's sword to his throat, taking him unawares. She had demanded he leave with her immediately. She had kept the weapon pointed at him this whole time and now her arm was aching with the weight of it. Was it safe to drop her sword now? Surely he wouldn't attempt to overpower her and take her back, not now they'd made it this far?

He had told her he wouldn't, that he would make sure she got to wherever she needed to get to safely. But she couldn't take the risk. If he dragged her back and told Teon what she'd done, his wrath would be the equivalent of Ragnarök. The end of her world.

As they finally reached the end of the tunnel and saw the narrow ladder leading up to the trapdoor, nerves erupted inside her. Would Harold's army be waiting for them on the other side? But right now, she thought she'd rather take her chance with the enemy than go back and face Teon.

She went to sheath her sword and put her foot on the first rung, when she felt Egeslic's hand on her arm. 'Let me go, my lady,' he said. 'I don't want you getting hurt.'

'It was my decision to come. I should go.'

'The Prince will have my head if anything should happen to you,' he countered. 'Please.'

She doubted it, but she relented anyway. 'You're a good man, Egeslic.'

Her heart in her mouth, she watched as the tiny rungs wobbled beneath his giant feet. She hoped the ladder would take his weight. There was no way out otherwise, unless they turned around and went back. When he reached the top and slowly lifted the door, a shaft of golden daylight slipped down into the tunnel. She bit her lip as he glanced all around, in every direction, before lowering the wood again.

'It's all clear,' he said. 'You can come up.'

Gingerly, she made her way up, her legs aching from the climb, her hands biting against the cold metal. When she reached the top, Egeslic lifted the door slightly again. He looked around once more, before pushing it open fully and clambering out. He held out his hand for her to take and he pulled her up and out.

'We need to lay low. Head for the fringe of fern trees over there.'

She nodded. Staying down, they crept towards the treeline of the forest. Her heart was pounding in her chest, rushing in her ears. It would be awful if they were to be caught now. Harold would use them as leverage in his battle with Teon, jeopardising the position of the stronghold. Teon would never forgive her.

When they reached the shelter of the tall pines, Revna couldn't believe it—large areas of the woods had been cleared. Had Harold hacked them down to make his deadly weapons? He was exhausting the land and anger stirred up inside her. He could not be allowed to be King. He was destroying everything in his path.

She looked ominously up at the rain clouds and then back towards the fortress of Kinborough. From here, she could see Harold's camp in the foreground and the lands surrounding the stronghold that had been scarred by the constant fighting scorched by fire. All the farmsteads that had lived in the shadow of Kinborough's walls were gone and she felt a lump rise in her throat. What had Harold done? And as for the fortress...

The palisades were blackened and it was surrounded by defensive earthworks, an army of men were scrambling over the walls and a cloud of arrows were hurtling over the ramparts, while giant structures were being rolled towards the walls. She'd lived such a sheltered life in the safety of the fortress these past eight winters and, in the space of a week, all that had changed. It was strange to be on the other side of the walls, looking from the outside in. It was how she imagined Niflheim would look—the Old Norse world of the dead.

Spending her nights with Teon, safe in his arms, it had been all too easy to think of the enemy being a long way away. She had hoped that they would never breach the walls and reach them. Seeing it from this perspective sent a fresh wave of fear through her for all the people barricaded inside. It suddenly hit home just how much danger they were in and she felt guilty that she had deserted them, for it didn't look as though Harold was about to give in any time soon.

In fact, it looked as though he was ramping up his assault. That he wanted this battle over with, once and for all. But perhaps now she was out, she could finally get them the help they needed. She knew Teon wouldn't want it, but sometimes he didn't know what was best for him. He was much too stubborn.

Right now, she was out of his reach. He could no longer control her. He couldn't do anything to stop her. She had made a promise to the King to do whatever she could to keep the people safe. If that meant asking her father for help, then so be it.

Egeslic placed a hand on her shoulder, making her jump. 'Come away, my lady,' he said. 'Don't look too close. This hell is not for a woman's eyes. We'd better go, before we're seen here.'

Pressing on, trekking through the bracken, she hurried forward, leading the way, wanting to reach her father's settlement before the storm set in.

'Does your name really mean terror, Egeslic?'

'Yes. And from the outside, I might look rather terrifying, but inside, I'm not all that bad.'

She smiled. 'I know that. You're a good man. Thank you for coming.'

'I don't know where it is you're going, or why we've left the fortress, but I do know that whatever has happened to make you feel you have to leave, you must know the Prince cares for you, my lady. He has never had me guarding the life of another woman, that's for sure.'

But it was his duty to protect his Queen, to save his people from falling into more danger, wasn't it? She couldn't believe, after everything he'd said last night, he was doing it because he cared. He had told her in no uncertain terms that he did not.

She was weary now. It had been an unbearably long journey on foot, after getting no sleep, and the cold was beginning to seep through her woollen cloak, chilling her to the marrow. But it wasn't the chill, or the thunder she feared most, it was Harold's soldiers if they were to catch them here.

Finally, she saw the two hills that marked the entrance to her father's settlement. They'd made it. As they drew closer, her eyes sought out the guards on the gates and she watched them confer before the sound of the ox horn bellowed out across the roofs of all the farmsteads. Moments later, her father appeared at the bridge and she almost sank to the ground in relief. Their same blue eyes clashed across the distance between them and he acknowledged her with the tilt of his head.

He looked just the same—he had the build of a warrior, a stern look on his features, and he still wore his hair long in rope-like strands, although it was greying slightly at the temples. He'd aged since she'd last seen him, his face had more lines, the piercing colour of his eyes slightly faded. She should have come more often, she thought.

As the tall wooden gates to the settlement began to open and he hurried down the steps to greet her, she suddenly didn't care who was watching. She raced forward and flung herself into her father's arms, needing his support and comfort.

'Revna!' he gasped, hugging her close, his brow furrowing in concern at her arrival and her unexpected rush of affection. When she eventually pulled away, he acknowledged Egeslic beside her, before turning back to her. 'What are you doing here? Is everything all right?'

'No,' she said, shaking her head. 'Father, Kinborough has been attacked. We need your help.'

His face hardened, growing serious, and he nodded. 'Of course. We will honour our agreement.' He turned to his chief man. 'Bjorn, ready the men.'

'Thank you, Father.'

'Now come inside out of the rain and dry yourselves by the fire. We'll get some food down you and you can tell me everything.'

'I will. But first, I need to speak to you alone. I need to ask you something. Something important…'

Chapter Ten

The storm matched Teon's dark mood—the foul, fierce wind whipping across the battlements, the rain pelting down, causing the men to brace against it, hindering their progress against the enemy. It was as if the sky was enraged—he could hear the distant growl of threatening thunder and the angry lashes of the lightning kept shattering on the horizon.

The land before them, crawling with Harold's men, was drained of colour—just like his life. And he felt as if the tide was turning. He had failed Revna and now he was failing his people. Today, it seemed as if his men were being overrun. They couldn't hold Harold's forces back.

Harold had ramped up his attack. There was no let-up between the constant barrage of arrows, as if he wanted this battle over with, too. As if he wanted to be sitting on the throne by nightfall. With a slow realisation of horror, Teon saw they had new structures. Giant breaching towers with many men inside were being pushed towards them. As the first one crashed against the stone walls, men climbed up and out of them, on to the fortress ramparts like scuttling rats, trying to reach their prey.

He and his men fought ferociously, taking on two, sometimes three men at a time, knowing what was at stake. They had their families to think of. And Teon had made his decision and his orders known. They had to make every possible effort, use all available resources at their disposal, to bring this to an end as soon as possible, for only then could he go in search of Revna. Some of his soldiers were pouring boiling hot ale over the walls and dropping bee skeps on to the enemy below, causing a wild swarm.

He commanded his father's army, who were bracing the gate, to support the soldiers on the ramparts. As he notched his arrow, Bordan lit the head of the spear up with fire and he sent it soaring into the heart of one of the siege towers, causing an almighty explosion, giant splinters of wood cascading all around them.

But through the swirling thick smoke and ripples of the heat of the fire, something in the distance caught his eye. Along the horizon, behind Harold's camp, he saw a wall of men gathering beneath the early rising moon. He swallowed in despair. He hoped to God they weren't on Harold's side, or the people of Kinborough would never make it out of this alive.

'It's Revna. It's Revna and her father's army!' a voice shouted in the distance. 'They've come to our aid.'

A rush of shock ripped through him. He raced

to the top of the ramparts, cutting men down in his wake, as he tried to get to the sycamore tree, wanting to get a better view. He had to see this with his own eyes. He had to know if it was true.

When he looked again, peering closer, he saw that it was her. She had gone against his command, leaving the fortress, calling on her father for help. He had never asked her to do so or wanted Ravn's aid…yet, right now, he knew they needed it. It could make all the difference between winning and losing his father's fortress today.

Revna had disobeyed him again, but he didn't care. The main thing was she was safe. She had made it out and she was alive. And it gave him cautious hope. If she'd come back to help him, maybe she hadn't totally hardened her heart against him.

Her unequivocal loyalty struck him between the ribs, harder than any blow from the enemy. It was suddenly clear to him that she had always been there for him. She had said she'd cared for him since the moment they'd first met, back when she was a child. And even when he'd left her, returning home eight winters later, she'd stood by him, willing to forgive him.

On the first day of the siege, she'd fought that brute on the ramparts, trying to protect him and his men. His warrior Queen. And then when he'd told her she could leave and evacuate the women and children, she'd said no. She had wanted to stay and help.

Perhaps he should have insisted. He should have sent her away to safer pastures. But she had been obstinate. She had offered herself up when Harold had made his demands, not caring for her own safety. And even when he had told her he didn't want children, she'd still been willing to stick by him—at a great sacrifice to herself.

He thought about how she had embraced his family as her own, taking care of his father and his sisters. They had relied on her and he was beginning to feel the same. She was always there with her courage and support at every turn. And now, despite all the awful things he'd said to her last night, she was still here, fighting for his cause.

Through jabs and tussles, fighting off man after man, he saw the leader of the heathen army throw a spear in the distance. It arced over the canvas tents of Harold's camp and into the enemy's men. Harold's army turned, readying themselves to face new opponents, drawing their attention away from Teon and his men. And Teon realised he had one last chance to redeem himself. He had to win this war, for her, so he could try to salvage their relationship.

If he got her back, he would take that wedding ring out of her trinket box and present it to her again. He would ask her to be his wife properly this time. He wanted to show her what she meant to him. She might say no, but he had to try. At that thought, his heart lifted a little and he threw himself back into the fray with a fresh determination.

'Gather the men, ready the horses,' Teon roared. 'We need to ride out and attack while they're at their weakest. They'll struggle to fight an enemy on two fronts.'

He mounted his horse in the courtyard and tightened his armour. He instructed the men at his side as the battering ram continued to strike the gate.

'Are you sure you want to do this?' Bordan asked. 'If we open the gates, we leave ourselves vulnerable to attack.'

'We must seize the advantage. This war ends today!' he said, holding his sword in the air and nodding to the men who were reinforcing the gate.

With an inrush of breath, the gate lifted for the first time in a week, surprising their attackers, who all fell inwards, like a dam bursting its banks, and Teon led the charge as he and his warriors met them head on.

Cutting down swathes of men, they pushed them back, out into the flatlands, and he saw the Greenlanders approach from the other side, hacking down the enemy, forcing Harold's men to split up and choose which army to fight first. Men came at him in all directions and Teon stood his ground, disposing of them one by one, but he was distracted. He could see Revna wielding her sword, slashing down men from her position on her horse, and he couldn't take his eyes off her.

Once more he was in awe. Who was this woman? She wore boots and breeches, a tunic and chainmail— and she took his breath away. He'd wanted her from the moment he laid eyes on her again, when she'd stood up to him in the church at his father's funeral. She had challenged him at every turn, highlighting his flaws, and he had fought his feelings, not want-

ing to care for her. He'd thought her beneath him—
that she wasn't good enough for him. But he had been
so wrong.

Watching her now, he realised he had never seen
a woman, apart from his mother, ride astride a horse
before—or fight so ferociously—and he was riveted.
She had told him she could fight, but he'd dismissed
her, not giving her her due. He had underestimated
her, yet again. And now he was inspired by her courage. Even after everything he'd done, she was here,
fighting for his people.

It was he who wasn't good enough for her. He didn't
deserve her—not that he ever had.

Yet, at the same time, he still didn't want her fighting. She could get hurt. It meant there was more than
his fortress and his crown at risk. He scoured the
battle scene, looking for Harold. He wanted to find
him and put an end to this. And he wanted to make
sure he kept him as far away from Revna as possible.

Between Teon and Ravn's men, they were winning, but then, with a wrenching twist to his gut, he
saw Revna fall from her horse and his heart stopped
dead. He charged towards her, pushing men out of
his way. He had almost reached her when he saw her
get back up and relief floored him. He looked heav-
enwards, sending up his thanks. Then he froze, his
whole body contracting in shock as he saw her face
pale to ash. He saw her drop her sword in defeat and
he suddenly realised why. Harold was pointing his
weapon at her. Aiming it at her heart.

No!

Teon suddenly felt sick at what could happen—at everything he could lose in an instant.

He threw himself through the warring bodies, emerging from the battling warriors to appear in front of his half-brother. Harold swung to look at him and sneered.

'Drop your weapon, or I shall run her through,' he said, edging his knife into her perfect chest.

Revna looked up at Teon, her blue eyes wide with fear, and he wanted to get her far, far away from here. Take her on one of her adventures she craved. Get her out of harm's reach. He wanted to return to yesterday, when she was safe in his arms.

Ravn burst through the crowds to appear in front of them, too, and Harold pressed the tip of his blade in harder, making Revna draw in a breath. 'Don't come any closer, heathen, or I shall kill her. Tell your men on both sides to lay down their weapons. Tell them I have won…'

Revna looked at him, shaking her head. 'Teon, don't,' she whispered. 'I'm not worth it.' Her stoic face belied the terror she must have been feeling as Harold roughly bound her wrists, the rope cutting into her skin. She tipped her chin up.

But Teon ignored her, giving a quick shake of his head. If he was going to give up his crown and his kingdom for someone, he couldn't imagine anyone more worthy. She was worth it.

The words he'd told her earlier this week, as they lay in bed, filtered back to him. *'Nothing could force me to ever abdicate. I wouldn't be able to live with myself.'*

But he would be able to live with himself if it meant saving her life. She meant more to him than anything. And he couldn't rule here without her. He couldn't live without her.

Turning to her father, his enemy of old, they shared a look and nodded in silent exchange.

'Your abdication can occur by force, or voluntarily, Brother. Now which will it be?'

'You are forcing me to give up my royal duty. Something granted by God.'

'So you have made your choice?'

'Yes,' he said, but he turned to speak to Revna. 'I said I would die defending my fortress. But I would rather die defending you.' And he slowly put down his weapon. He watched as, beside him, Ravn did the same.

'No,' Revna gasped.

'Now on your knees and tell your men,' Harold said. 'Do it,' he urged, as the tip of his blade cut into her leather vest at her breast.

'Hurt a hair on her head and I swear to God, I'll kill you,' Teon said to Harold.

'You are in no position to bargain. You have lost this battle and your crown. Now tell your men.'

Teon felt a muscle flicker in his jaw, anger raging through him, as he sank down to his knees. He turned around to his men, who were still fighting. 'Men of Kinborough, lower your weapons,' he announced. And Ravn followed suit, telling his tribe the same.

Harold motioned for one of his men to bind Teon's and Ravn's hands and their weapons were removed and destroyed. Some of the men were unwilling to lay down their arms and, when they protested, Harold had them run through. Teon wanted to kill him.

'There. I have done what you asked. You can take my crown and my fortress, now let her go.'

And then, as if all his worst fears were coming true, he watched as Harold pulled himself up on to his horse and tried to drag Revna with him. She began to lash out, struggling in the man's arms, like the woman he'd come to know and care for, not giving up without a fight. But Harold responded with force, hitting her, silencing her. Bile rose in Teon's throat.

'You misunderstand me, Brother. Did I not tell you that first day that I meant to take possession of your wife, your throne and your fortress?' he said darkly. 'Whatever made you think I wouldn't claim all three? And if you want her to live, I suggest you and your men leave these lands for good. Come within an inch of *my* stronghold and she'll die a slow and painful death.'

He kicked his heels into his horse's sides and they galloped away, heading to the gates of Kinborough.

Teon saw red.

He roared with anger and began to struggle against his bonds, desperate to be free of them. If something happened to her...if Harold lay a finger on her...he shuddered.

He felt nothing but shame. For a man who had been in total control for the past eight winters, he wondered how he had lost his kingdom, his crown and his wife, all in the space of one week.

He was determined to put things right, yet right now he could think of nothing but Revna. He had given everything up to save her, but still she was in danger. And he had to get her back.

'He won't hurt her—not yet anyway,' a deep voice beside him said.

He swung to look at Ravn, wondering if the fear he was feeling for her was etched across his face, clear for everyone to see. How could the man look so calm? Harold had his daughter! 'How do you know?'

'Because the throne is the most important thing to him. He can't wait to sit on it. He can't wait for us all to *see* him sitting on it. It's after that we need to worry. I raised her to be tough, she'll be all right until we can get to her.'

Teon felt sick.

'And we *will* get to her.'

'Yes,' Teon said, his mind beginning to whir, wondering how he could get back inside.

'How?' Ravn asked.

'We need to go through the tunnels. Harold won't know about them yet.'

The Greenlander nodded. 'Let's go,' he said, removing a hidden knife from his boot and slicing Teon's bonds open. 'Now cut mine,' he said, but Teon hesitated.

'I didn't kill your mother,' Ravn said, giving him a steady stare.

Teon looked into his blue eyes and it was like looking into Revna's icy depths. Crystal-clear. Honest.

'Revna told me all about it. What you believe. It's not true,' Ravn said.

Teon thought he must be in shock. He'd just lost everything he ever cared about and now his enemy was heading to his home. He couldn't be sure what Harold would do when he got there—to Revna and to the other women and children. And now the man he'd always hated, who he'd always blamed for his mother's death, was trying to talk to him, trying to persuade him he wasn't responsible. Of all the moments. Anger caused his eyebrows to gather together.

'I saw you. I watched as you carried her lifeless body to the gates.'

'Ey, I did that. But what you saw—it's not what you think.'

'No?'

'No. Do you want to hear the truth? Untie me and I'll tell you on the way to the tunnels. Let's not waste another moment here. That man's got our girl and we need to get her back.'

Making his decision, Teon cut the ropes.

They stood and turned, watching Harold's army approaching the fortress. Their men stood around, looking at their leaders for guidance, wondering how this could have happened. Teon knew they must all be fearful for their women and children, as he was for Revna. He had to give them hope.

'This isn't over. Ravn, your men need to lead the charge on the fortress. My men, you'll come with me through the tunnels. We need to move. Fast.'

The heathen men began to beat their weapons

against their shields, chanting their chilling battle cry, before surging forward.

Then Teon was running, his heart pounding in his chest. Ravn was right beside him, surprisingly keeping pace with him for an older man. 'Your mother and I...we were lovers,' Ravn said.

Teon's head snapped round to look at him, stopping dead in his tracks. 'What?'

'She came to visit us at the settlement, that's how it all began. She helped with the sowing of the crop. She was interested in our customs and we...we eventually fell into bed.'

Teon shook his head, bending over, trying to catch his breath, his hands on his knees. 'I don't believe you.'

The man shrugged. 'That's your choice. I know it must be hard to hear. But it's the truth none the less.'

As they started to run again, Teon called back to his soldiers, rallying the men to keep following.

'I was grieving my wife, struggling with a daughter I didn't know how to raise. Your mother, Edith, was hurt after your father had his affair and she was trying to console a son who was angry about it all. She jested that you and Revna would one day be perfect for one another. She had an eye for these things, I tell ye. Meanwhile, our feelings grew...'

'You're lying,' Teon spat out. He couldn't believe his mother would do such a thing. Yet he of all people knew no one was infallible.

'Why would I lie?'

'So if this is true, what happened? How did she die?'

'The truth is, I don't know,' he said gravely. 'I

can't give you that answer. We had made an arrangement to meet one night, but when she arrived, she had been hurt. She had a deep stab wound to her stomach. There was a lot of blood. I was horrified. She slipped off her horse, into my arms and...' The man swallowed. 'I was devastated, crushed. I loved my first wife, but Edith...she was everything I ever wanted and couldn't have. Of course she could never leave your father, but still, we made each other happy for that short time.'

Teon shook his head, struggling to comprehend all this. This man was telling him that his mother had also been unfaithful. That she'd cheated on his father with a man who came from the isles of mountains and ice. 'Why did you bring her back to Kinborough?'

'I was hurting. In my rage, I wondered if your father had found out about us and arranged the killing. I wanted to confront him. But when he saw her, he was a wreck, like me. He saw I was a broken man and took pity on me. He felt to blame for what had happened. He knew he'd pushed her away, into my arms. He asked that I keep our affair a secret, for the sake of his realm. But then you attacked us... It all makes sense now. I didn't know you had seen me that night.'

'I wanted vengeance,' Teon snarled.

'I understand. But it wasn't mine or my people's doing. I approached your father, asking him to stop the battle you were waging, and he agreed. It was then that I suggested a marriage alliance between you and Revna...'

'Why?' Teon said.

'I told him how alike you both were, what your mother had said about the two of you being a good match. Of course I had an ulterior motive. I wanted a secure home for my daughter—for her to make a successful match. Where we had come from in Greenland, we had had everything. Here, we had nothing. But I also thought it would bring peace to both our peoples.'

'And you wanted to secure your lineage in these lands,' Teon raged.

'Is that so wrong? All men want a legacy, do they not? But I love my daughter, more than anything. I did hope you and Revna could have what me and Edith did. That crazy type of attraction, where you can't think about anything but the other person. It seems to me I was right?'

Teon studied the man beside him. He was a warrior, with long dark hair and a muscular frame. He had brilliant piercing blue eyes, just like Revna's. He could see how his mother might have found a man such as him powerfully attractive.

'You and my father allowed me to think Revna was the enemy…what hope did the two of us have? I blamed her for everything. I made us both miserable.'

Ravn shook his head. 'I didn't know you thought I was responsible for your mother's death. I thought you just had a dislike for us coming to your lands and settling here, along with many others. But when I heard you'd left on your wedding night, to go and fight on the borders, I realised I'd miscalculated your hatred of us…but what was done was done then. There was no going back. I hoped one day you would come to think differently. That you'd come home to her.'

They were inside the tunnels now and Teon knew he needed to think, to come up with a way out of this mess when they reached the other end. But first, he had to finish this talk with Revna's father. To try to lay his mother's ghost to rest.

'How did you come to have her necklace?'

'I got that for your mother at a market… I thought it matched the colour of her hair. It was radiant. She, of course, told me she couldn't accept it—that she wouldn't be able to explain where she got it from. She told me I should keep it and give it to Revna instead. But I insisted…'

Teon swallowed. 'She wore it all the time.'

'When she died in my arms, I saw she was wearing it. I wanted to keep something to remind me of her, so I took it back. But I found I was unable to look at it. It brought my grief to the surface. They were dark days, they were. Still are sometimes. So I gave it to Revna, told her to trade it. She obviously didn't.' He shrugged.

Teon nodded. It was quite an elaborate story to make up. 'I can't believe my father forgave you.'

The man laughed then, the sound echoing round the fortress. 'Neither can I. He was a good man, your father. And an even better King. I think he saw he was as much at fault. He didn't see the point in wasting time being angry.'

Teon felt a searing sensation in his chest. Perhaps his father was right. He was starting to feel as if he'd wasted too much time on rage, too much time being angry about his father's infidelity, too much time wanting revenge for his mother's death and the raids on their villages. It had taken him away from spending time with his father in his final years. It had taken him away from his sisters and his people. But his main regret was that it had taken him away from Revna. He'd wasted eight years…and he didn't want to waste another moment. He had to get her back.

'It seems my father was a much wiser king than me. He would never have let any of this happen.'

'Let's not forget who started this war. It's your father's bastard son who's doing all this. Your father wasn't perfect either, Teon. All we can do is learn from the past and choose to make better decisions in our future.'

He nodded. 'Thank you, for explaining it to me. And thank you for coming to our aid today. I appreciate it. Now I have to ask you for your help in getting my fortress and Revna back. But it does leave one question…' he said, as they continued to run along the dark tunnel. 'If you didn't murder my mother, who did?'

Chapter Eleven

Harold and his soldiers entered the fortress and there were barely any men left to resist them. With a sinking feeling of dread, Revna realised they'd all taken up arms on the battlefield to fight alongside Teon. The place felt deserted—the men on the ramparts gone, the courtyard empty. It felt strange to be back here without them. Without Teon. And she had to hold her chin up to stop her from sinking to the ground in a heap, wanting to give up.

She couldn't believe he'd given up his fortress and his throne for her, hoping to save her. Yet he'd lost it all anyway, she despaired. How had it all gone so wrong? Was she to blame? Had she brought this upon them, by asking her father to come to their aid?

Reining his horse up in the courtyard, Harold looked around at the devastation he'd caused and smiled. 'I'm amazed you stuck it out so long.' He smirked and she wriggled, wanting to get away from him. He dismounted from the horse and grabbed

Revna by her bonded wrists, dragging her to her feet and towards the doors of the keep.

'Barricade the gates, man the walls. Don't let those men back in here. Do this for me and their wives will be your spoils,' he said to some of his commanders, who grinned and remained outside, taking up their positions, drawing their weapons.

When he kicked the doors open, a small band of men behind him, the women and children screamed and wailed in fear, seeing Revna as Harold's captive, and they cowered backwards against the walls.

'Ah, our reward, to celebrate our victory.'

'Don't you dare lay a finger on them,' Revna warned.

'Or what?' he sneered. 'I'm in control now. I can do as I please. And my, what a grand hall,' he said, looking around, pulling her past the people in the hall, up towards the top table. 'To think my brother gave all this up for you. A heathen,' he said. 'I'm looking forward to finding out what all the fuss is about.'

Revna's stomach rolled. 'Come near me and I'll kill you,' she said, livid.

'Without a weapon? That should be fun. I do like women who put up a fight.'

His rough hands cast her down into one of the chairs and she felt sick. For herself. For the people. Everyone. Just yesterday morning she'd been lying beneath Teon's warm body as he'd kissed and touched her so tenderly. She'd been able to cope with the monotonous days and the brutality of the war they'd been fighting, as she'd had him. He had been her hope.

She would give anything to be back in that moment with him. Even arguing with him last night was preferential to this. Because despite the things he had said she still knew he was a good man. The best. And the fact that he had saved her, it made her think perhaps he hadn't meant the words he'd said. Perhaps he had just lashed out. But now he was gone. Now everything was wrong.

Harold ordered his men to stake out the labyrinth of corridors and rooms, to check no one was hiding in there. Anyone they found was brought back into the hall and tossed to the floor. When Revna saw a man dragging in Edlynne and Eldrida, she went still, feeling the blood drain from her face. She hoped Harold wouldn't realise they were the Princesses. She didn't think he'd be kind.

'And what do we have here? My sisters,' he said, clapping his hands together in a strange type of glee. 'Isn't it wonderful to meet each other at last? And on such happy terms.' He took their faces in his hands one by one, studying them. 'You know, I don't see any resemblance between us, but I'm sure you will much prefer living with me than your brother. What fun we will have.'

'Leave them alone,' Revna said.

And he turned round and slapped her hard across the cheek. 'Don't talk to your King like that,' he said.

'You will never be our King. None of us will ever bow down to you.'

'No?' he sneered. 'Then I'll just have to make you.'

He hit her again and she fell on to her knees before him and he loomed over her. 'See how easy it is?'

And then her mouth filled with bile as she saw him unbuckle his belt, undoing his trousers. Dread pounded through her veins at what he was going to do. 'Perhaps I need to show you what submission to your King looks like...'

Teon pushed open the trapdoor and launched himself up into the courtyard. He was strangely glad to be back, despite having been cooped up in here for days. Upon hearing the sounds of women and children wailing, coming from the hall, he just hoped he wasn't too late.

Scouting out the locations of all Harold's men, he directed his own warriors to where they needed to go to launch their stealth attack as each one came up through the trapdoor behind him. Seeing no sign of his sisters or Revna, his heart hammered in his chest. They needed to hurry up.

As the last of the men headed out to the courtyard, he gave the signal to attack, as he, Ravn and Bordan opened the door to the keep and threw themselves inside.

His eyes scoured the room and his eyes collided with Revna's and she sagged in relief when she saw him. Knelt on the floor before Harold, his trousers undone, Teon saw that her lip was bleeding and his anger was extreme. He wanted Harold dead.

'Welcome, Brother!' Harold said, shocked to see him there. 'I don't know how you made it back here so fast, but you're right on time to see me sit on the throne.' He laughed and he lowered himself down into the grand seat. 'Any later and you would have seen me sitting on your wife, making her mine,' he said, stroking a finger down her face.

Seeing his hands on her was sickening.

'I would never be yours,' Revna snapped at him.

'Quiet, infidel!' he said. 'Now tell me, Brother, what have you come back for? Your crown or your heathen?'

'My Queen, my people, my home and my crown— in that order. It is over, Harold. Continue any further along this path and I shall have your head.'

'But you have abdicated, Brother. We all heard it. Did you not give up your throne, relinquish your power to me out on the battlefield, before God?'

'The people will protest. They will rise up against you.'

'They will object to you putting a heathen on the throne, too.'

'You're wrong. Revna is beloved by all the people. She is loved by me…'

She swung to look at him, her eyes wide.

'She will make the best Queen this kingdom has ever seen.'

'Pity it will never happen then,' Harold said, cupping her chin, and she tried to turn away in disgust. 'I'm in charge now. But I should like to tell you that she'll be the second Queen I've stolen from you.'

No! Teon thought, his body going still in shock. He didn't. He wouldn't have… He stepped towards him, anger vibrating through his body. 'It was you?'

'What? Who stabbed your mother? Yes, I'm afraid so.'

Teon felt Ravn launch forward at his side and he used his arm to hold him back. This wasn't his fight.

'I felt it was so unfair that you and your mother got to live in this huge fortress, while I had to live in what was barely a hut on the flatlands. I had to sit in a room and listen to our father, the mighty King, come and take my mother whenever he wanted, then do up his trousers and leave again, barely giving me the time of day.

'You had everything. I had nothing. So I thought why not kill your whore of a queen mother while she was out on a secret love tryst of her own, making it look as though one of the heathens did it. It was genius, you see. I thought our father might move my own mother and me into the fortress then, but no… clearly he didn't think we were good enough for that.

'Somehow, he realised it was me who had taken his wife from him and then he wanted to disinherit me. But I've made it here now. I hope he's looking down on me, feeling proud.'

Teon swallowed. Their father knew? Had he been so ashamed that he had kept it to himself?

'The people will never accept you as their King,' Teon said.

'They don't need to accept it, I shall rule with force,' he said, spittle forming at the corners of his mouth.

'The same force that's currently being taken down by my men out in the courtyard?'

For the first time, he saw Harold waver and he knew he was finally getting to him.

'Fight me, man to man.'

Harold laughed. 'And why would I want or need to do that?'

'Because if you don't, your whole kingdom will know you're a coward. The lesser brother. They've known it all along, but perhaps you want a chance to prove it's not true?'

A muscle flickered in Harold's cheek.

'Beat me and no one will ever doubt your title here. My men outside will stand down...'

'To the death?' Harold smirked.

'Absolutely,' Teon said.

'Teon, no!' Revna gasped, her beautiful blue eyes misting over like a cloud-filled sky. But he ignored her protests.

He had to see this through now. He had to finish what his father had started.

The tables were moved, holed up in nooks and crannies around the room, to create space for them to fight. Revna's heart was in her mouth. She didn't want him to do this. What if he lost?

She watched as Harold took off his cloak and withdrew his sword, and she retched. How could she stand by and watch this man try to kill her lover, her husband, her everything?

Edlynne, who had raced to their father's study, came rushing back in with the King's heavy sword and handed it to Teon. He muttered his thanks, accepting Edlynne's quick embrace, while rolling up his sleeves. And Revna thought her heart might break.

She hadn't moved from her position on the floor, her hands still tied, and she wasn't sure what to do.

Should she try to convince him not to do this? Beg him not to fight? Or should she let him be the stubborn man who needed to end all this? Had he really said he loved her, in front of all these people? Could it be true?

His gaze settled on her across the room and he inclined his head, as if to say, we'll speak afterwards. And she really hoped so. She couldn't bear it if something were to happen to him. In the space of a week he had become her whole world.

Men from both sides, who had been fighting out on the ramparts began to file in, crowding around the edge of the hall, eager to see the fight unfold, keen to see this battle that had affected them all settled, once and for all.

Harold struck the first blow and Revna caught her breath, unable to take her eyes off his sword as he thrust it forward, trying to stab Teon in the chest. But Teon was quick, darting sideways, just missing the edge of the blade. He circled his opponent— his brother, who bore no resemblance to him—and jabbed his father's sword, but Harold backed away, out of reach of the tip. The blows were lethal, each one with the same deadly aim—to cause the other person harm.

Then the clashing of the metal became quicker, more brutal, as both men wanted to see this over with. Teon's sword grazed Harold's neck, drawing first blood, but then Harold sliced his blade into Teon's side, making Revna cry out, but he ignored the injury, as if it hadn't even stung. He fought bravely, all power and lithe legs, and the people in the hall watched on in horror and awe, hoping for the right outcome.

When Teon's sword suddenly cut across Harold's middle, slicing through his armour, the man floundered, losing his weapon, and he threw himself on the floor to try to get to it. But Teon got there first, pressing his foot down on the sword so Harold couldn't grab it.

Then, to everyone's alarm, the Prince cast his own sword to one side, too, and a savage struggle ensued, with each man throwing punches, using their bare fists, viciously wrestling. It was primal—brutal and bloody and raw. Teon was like something possessed, as if all his rage and grief was being let loose upon his brother, the man who had murdered his mother.

She knew he needed his vengeance, but Harold was fighting back, just as wildly, and Revna squeezed her eyes shut, but then opened them again, needing to know Teon was all right. She was willing him to win, praying to her gods to keep him safe. Then, finally, Teon dealt Harold the final blow, sending him into a crumpled heap, so he was groaning on the floor, trying to crawl away.

'Take him,' Teon said to his men, dropping down to his knees on the floor, commanding them through his bloodied face. 'Take him before I do something I regret.' Bordan and another man grabbed Harold by the arms and dragged him outside.

As soon as Harold was gone, his men put down their weapons, surrendering, almost as though they were relieved it was over. When Teon tried to stand, Revna rushed over to him. He untied her bonds with his trembling, bloodied fingers and then she helped him, gripping him under his arms as he rose. When he was on his feet, he hauled her to him, wrapping his arms around her neck, holding her tight, and it felt so good to be back in his arms again.

It was over. They were safe. She felt as if the whole hall let out a collective sigh in union with her.

'Are you hurt?' he asked, pulling away from her slightly to inspect her face, his thumb smoothing over her split lip. He rested his head against her forehead.

'The thought of him laying a finger on you...' He shuddered.

She shook her head against his shoulder. 'I'm all right. It's you I'm worried about. How bad are your wounds?' she whispered, looking up at him, her eyes tearing up. He looked rumpled, unkempt, as though he hadn't slept in days, and bruises were already appearing on his cheek.

'It's nothing you can't heal,' he said, kissing her eyes, her nose, her mouth, in front of everyone in the hall. His hands curved over her shoulders. 'I really thought I'd lost you,' he said, his voice cracking.

'You could never,' she said. 'But, Teon, I need you to know... I didn't have anything to do with your mother's death or stealing her necklace.'

'I know,' he said. 'And we'll talk about it.'
She nodded.
Keeping Revna tucked under his arm, Teon turned to face his people in the hall, his loyal subjects, who

had stuck by him when things had looked so bleak. He was incredibly grateful. Slowly, his men were working their way back inside and there were reunions going on all around the room.

'Is everyone all right?' he asked.

There were utterings and mumblings and then everyone started to clap and stamp their feet, turn around and hug each other. It was a glorious sight.

He looked over at Bordan and Ravn and he nodded his thanks to them both, and they did the same, acknowledging him in return. There would be time to thank everyone properly later, but right now, he just wanted to hold Revna and be by her side, where he should have been all along. He needed to apologise and tell her how he felt about her. He gripped her tightly and pulled her into his chest again, closing his eyes and sending a silent thanks up above.

He told Edlynne and Eldrida to start pouring the ale and dig out any food the men and their families could eat. 'Tonight, we shall feast in celebration of us defending our stronghold. I will make a toast in your honour, for your loyalty.' And then he took Revna's hand in his and led her to his room.

She helped to lower him down on to the bed, his hand curled across his side that was bleeding profusely now. Then she lit the fire so she would be able to see his wounds properly. But when she came back to the bed, he turned her own face into the firelight and checked her over again. 'Are you sure you're all right?' he asked, concerned.

'I'm honestly fine,' she said, rolling her eyes. 'But you...you look a bit of a mess.'

He laughed, and then grimaced at the pain the movement had caused. 'Thanks! I think I can feel my eye swelling up. I probably won't be able to see out of it tomorrow.'

'It's the cut to your side I'm more concerned about. Let's take that off,' she said, nodding to his damaged chainmail and tunic. 'I'd better see how bad it is.'

He pulled off his leather vest, gently easing it away from his skin and removing his arms from the holes. But the material of the tunic was soaked with blood and stuck in his wound. He winced as he tried to peel it away and she helped him, lifting it gently from his body.

He raised his arm and tried to look at the wound. It was just above the one he'd got the other day. 'Please, no more stitches,' he said. 'Not tonight. I just want to hold you,' he groaned.

'I must do it, I'm afraid. I don't want it getting infected.'

He moaned and lay back on the bed.

'I'll be back in a moment.'

He gripped her hand. 'Don't go.'

'Teon!' she chided. 'Would you rather I got Edlynne to do it?'

'No,' he said.

'Then let me go,' she said sternly.

When she returned moments later, she came to sit next to him on the bed and he groaned. 'No more pain!' he jested. But he let her do it anyway, throwing his arm over his face until it was done and she discarded the needle and thread.

She dipped some wool into a bowl of water and began to clean the cuts and bruises to his eyes and jaw. She hated that that man had blackened his beautiful face. She was so glad Teon's men had apprehended him and had placed him under guard. She hoped Teon would see him punished appropriately.

'I don't know how you refrained from killing him.' He was a good, strong man.

'No matter what he's done, it didn't seem right killing my own flesh and blood. But I'm thinking he should be exiled…a long, long way from here. I never want to see him again.'

'Me either.'

She moved the bowl aside, making room for herself on the furs, and lay down beside him, resting her head on his shoulder, careful not to touch his wounds.

He took her chin between his fingers and tipped her face up to look at him. 'I'm glad you're here. I'm glad you came back…despite all the awful things I said. I'm so sorry I didn't believe you straight away, Revna—about the necklace or your father. You told me he was innocent and I should have listened.'

She shrugged her shoulder, so willing to forgive him. 'I guess the evidence was against us.'

'I will never jump to conclusions again,' he said. 'You have my word.'

She bit her lip. 'What made you change your mind? Did you speak to him?'

'I think I knew deep down it had nothing to do

with you as soon as you left my room that night. I'd taken my anger towards myself out on you.'

She frowned. 'Why were you angry with yourself?

'I saw the necklace and I felt disgusted at myself for forgetting about my mother. I had wanted you so badly, I'd forgotten my vow to her to seek vengeance. I thought your father was to blame and, in that moment, I saw myself as weak. That I'd put my own needs, my own wants and desires before my need to avenge her death. I was livid with myself, not you.

'I didn't mean any of those things I said. I lashed out, afraid of everything I was feeling. I guess I've thought of you as the enemy for so long, it sounds foolish, but it was almost easier to think of you that way, rather than deal with the disturbing feelings I was having for you. I didn't want to like you, but I ended up falling in love with you... And it terrified me. I've seen what happens when relationships go wrong. How much hurt it can cause.'

She swallowed upon hearing his words. 'Teon...'

'Let me finish,' he said. 'I need to explain myself. I need you to know how sorry I am. That comment I made about you not being able to keep me interested for long, it couldn't be further from the truth. I have never wanted anyone like I want you. I will never want anyone other than you ever again. I will always be faithful to you, Revna.

'You see, when you left me, I got a taste of what it must have felt like when I left you on our wedding night and when I've hurt you time and time again since. It was the worst. I hated myself. I was so worried I'd ruined everything and you wouldn't forgive me, just wanting you back, knowing that I didn't want to be here without you. And then when I saw you there, on the battlefield, I could scarcely believe it, I hoped it meant you still cared for me. That you hadn't given up on me.'

'I have never given up on you, Teon. And I will never...'

'If you take me back, I promise I'll never, ever leave you again. I want us to be together, always. I never even want to let you out of my sight, not for a moment.'

She laughed at that. 'I think you might get a little tired of me.'

'I doubt it.'

She shook her head, propping herself up on one elbow, staring down at him. 'I can't believe you gave up your fortress for me.'

'When Harold pointed that blade at your chest, my life flashed before my eyes. In the space of a week you have become the single most important thing to me. You come before my crown, my home—everything. Without you, none of it means anything.'

She leaned down and placed a soft kiss on his lips. And his hand came up to curl into her hair and pull her head down and he kissed her back, fully, genuinely.

'Does that hurt?' she asked, pulling her head back a little.

'It's worth it,' he said. 'Did your father tell you about him and my mother?'

'Yes,' she said honestly. 'I couldn't believe it at first, then I thought back to all the times she'd visited our settlement, helping with the crops and showing an interest in me. And it did seem to make sense. It certainly explained why he never came to our wedding, or to visit me. It would have been far too awkward between him and your father. How do you feel about it?'

'I'm not sure,' he said. 'Like you I was shocked at first, then I guess I could see them together, like you and me. It seems my mother even said we would make a good match, that's why your father had suggested our union in the first place. Perhaps all this happened for a reason, to bring us to this moment, right here and now.

'Here,' he said, wincing as he reached over to the small table by the side of the bed to pick something up. 'I was looking inside your trinket box that night as I was searching for your wedding ring, wondering if you still had it. I know I should have asked you, rather than rummaging through your belongings, but I wanted it to be a surprise.' He took her hand in his and pushed the dainty gold band on to her finger, easing it down halfway. 'I never got to ask you this eight years ago, but...will you be my wife, Revna? I want to be bound as one, for real this time. For ever.'

'Yes,' she said. 'Of course I will.'

'When things have settled down, I'd like us to renew our vows.' He pushed the band down the rest of the way. 'Does that mean you love me?' he asked. 'The way I love you?'

'I love you, Teon. I always have and I always will.'

She kissed him again, smiling.

'I want to show you how much I love you. But I'm not sure I can right now,' he groaned. 'I can barely move. But I promise I'll make it up to you later.'

'I'll look forward to it,' she said and laughed.

Revna woke in the middle of the night and could still hear the celebrations going on in the hall. She hoped they were all having fun, her father included, but she didn't want to be anywhere other than right here, by Teon's side.

The fire was on its way out, but she could just make out the lines of his face in the darkness and his chest slowly rising and falling beneath her hand. She was so happy he'd asked her to marry him, by his own accord. First time round, he'd had no say in the matter, it had been forced upon him, but now she knew he wanted her. In every sense of the word.

He had told her he loved her, in front of all his subjects in the hall, and kissed her in front of them all, too, showing them how much he cared. He said she would make a good queen, proving he was no longer ashamed of her heritage. He wanted her seemingly as much as she wanted him and it felt incredible to know he cared for her in that way. She had almost everything she wanted.

But a niggling thought was still eating away at her. When he'd been apologising, he hadn't brought up the fact he'd told her he didn't want to father her children. She hoped that he had just been lashing out, that it hadn't been true, but she still wasn't sure what his thoughts were on becoming a father and having a family one day. Not that there was any rush. But trailing her fingers over his stomach, her palms up over his chest, she knew she wanted him to make love to her again as he had the other morning. Did he want that, too?

She felt so excited just lying next to him and tossed her hair back over her shoulders, out of the way, so she could explore all the lines and ridges of his incredible body.

She curved her hand over his broad shoulders, running her fingertips over the little scars there, and down, over his sculpted arms. She placed her hand over his chest and swirled her fingertips over his nipples. His arm around her waist tightened its grip in his sleep and he moaned.

She wrapped her knee over his thigh as she drew her knuckles down over his hard stomach, down his trail of dark hair and over the ridge in his trousers. He stirred, turning his head towards her, and she curved her hand over him. She was fascinated when he grew hard beneath her touch.

'Revna,' he whispered.

She kissed him softly on the mouth, trying not to brush against his injuries, as her fingers found the waistband of his trousers and roamed underneath, wanting to take him in her hand again, but her movement was restricted.

He groaned. 'What are you—?'

'Shh,' she whispered. 'Just rest. Relax.'

All the times they'd been together in the past, he

had instigated it. But he knew she was a woman who fought for what she wanted and, right now, she wanted his body. She wanted to help him forget his wounds and his pain, by replacing it with pleasure.

Sitting up, she tugged down his trousers and he raised his bottom off the furs to help her, awake now. Fully alert. She rolled the material down his legs and threw them on to the floor.

She had what she wanted. He was lying naked before her. And she knew he was watching her through the open slits of his eyes, his dark gaze glittering with interest.

'Are you trying to seduce me?' He grinned.

'Maybe. Is that all right?'

'Always. But I warn you I can barely move.'

'Good, you're mine for the taking then.' She grinned.

She swung her legs off the bed and stood, tugging down her breeches and removing the armour her father had lent her, before peeling off her tunic.

'Revna...' he groaned.

Standing beside him, she took his hand and moved it to the apex of her thighs. 'I want you to touch me,' she said. 'I'll go mad if you don't.'

And his hand cupped her heat, the palm of his hand rubbing against her tiny nub as his fingertips inched inside her, driving her wild.

But after a couple of strokes, she removed his hand and got back on to the bed, kneeling at his feet, nudging his legs apart with her knees as she came nearer. Then she leaned over him, stretched out over his body, careful not to press any weight on him by using her elbows to hold her up. She kissed him, her breasts brushing against his chest and her mound rubbing over his shaft.

His arms came up around her back, pulling her close, trying to hold her fast, his lips dipping to her cleavage, to trace the soft swells of her breasts. But then she was wriggling downwards, her mouth on his stomach, placing hot, hard kisses over his skin. She took his shaft in the palm of her hand and stroked him up and down, before placing a soft kiss to the tip.

'Dear God, what are you doing to me?' he said. 'I want you so much.'

'How much?'

'So much I think I might explode at any moment.'

She enjoyed the feeling of being in total control, of having power over him for once. And as she wrapped her mouth around the tip, she moved her hand over his thighs, between his legs, wanting to touch him everywhere.

'Revna…'

Slowly, she licked and sucked at him, dragging her tongue down the length of him and back up, before taking him in her mouth again.

'Does that feel good?'

'Yes. More,' he said. 'Deeper.'

And she slid him inside her mouth, as deep as she could, and he swore. He bucked, his groin gently thrusting towards her, filling her mouth.

She knew he was close, that she was driving him wild, but she didn't want it to be over. Not yet. She wanted him inside her. Badly. So she tore her mouth away and he bit out his protest.

'Stop teasing me,' he groaned.

'What do you want?' she asked.

'I want to taste you, too,' he said, urging her up his body. 'Come closer.'

She knew what he was asking, but she wasn't sure she could do it. It was so brazen. So intimate. But he was increasing his pressure on the back of her thighs, coaxing her towards him, and she moved her body, straddling him, up to his chest.

She bit her lip.

'Closer, Revna.'

And he gripped her buttocks, pulling her towards him the final way, and she brought her knees down to rest on his shoulders. He raised his head, his eyes looking up at her, his mouth closing over her, and she cried out.

She looked down at him, at the centre of her world. 'Teon,' she choked out. 'Oh, Teon.' She tried to move away, but he held her fast.

His tongue glided along her opening, flicking over her little bud, and she splayed her hands out on the wall. Every stroke of his wicked tongue was intended to elicit her gasps of pleasure. She writhed on top of him. She had wanted them to find their release together, but she was too close now, she knew she wouldn't make it, and as his tongue rolled over her in waves, she came apart on top of him, sobbing out her powerful climax.

He held her thighs as she tumbled back down to

earth and he was looking up at her with burning heat in his eyes.

'I want to be inside you,' he said. 'Do you want that, too?'

'Yes,' she said, wiping her tear-stained cheeks.

She lifted herself away and then came back to lay down beside him, taking him in her hand again.

'Come back on top of me,' he said.

Straddling his thighs, she gripped his face between her hands and kissed him, hard, her tongue entwining with his. And she could smell her own raw scent on his lips. She guided him to her entrance and lowered herself down on top of him. She was so wet from his mouth and her excitement his silky tip eased inside her opening.

Then she lowered herself, fully impaling herself on him, and she cried out at how amazing it felt. He was huge, filling her up. He began to thrust beneath her, torturously slowly, as much as his wound would allow, and she moved her hips up and down, back and forth, riding him, trying to match his unhurried pace. She brought her hands up to lift her hair, to stroke her breasts, knowing he was watching her, and she got the response she wanted.

He growled and gripped her buttocks, pulling her down on top of him harder, burying himself deeper, quickening his pace, forcing her to move frantically, until she could take it no longer. She felt her body splinter into pieces of blinding pleasure and she felt his own explosive release.

'That was incredible,' he whispered as she collapsed on top of him and he cradled her in his arms.

'You're incredible,' she said.

'We're incredible. I love you, Revna. I love you so much.'

Epilogue

It had been a month since they'd taken back control of the fortress and the stronghold was a hive of activity as they prepared for the coronation ceremony and feast. Finally, Teon was going to be made King. They had spent the days rebuilding—restoring their homes and their relationships.

Harold had caused widespread devastation, but they had destroyed all of his war machines, cleared his camp and begun to level the earth, turning over the soil. The dark winter days were making way for summer and the plains would soon be filled with men, women and children happily planting barley and corn. Buds were bursting into life on the trees and the people were pulling together to mend the broken walls and gates and restocking the food stores. The atrocities they'd suffered had somehow brought everyone closer together.

Teon had ensured that Harold had been sent to Frankia on a ship with his mother, forced to live out his days in exile, and everyone was glad they would never have to see him again. It turned out Harold's men had indeed lost their houses and had their families threatened. They'd been told their families would be killed unless they fought alongside him. They had been given a royal pardon, as long as they all bent the knee.

And Teon remained true to his word…he had promised to richly reward those who stood by him and he had given all those men and their families new land to farm and gold and silver to help them start afresh. He had been more than fair.

Revna was delighted her father and his men had remained to help, wanting to see Prince Teon be crowned King. She had been enjoying spending her days with her father again and she loved seeing him and Teon converse, laughing together. Finally, the Saxons and Greenlanders were allies and it made her heart overflow with joy.

Edlynne and Eldrida had made new dresses for the coronation and Edlynne had told Revna in confidence that she was hopeful she might get to sit next to the handsome warrior Bordan, for she had taken quite a liking to him. And Darrelle and her family were thriving, looking forward to moving into their newly built farmstead. Revna had promised to come and help them, especially during the lambing season.

Teon's wounds were healing well—he said it was because he had the best nurse. Revna was enjoying seeing how much they were improving at night-time, by discovering that his stamina was increasing. From dusk till dawn, they just couldn't seem to get enough of each other.

The eve before, in the middle of the night, she had been awoken by him picking her up and carrying her in his arms, pressed against his bare chest, along the corridor.

'Where are we going?' she'd whispered.

'You'll see.'

The hall was deserted, the people having now decamped to new homes with their families, and she looked around and saw there was a fire burning near the top table, but the rest of the keep was still.

He gently set her down on her feet in front of his grand chair—the one they were using at the enthronement today.

He knelt before her and silently began to undress her. Her heart rate had picked up, as it always did when his eyes burned into her, telling her he wanted her. She always wanted his hands on her, too. She would never say no to him. He smoothed her clothes off her, so she stood naked before him in the hall. And she felt so small in this vast room. It reminded her of their first intimate moments together, but she no longer felt shy with him. She no longer wanted to hide from his heated gaze.

'I've wanted to do this to you for a long time now. I want to worship my Queen, sitting on her throne, in this grand hall. I want to make you feel powerful, for you to see yourself in my eyes, as the Queen you've come to be. Will you let me?'

'Yes.'

He gently pushed her back into the seat, and coming down before her, bowing down on his knees, he ruthlessly pressed her knees apart with his hands, spreading her thighs wide.

'Teon.' She blushed. She would never get used to him wanting to look at her. 'What if someone comes in?'

'We won't be disturbed. I asked my men to make sure of it.'

It excited her that he had planned it. That he'd thought ahead about how he could give her pleasure.

He gripped her by the bottom and pulled her towards him, before he set to placing delicate little kisses all along her inner thighs. And when he began to whisper his oath to her, the one he'd shouted to her from the treetops, she tipped her head back in wonder.

'According to the laws of God, I,' he whispered, trailing his tongue along her soft skin, 'Teon, Edmund's son, Prince of Kinborough…' he looked up at her, grinning '…swear that I will be loyal and faithful and bear true allegiance to Revna…' he turned his head and did the same along the other thigh '…my warrior Queen, according to the Almighty Lord's law…' His mouth hovered at the junction of her thighs, his breath whispering across her. 'I will uphold justice and mercy where she is concerned, fulfil *all* my duties…' his tongue parted her crease, licking her open '…and hold the peace for the length of her rule.'

Then he laid claim to her with his tongue. She cradled his head as his tongue found her nub and circled it, intimately, explicitly. And her cries of pleasure made him want more, half-mad for her as always. He hooked one leg over his shoulder and the other over the side of the chair, spreading her even wider, feasting on her, and she screamed out her insane swirling climax.

She sank down on to his lap, straddling his thighs, and gripping her bottom, he lay her down on the floor as he came down on top of her. 'I want to make love to you in this great hall of kings, where realms are built and legacies are made.'

And she knew she should have brought it up then. She had wanted to ask him if he wanted to create a legacy with her. They still hadn't spoken about it and she felt as if it was becoming this enormous, difficult subject that both of them were reluctant to talk about again.

She was afraid, knowing he might not want to discuss it, fearful of what he would say. She didn't want to ruin the way things were between them. And perhaps, given he was about to make his pledge to the realm the following day and he had a lot on his mind, it probably wasn't the right time to bring it up. It could wait… Because everything was perfect otherwise.

So she kept quiet, instead giving in to the incredible sensations he was creating as he thrust inside her.

'Will it always be like this?' she'd asked him afterwards, as she lay beneath his trembling, sweat-slicked body.

'Maybe not when we're much older,' he'd jested. 'So we'd better make the most of it now. But I will always want you by my side, Revna, whether in bed or otherwise.'

* * *

The coronation service got underway as the sun was at its highest point in the sky, first in the church, where Teon said his oath and was anointed, and then they all walked up to the great hall. The weather and the mood were so different to that of the funeral and she realised how far they had all come. The room had never looked grander, with the fires burning brightly and stag banners flying.

Revna couldn't have been prouder, watching Teon be crowned and enthroned, with everyone cheering from the side lines. He stood up to make a speech, thanking all his people for standing by him and saying he hoped to live out the rest of his reign in peace. And then, to her astonishment, he announced that he would like to crown Revna as Queen, bringing her up on to the platform, pressing a kiss to her lips to show everyone how much he loved his wife. And she was overwhelmed with the crowd cheering and the love shining down from his eyes.

'I told you, I don't need a crown, Teon,' she whispered.

'I know. But I refuse to be crowned unless you are, too.' He grinned. 'We are in this together, remember? We will have equal responsibility over our rule here. Equal power. I have also discussed this with the witan and they feel it necessary that the King and Queen embark on a royal tour. Official engagements, if you like, to see the rest of our kingdom and other lands, if that is what you would wish.' He winked. 'I'm sure Bordan and Edlynne could hold the fort for a while.'

Revna couldn't believe it. What an unexpected, thoughtful and surprising thing for him to arrange. He was trying to make all her dreams come true.

Then Father Cuthbert brought a sword out on a purple cushion and Teon got down on one knee. She stared at him, wondering what was going on. Was it all part of the ceremony?

'You told me, where you come from, families exchange swords, not rings, when they marry. And so I want you to have my father's sword, Revna,' he said, offering the blade to her. 'He would have wanted you to have it.'

Her hand came up to cover her chest, moved.

'And as you have come to learn our customs so well, I have been doing a little research of my own about your cultures and traditions.' He turned to look at her father and nodded his thanks. 'I've learned that where you come from, if a man gives his father's sword to his woman, it represents the continuity of his bloodline. And I want that, Revna, with you.'

Her breath hitched and her eyes watered. Was he really telling her, and all his subjects in his hall, that he wanted children with her?

'Really?' she said. And then she lowered her voice. 'Even though I'm a heathen?'

He grinned. 'I think it's the heathen part of you that I love the most,' he said. 'The wild, beautiful exotic side. The unpredictable, outspoken and honest side. The insatiable side! And I hope our children have all of those things and more.'

'I'm glad you said that,' she said, 'as I have something to tell you.'

And then she drew him closer and whispered in his ear that she thought she was, in fact, already with child.

He pulled back to look at her, startled. 'Really?' he asked.

'Yes.' She nodded.

He ran his hand down over her stomach in wonder. 'Are you feeling all right?'

'Yes.' She laughed.

And as if he couldn't help himself, he pulled her towards him, kissing her, passionately, deeply, in front of everyone, letting her know he really did want the child that was growing in her belly. The child they'd made together out of love.

When he finally broke away, leaving her breathless, he turned and announced their happy news to their loyal subjects in the hall and everyone erupted in more clapping and cheering.

He gathered her to him again. 'Thank you, Revna, for giving me everything I dreamed of and more. For not giving up on me. For giving me a second chance...'

She wrapped her arms around his neck. 'I knew you'd be worth the wait,' she said. Then she pulled his mouth down on hers for a kiss from her King.

* * * * *

COMING NEXT MONTH FROM

⊞ HARLEQUIN
HISTORICAL

All available in print and ebook via Reader Service and online

BECOMING THE EARL'S CONVENIENT WIFE (Regency)
by Louise Allen
If Isobel becomes Leo's convenient countess, she can escape her unhappy home...and he can inherit his fortune! But can Isobel escape the feelings that she's long had for him?

MISS ROSE AND THE VEXING VISCOUNT (Regency)
The Triplet Orphans • by Catherine Tinley
Bookworm Rose has no interest in making her debut. Her sponsor's nephew, James, is equally cynical about the marriage mart. But sparks of animosity soon become flames of attraction!

A GILDED AGE CHRISTMAS (Gilded Age)
by Amanda McCabe and Lauri Robinson
In *A Convenient Winter Wedding*, Connor is far from May's dream of a passionate husband...except for that scorching kiss! In *The Railroad Baron's Mistletoe Bride*, romance blooms when Kurt invites Harper and their shared niece to spend Christmas at his mansion...

THE LADY'S SCANDALOUS PROPOSITION (Victorian)
by Paulia Belgado
Persephone is a hopeless debutante! This will be her last season—and best chance to experience sensual pleasure...so she decides to shock Ransom with a daring proposition!

HER WARRIOR'S SURPRISE RETURN (Medieval)
Brothers and Rivals • by Ella Matthews
It's been years since Ruaidhri abandoned Sorcha, and she's not the woman she once was. His past betrayal still burns, even if their desire burns as strong as ever...

A DUKE FOR THE WALLFLOWER'S REVENGE (Regency)
by Casey Dubose
Eliza's plan: beg Gabriel, Duke of Vane, to help execute her revenge on the lecher who ruined her... while not *in any way* falling for her commitment-shy accomplice!

Get 3 FREE REWARDS!

We'll send you 2 FREE Books plus a FREE Mystery Gift.

Both the **Harlequin® Desire** and **Harlequin Presents®** series feature compelling novels filled with passion, sensuality and intriguing scandals.

YES! Please send me 2 FREE novels from the Harlequin Desire or Harlequin Presents series and my FREE gift (gift is worth about $10 retail). After receiving them, if I don't wish to receive any more books, I can return the shipping statement marked "cancel." If I don't cancel, I will receive 6 brand-new Harlequin Presents Larger-Print books every month and be billed just $6.30 each in the U.S. or $6.49 each in Canada, a savings of at least 10% off the cover price, or 3 Harlequin Desire books (2-in-1 story editions) every month and be billed just $7.83 each in the U.S. or $8.43 each in Canada, a savings of at least 12% off the cover price. It's quite a bargain! Shipping and handling is just 50¢ per book in the U.S. and $1.25 per book in Canada.* I understand that accepting the 2 free books and gift places me under no obligation to buy anything. I can always return a shipment and cancel at any time by calling the number below. The free books and gift are mine to keep no matter what I decide.

Choose one: ☐ **Harlequin Desire**   ☐ **Harlequin**   ☐ **Or Try Both!**
                  (225/326 BPA GRNA)   **Presents**   (225/326 & 176/376
                                                Larger-Print   BPA GRQP)
                                                (176/376 BPA GRNA)

Name (please print)

Address   Apt. #

City   State/Province   Zip/Postal Code

Email: Please check this box ☐ if you would like to receive newsletters and promotional emails from Harlequin Enterprises ULC and its affiliates. You can unsubscribe anytime.

Mail to the **Harlequin Reader Service:**
IN U.S.A.: P.O. Box 1341, Buffalo, NY 14240-8531
IN CANADA: P.O. Box 603, Fort Erie, Ontario L2A 5X3

Want to try 2 free books from another series! Call 1-800-873-8635 or visit www.ReaderService.com.

HARLEQUIN
PLUS

Try the best multimedia subscription service for romance readers like you!

Read, Watch and Play.

Experience the easiest way to get the romance content you crave.

Start your **FREE TRIAL** at
<u>www.harlequinplus.com/freetrial</u>.